SLIPPERY CREATURES

KJ CHARLES

Slippery Creatures

Published by KJC Books

Copyright © 2020 by KJ Charles

Edited by Veronica Vega

Cover design by Tiferet Design

ISBN: 978-1-912688-16-6

READER ADVISORY

This book contains references to a pandemic and the spread
of infectious disease.

A full list of content warnings is available at:
http://kjcharleswriter.com/content-warnings/

For the essential workers keeping us going
and for everyone who's supporting them by staying home

Pippa Harpster

April 7, 2022

ONE

Will Darling was outnumbered by books.

It hadn't always felt this way. When he'd first visited his uncle at Darling's Used & Antiquarian, he'd simply thought, *That's a lot of books,* and when he'd started helping here, they were just work. As he took over the running of the place in his uncle's last illness, though, he became increasingly aware of them looming around him, full of knowledge and secrets and lies. So much that, when Uncle William had died, Will remembered an ancient piece of lore about bees, and he'd cleared his throat and told the books, "He's gone."

He was dead, and Will, his sole heir, had inherited Darling's Used & Antiquarian: the premises on May's Buildings off St. Martin's Lane, the goodwill such as it was, and the stock. He was master of an entire building with a shop floor, two upstairs rooms, and a cubbyhole at the ground floor back which was all the space his uncle had allowed for human life. He'd have Uncle William's savings too, once probate had been sorted out. And he owned a lot of books,

This is me but in a positive way ↙

although just now and then, when it got dark and the shelves loomed over him, he got the feeling that they owned him.

He occupied some of the extremely long periods when nobody came into the shop by trying to calculate how many volumes his uncle had stuck him with, and had concluded it could easily be forty thousand. He had yet to find an inventory, and was increasingly convinced the old bugger had kept his records in his head. So here he was, at the shop desk with books double stacked in the floor-to-ceiling shelves that turned the room into a maze, books piled on every flat surface and against every vertical one, books half-obscuring the windows. Bloody books.

The place reeked of old paper over the fainter odours of damp, dust, and rodents. He'd put down traps, checked the walls, and taken a broom to what floor was visible as well as to the accumulating cobwebs on the fog-stained ceiling. It had had very little effect. He'd probably get used to the smell of second-hand books one day, just stop noticing it, and then he'd be doomed.

On that gloomy thought, he swung his feet up onto his desk and leaned back in his chair. Uncle William had spent good money on this chair once, and though the red leather was cracked, it was still comfortable. That was good enough for Will.

He was damned lucky to be here, even if he lived in danger of being crushed by a book landslide. Will had gone to the War at eighteen, and come back five years later to find himself useless and unwanted. In Flanders he'd been a grizzled veteran, a fount of professional expertise who knew the ropes and had seen it all. Back in Blighty he'd become a young man again, one with little training and no experience. He'd been apprenticed to a joiner before the war, but that felt like decades ago: all he was good at now was killing people, which was discouraged.

Britain was full of men like him, trying to find something to do in a country that had managed perfectly well without them. He'd gone home first, but his mother had died from the Spanish 'flu while he'd waited to be demobbed, and Northamptonshire was full of hollowed-out villages and hollow-eyed men. So, like everyone else, he'd come to London to look for work, paying his way with his war gratuity and the little his mother had left him. He'd taken whatever jobs he could find, tramped the streets for hours making increasingly desperate applications, and realised with slow-mounting fear as the months passed that his slide into poverty was unstoppable, no matter how willing he was to work.

He'd written to his unknown uncle when he'd reached the stage of rationing himself to one meal a day and calculating when his shoe leather would wear quite through. He hadn't expected an answer, let alone a welcome: it had been a last throw of the dice, and he'd rolled a double six. Uncle William had welcomed him as long-lost family, which alone would have made Will weak with thankfulness, but far more, he'd given him money, and let him work to earn it.

Will wouldn't have been able to repay that debt of gratitude in years. In the event, he'd only had a couple of months before the old man passed on, but at least he'd been there to care for him, make his final days as comfortable as they could be, ensure he didn't die alone. And now Will had an established business and an unmortgaged roof over his head. The change in his circumstances still made him dizzy.

The thought of rates reminded him that a good way to deal with the towering oppression of books might be to sell some of them. He had several plans toward that end, including finding out what he owned, making the shop less cluttered and more attractive, seeking out buyers instead of waiting for them to arrive by chance, and overall not behaving like a gnome protecting his hoard, in contrast to every other second-hand book dealer he'd met so far.

In pursuit of this aim he picked up Norden on book-dealing, found his page, and was skimming the chapter on music publishing when the door chime sounded.

Will glanced up, pointlessly because the view of the door from the desk was obscured by bookshelves. That was something he'd change as soon as he'd worked out the logistics of shifting about two tons of books to do it. He could easily not see people who came in for a good half-hour, or even at all, since many browsers preferred to lurk out of sight.

That had been deliberate on his uncle's part. He'd advised Will never to be a shop-walker, pouncing on customers and bothering them. Will suspected that his uncle had preferred not to sell books if he could avoid doing so, and had been keen to take a more active approach, but when he tried greeting browsers, they mostly stared as if he'd made an indecent proposition, or panicked and fled. In truth, he had very little idea of where to find books on Oriental porcelain or the Hundred Years' War in the chaos anyway, so he'd quickly given up.

He swung his feet back off the desk as a sop to customer service, and went back to his book.

Surprisingly, after a short hesitation, the footsteps came up to the desk. That suggested an initiative and sociability that were rare in his customers. Will looked up with a smile carefully adjusted not to seem too eager, and saw a man in his forties, wearing a light mackintosh and a hard, silent, unsmiling expression.

Eccentricity was rather the rule than the exception in Will's experience to date, so he didn't ask the fellow what he thought he was gawping at, but instead tried, "Good morning, sir. May I help you?"

"William Darling?"

"Yes..." Will said cautiously. Oh God, was it bailiffs? If he was being dunned on his uncle's behalf, that could tip his precarious financial balance disastrously. "What can I do for you?"

"I want the information."

Not an overdue bill, then. Will let out a long breath of relief. "Good! Good, excellent, I'm sure I can help. What information was that?"

"*The* information. The word is daffodil."

That was the strangest way Will could imagine of asking for a gardening book, but then, this was a business where people thought "it has a blue cover" was sufficient description to identify any novel from the last twenty years. "A book on flowers? I'm sure I can help. Are you after something specific, or—?"

The man's expression hardened. "You know what I want."

Doubtless he had written to Uncle William and the letter had vanished into the papery abyss of his records. "Did you ask for it to be put aside?" Will hazarded.

"Don't toy with me, Mr. Darling. The information was sent to you. I will pay you for it, very generously, but I must and will have it. Do you understand?"

He understood the bit about generous payment; the rest was less clear. "I'll be delighted to help once I've grasped what you're after. Who is it by?"

The man smacked his hand onto the desk, making the dust rise. It made Will rise as well, leaping to his feet in shock. "What the—"

"I told you not to toy with me, you jumped-up shop-keeper. I know you have it. Give it up, or we'll crush you underfoot."

"Get out of my shop," Will said. "Right now. I will not be spoken to like that. Who the devil do you think you are?"

The man simply sneered. He was a few inches taller than

Will, which put him over six foot, muscular and solidly built. The sort of man who wasn't often told where to get off. Today would be an exciting experience for him, then.

Will skirted round the desk to face up to him, blood singing. "I said, out. I don't have your damned daffodil book to my knowledge, and if I find it I'll feel free to sell it to someone more civil. Go on, clear off."

The man paused a second, arm muscles bulging. There was one slow tick of the clock during which Will was absolutely sure he was going to attack, and then he held up a hand, palm out. The action pulled back his coat sleeve and shirt cuff a little. "Take a moment to consider, Mr. Darling, before you make a very bad mistake. You would be well advised to think again."

"About what? Sling your hook before I make you."

"You will regret this," the man said in a growl.

"Pretty sure I won't," Will told him, and stalked behind him until his peculiar visitor slammed the door on his way out. He stayed near the shop entrance a little while, pretending to tidy the shelves and watching for the fellow's return, and finally calmed down enough to laugh at himself.

Throwing out a customer with money in his pocket! How quickly he'd adjusted to life as an antiquarian bookseller. It had been satisfying, but hardly the way to go if he wanted to keep eating. He got some very odd fish in here and he couldn't evict them all.

Still, he didn't need to swallow insults. You only had to do that when you were really hungry, and he had a packet of sausages in the back room waiting to go on the gas ring for lunch, a thought that drove the ill-mannered customer from his mind.

He did some tidying up to kill time before that blessed hour, sold a few three-shilling modern novels plus a fine edition of Macaulay's *Lays of Ancient Rome* for two pounds two shillings and sixpence, and ate his sausages in the happy consciousness of a good morning's work. The afternoon brought another flurry of customers, all perfectly rational by bookshop standards, and by the time he went to bed, he'd forgotten about the ill-mannered man in the mac.

He woke in the middle of the night.

Four years of war had left him able to sleep through a bombardment, but primed to wake at the slightest hint of stealthy movement—a rat, say, or the human equivalent trying to pinch his cigarettes. Will went from deep dreamless sleep to open-eyed alertness in the pitch dark, and for a minute wasn't quite sure where he was, or why he couldn't hear the bustle of movement and distant thunder of guns.

He was in the back room of the bookshop, of course. It had a door to the tiny yard and outhouse, a small window that looked onto the yard, and an internal door that opened on the shop floor. Will lay, first orienting himself, then trying to angle his hearing in the direction the sound had come from. As he strained his ears, he heard a very gentle but unmistakable riffle of paper.

Someone was in the shop. He sat up, and saw the faintest glimmer of light under the door. It wasn't from the street, since electric street lighting had yet to reach May's Buildings: a moment more saw it flicker in a way that confirmed his suspicions. Someone was in his shop, with a flashlight.

Will swung himself silently out of bed, careful not to make the rickety frame creak. He was wearing sufficiently robust flannel pyjamas that he could be confident in going out; he'd have been even more confident with his service revolver. Instead, he groped for the knife he used for onions, and felt a brief nostalgia as he grasped the handle in the dark. It was just like old times.

His uncle, in a rare burst of modernity, had had electricity put into the shop. There was a switch next to the back-room door. Will worked out his movements first, then eased the door handle round and the door open, and got his hand to the switch.

He shut his eyes as he flicked it and kicked the door fully open. There was a shout of surprise and, an instant later, a very familiar cascade of papery thumps.

Will opened his eyes to see two men, both black-clad and masked. One had gone headlong over a pile of books, sending them and himself to the floor; the other, holding an electric flashlight, was trying to pull him up.

"Hoi! You! Get out!" Will bellowed, and brandished the knife.

He'd expected them to flee. Instead, to his utter astonishment, the standing burglar swung round, dropped into a defensive crouch, and whipped out a knife of his own.

Who the hell came armed to rob a bookshop? Will dropped low, slicing out at the fellow's arm. His opponent blocked the attack while feinting with his own weapon, in a move practised enough to make Will very unhappy at his makeshift weapon.

The second man had now scrambled to his feet. Will shouted, "Thieves!" at the top of his voice, hoping to God there was a constable passing. He didn't want to take on two proficient fighters alone and in his pyjamas.

The second man was retreating, though, and as he did he snapped, "Come on!"

The knifeman lunged at Will again. Will twisted past the move and sliced through the cloth over bastard's cheek with his little blade, missing the eye but eliciting a curse. The second man snapped a word that sounded vaguely foreign, though his accent was English, then added, "Now, damn you!" in a commanding tone. The first turned, reluctantly, and they both ran for the door.

Will hurdled the spilled books and raced after them. They slammed the door in his face as they fled; he wrenched it open, setting the bell jangling wildly, to see them haring up the street. He followed for a few steps, then his bare foot landed on something sharp, slicing the skin and making him stumble, slip, and fall badly on the wet, uneven road, cracking his knee. "Jesus!"

He breathed down the variety of pains, hauled himself up, and looked around. The men were gone. May's Buildings was empty, dark and still. If anyone had heard the racket, they weren't turning on the lights or coming out to help.

He made his way back inside over the cold, wet pavement, limping and thinking.

Will didn't find it easy to get back to sleep and thus didn't approach the next morning with a great deal of grace. He went to the police station to report the break-in, and spent an infuriating hour with a desk sergeant who seemed to regard it as highly suspicious that he hadn't roamed the streets at three in the morning, searching for a constable. Even more suspicious was Will's assertion that the lock had been picked rather than the door forced, leaving no damage, and that nothing to his knowledge had been stolen.

"A burglary with no evidence of a break-in and nothing missing, Mr. Darling? Are you sure you didn't leave the door unlocked? No? Well, I'm afraid we're very busy here but I'll ask someone to come round and take your statement in due course."

Will requested firmly that he should give a statement at once for the record, and the whole tedious business took up nearly two hours of his morning. He returned to the shop to find a rude note from a customer outraged that he was closed, and another from a neighbour requesting that he refrain from raucous drunkenness in the small hours. After that he discovered that the tea-caddy was empty so had to go out *again* on his painfully cut foot, and overall he was in a decidedly poor state of mind by three o'clock, when the bell jangled and two men approached his desk.

Brass, was his instant thought. They wore suits and carried umbrellas, but he could tell brass when he saw it, even in mufti. He knew an impulse to stand and salute, which he resisted.

The first officer—gentleman, rather—was in his fifties, with a little grey toothbrush moustache. The second was pink, round-faced and curly-haired, which rather gave him the air of a large baby.

"Mr. William Darling?" the older said. "My name is Ingoldsby. This is Mr. Price. May I have a few minutes of your time?"

"Certainly. What can I do for you?"

Ingoldsby nodded to Price, who slipped away. Will raised a brow. "The door," Ingoldsby said. "This is a private conversation. Is there anyone else on the premises?"

"Not unless I'm being burgled."

"I heard about that." Ingoldsby looked around for a chair. With a little reluctance, Will removed a stack of books from the spare and gestured to him to sit down. "Thank you. As I said, I am Captain Charles Ingoldsby, and I am with the War Office."

Will sat straight up at that, an automatic response. "Sir."

"And I dare say you know what this is about."

Will considered that from several angles. "No, sir. I don't."

Ingoldsby's brows rose in that upper-class way they seemed to teach at Eton. "Really, Darling?"

That's Mr. Darling to you, I'm not in uniform, Will thought, but didn't quite say. "I have no idea. All I know— Hold on, just a second. What do you mean you heard about my burglary?"

"The War Office is interested in you, for reasons that should be very obvious."

"What? Why?"

Ingoldsby shot him a scathing glance. "This is official business. You would be ill advised to waste my time."

"I've absolutely no idea what you're talking about. You'll have to explain."

Ingoldsby huffed with irritation. "Draven's letter."

Will waited for more. It didn't come. "Who?"

"Stop playing the fool! You have corresponded with him for years. We know what he sent you, it is ours, we want it back, and your refusal to cooperate will have extremely serious consequences. Draven sent you a communication six weeks ago—"

"The information," Will said, light dawning at last. "This character Draven sent the information."

Ingoldsby sat back, calming down a little. "Yes. The information. That is what I want, and at once."

"Bad luck," Will said. "You've got the wrong Darling."

Ingoldsby took that in for an unblinking moment. "I beg your pardon?"

"My uncle, Mr. William Darling, owned this place until he died a fortnight ago. Monday before last. I'd worked here for a few weeks before he was taken ill. I moved in to look after him when he had a stroke, ten days before his death. If Draven was communicating with a William Darling, it was him, not me. I've never heard of the fellow, and I have no idea what he sent, far less where it is."

"You mentioned it. You know that it exists."

"No, I don't know that. All I know is that you're not the first person to ask for it. I had a bad-tempered sort in here yesterday, demanding some sort of information with veiled threats. I thought he meant a book he'd ordered. He got very shirty about it. And, as noted, I also had a burglary last night, two men who seemed to be searching my desk but didn't touch the petty cash box. One of them had a knife. What's all this about, Captain Ingoldsby?"

"Can you describe the man you spoke to yesterday?"

"About six foot one, perhaps, well built, muscular. Brown hair, receding a little. Light eyes—grey or blue, perhaps. And I'll bet he's got a shallow cut on his face where I caught him with a knife last night, because I'm pretty sure it was him burgling the place."

"Your police report said the burglar was masked."

Ingoldsby had read the report he'd filed just that morning. Will found that vaguely worrying. "He was, but he had the same build and pale eyes. And the man I spoke to yesterday had a little tattoo on the underside of his wrist, where a watch-strap might go." Will indicated the point on his own wrist. "I couldn't make out what it was, I only saw it for a second. Perhaps a sailboat? There was a triangular shape to it. But I definitely saw a tattoo in the same spot when I engaged with the enemy—the burglar, rather, last night."

"Did you." Ingoldsby sounded calm, but his eyes were far away. "Libra."

The last word was almost under his breath. Will said, "What?

"No concern of yours."

"It's my concern if he broke in here and pulled a knife on

me. And *libra* sounds like what the other man said to him. Isn't it the Latin for book?"

Ingoldsby pressed his lips together in thought, and didn't answer. That was becoming irritating. "This is very informative, but not the information I came for. Where is that?"

"I told you. I don't have the foggiest."

"You must know." Ingoldsby sounded frustrated. "Did your uncle destroy any papers?"

"If he did, it wasn't in my presence. He never asked me to destroy any papers for him."

"Have you gone through his recent correspondence?"

"Only to look for bills and orders. I've a job on to get this place sorted out."

Ingoldsby took a slow survey of the shop, a sneer raising his upper lip and Will's hackles. "So I see. We can save you that task."

"Sorry?"

"My men will search your uncle's correspondence and all private papers. If they don't find it there, they will have to extend the search. Considering the conditions of this establishment, we may well need to take charge of the property until it's found. You should go to a hotel."

"Right, good idea," Will said. "Just one thing. Where's your warrant?"

"I beg your pardon?"

"Warrant. Magna Carta, remember? You don't just walk in here and tell me you'll be going through my private papers. We've got laws in this country."

Ingoldsby sighed pointedly. "There is no need for a warrant if you grant your permission for the search to take place."

"Why should I do that?"

"As a soldier, Darling, you should understand that some

orders must be given without explanation and obeyed without question. This is one of those."

"I remember those orders," Will said. "They usually killed a lot of men. And by the way, I'm not a soldier any more, and it's Mr. Darling, thank you. Come back with a warrant and I'll have a look at it."

"Do you—" Ingoldsby cut himself off. "Let me impress on you, *Mr.* Darling, that this is a matter of grave importance. The War Office needs this information."

"But you won't tell me what it is or why."

"It's a classified matter."

"So you want me to take your word for it and hand over my business without explanation." Will was extremely angry, he realised, so angry he could feel the tremor in his muscles. "We aren't at war any more. I have *rights*."

"Are you a Socialist, Mr. Darling? An anarchist?"

Will almost laughed. "Oh, here we go. If I don't do exactly what you say, I must be trying to bring down the state. No, I'm not an anarchist. I believe in the rule of law and the rights of an Englishman's home to be his castle, which is more than you seem to do, because this is my home and the papers you want to search are my property. You have no right to walk in here and demand them."

"I have a need. Your *country* has a need, and as a soldier, I would expect you to extend every assistance."

"For crying out loud," Will said. "My uncle was an anti-quarian bookseller! What possible information could he have had? No, don't tell me, it's classified," he added, before Ingoldsby could say it himself. "If you share your information with me, I'll consider sharing mine with you. If not, you can come back with a warrant from a judge once you've explained to him why you're entitled to search the house of a private citizen who isn't suspected of any wrongdoing. Now, the door's over there. I've a business to run."

He enjoyed ushering Ingoldsby out. He'd been a working part in the State machine for years, a tool to be used, easily replaceable if he broke. He hadn't particularly minded it at the time—there was a job to be done, one at which he'd proved rather good. But he wasn't a tool any more, and he was damned if he'd be put back in that box without a by-your-leave.

It felt less good by nightfall, as he locked up. He'd added bolts to the door as part of his day's work, but there were no shutters to stop anyone who wanted to smash a window. He didn't have a gun and rather regretted that.

What he did have at the bottom of his box was a German Nahkampfmesser, a trench knife with an eight-inch blade and a nicely carved wooden grip that its previous owner had put a lot of effort into. Will had taken it off that owner once he was no longer in a position to use it. The German Army had issued damned good knives, and it was a lot better than the sharpened barbed-wire stakes or cut-down bayonets his battalion had been reduced to. He'd brought the Messer back to Blighty, and it was one of the few possessions he'd never pawned. That wasn't a sentimental attachment: he'd known he'd want it if he ended up on the streets.

He dug the Messer out now, making a note to find a knife-grinder to put a better edge on it, and placed it by his bed in its leather sheath.

It seemed mildly ridiculous as a precaution, but the whole business was absurd. What had Uncle William to do with the War Office, or with the sort of men who threatened and burgled? Will would have assumed the whole thing was a mistake, except that Ingoldsby had unquestionably recognised the description he'd given of the man with the wrist tattoo.

It had to be a misunderstanding. Anyone who'd had deal-ings with the War Office knew exactly how shambolic they could be. Probably Uncle William was this Draven chap's old school chum, and the missing communication would turn out to be a Christmas card.

He told himself that. But he still lay awake until the small hours, listening to every creak and rustle.

TWO

Will went to see his friend Maisie Jones the next day.

Maisie was a smart young lady, with a lilting Welsh accent. They'd met when Will got a job fetching and carrying for her previous employer, and struck up a conversation over their un-London voices—Maisie had left Cardiff after the Tiger Bay race riots, seeing no more future there than Will had in Northamptonshire, though neither had found London's streets paved with gold. She was round-faced and bright-eyed, with brown skin, black hair ruthlessly marcelled into waves, a quick mind, and a smile that lit rooms.

Will had asked her dancing early on in their acquaintance, and they'd had some very pleasant evenings. Then he had walked into a storeroom at work, and found the senior shop-floor clerk trapping her there. He'd removed the man without ceremony, using his boot, and been summarily dismissed.

That had put a stop to dancing, because he'd had to save his pennies and his shoe leather. It had also changed his relations with Maisie over the months that followed. She'd refused to let him slip out of sight, demanded he come round for tea, bought him meals when he'd accept them, pressed him to accept a loan of ten shillings that kept a dosshouse roof over his head in a week of desperation, and bullied him into writing to his long-estranged uncle. That last had changed his life.

He'd set any thought of romance firmly aside—it was bad enough to be scrounging off her without being a bloody gigolo about it—and they'd come to be friends in a way you couldn't be with a girl if your intention was to get her on her back. That was a pity in its way because Will liked her a great deal, but friendship was no sort of second best in this lonely, teeming city.

Maisie worked at a milliner's on Lexington Street, which had a fancy French name and served women who, she said, needed to look at exciting hats while they bought boring ones. He waited for her to come out at lunchtime, took her to a Lyon's Corner House, and launched into his story.

Maisie listened, frowning. "What an extraordinary business. Have you searched for this paper or letter, or whatever it is?"

"I started going through my uncle's correspondence this morning. The problem is, I don't know what I'm trying to find, and my uncle left more paper than you can shake a stick at. There's boxes and boxes with letters just thrown in any old how, and I moved a lot of it around to make a space to sleep in when I was taking care of him. So if it was ordered once, it isn't now."

"Hmm. Would you consider letting one of them have a go? The War Office fellow, or the one who offered to pay you?" Her eyes lit with laughter. "Look at you, as if I'd said you should stand on your head. You are the stubbornest man, Will Darling."

"I don't like being pushed around. The fellow with the

threats can go whistle. Breaking in and pulling a knife on me."

"You pulled a knife on him first, and I don't need to say what I think about *that*. Why not let the War Office look, though, if it's important? Isn't that something you ought to do?"

"Because..." He struggled to put his feelings into words. Maisie was very good at asking difficult questions. "Because if someone sent it to my uncle, then shouldn't I be sure what it is before I give it away? Maybe my uncle was supposed to keep it safe for this Draven character."

"Your uncle didn't say anything about it?"

Will shook his head. "He couldn't speak after the stroke. He was trying, I'm sure of that, but whether it was to tell me important secrets or just wanting his voice back, I've no way of knowing."

"No." Maisie traced a pattern on the tabletop in spilled tea. "I don't mean to say anything against your uncle, Will, but people don't behave like this over honest business."

"No."

"If this Mr. Draven had sent your uncle a rare book to take care of, whoever wanted it back would just say so, wouldn't they?"

"Yes."

"But information that people threaten you about, and gentlemen come in search of it and even break in, and not one of them will say what it is—"

"I know. I was thinking extortion," Will said. "I'd rather not believe that of my uncle. I didn't know him well enough to be sure, but I'd have called him a good man. He fell out with my father on some point of principle, since they were both pretty obstinate—"

"Runs in the family, does it?"

"—but Ma never suggested that that he did anything bad.

And I certainly haven't found piles of money lying around, which you might expect if he was a blackmailer."

"But he wouldn't need to be doing it himself," Maisie said. "What if Draven is the blackmailer, and he wanted your uncle to keep something incriminating safe for him? Because if that's the case, you should let them have it back."

"That's true. But which 'them'? Because there's two lots of people who want it, and it can't belong to them both. And if I give it to the wrong one—"

"Yes, of course. Ugh, this is a tangle. Is it your job to untangle it?"

"My uncle left me everything," Will said. "I was on my uppers, and now I have a shop and an income and a decent bit of money coming my way. That makes me responsible, surely. If Uncle promised Draven to hold on to this thing, or if he had a good reason to keep the information secret, shouldn't I respect his wish?"

"I suppose so. Well, it's simple then."

"Is it?"

"You have to find it," Maisie decreed. "You can't make a sensible decision till you know what you're deciding about, and we're only guessing it's blackmail. Maybe it's the birth certificate of a child from a secret marriage who'll disinherit the War Office fellow from an earldom. I expect the burglar man is his illegitimate elder brother, only it turns out he's really the legitimate one. The fate of an English noble house hangs on this, Will Darling."

"It does?"

"Of course it does. Or maybe—"

Maisie was an avid reader of the romantic story papers. Will threw in a few of the more implausible ideas he'd come up with, and the rest of the lunch passed in increasingly silly speculation.

It wasn't useful, as such but it made Will feel a lot less

alone, and a fair bit clearer in his head. Maisie was right: he had to find the thing first. He shouldn't hand over anything to anyone before he knew that was the proper thing to do. Why, he only had Ingoldsby's word for it that he was War Office at all. He'd obey a warrant; otherwise the fellow could go whistle. And meanwhile, he'd have a look through the boxes of papers and see what he could find. It all needed doing at some point anyway, God help him.

Will was methodically working on a pile of papers a foot high, the first of many, when the shop bell jangled. He was less than pleased to see Captain Ingoldsby again.

"Got your warrant?" he enquired in lieu of greeting.

Ingoldsby gave a tight, unamused smile. "I hoped to find you in a more reasonable frame of mind, Mr. Darling. You've had time to consider your position. You must see that the only sensible and responsible course of action is to offer the assistance your country requires."

"No warrant, then."

"This isn't a joke," Ingoldsby snapped. "Your refusal to cooperate—"

"I don't even know who you are," Will said. "You haven't shown me proof you're from the War Office, let alone told me why I should help you. If this information is so important, you should be grateful I didn't give it over to the first man who asked."

"So you do have it," Ingoldsby said swiftly.

"What? No. Figure of speech. I'll judge what's right and do it, and I won't be bullied into acting before I'm ready."

"And what if—the other party—breaks in again? What if they find it first?"

Will gestured around the shop. "You think you can find anything in here?"

"Notwithstanding—"

"No. My uncle left me everything he had. If that includes a promise or a responsibility, I'll deal with that in my own way. Barracking me won't help you."

"You are an extremely stubborn man, Mr. Darling."

"That's the second time I've heard that today."

Ingoldsby's lip curled. "If this is a matter of, shall we say, compensation for your cooperation—"

"It isn't."

"Holding out for the highest bidder can be dangerous. I would not advise you to do it."

"I told you," Will said. "I'll give this thing, whatever it is, to its rightful owner. If that's you, you've nothing to worry about."

Ingoldsby turned on his heel, then looked back. "You should be careful in whatever game you're playing, Mr. Darling. Very careful indeed."

Will stayed up late, clearing out two boxes of papers without finding any sort of communication from Draven, or anything that might be a secret. He started again the next morning after a night without incident, kneeling on the floor of the back room as he went through ancient delivery notes, payment requests, covering letters, invoices. He tried not to curse his uncle for administrative incompetence, but it was difficult.

By early afternoon, he wanted to curse a lot of people. The shop door bell had only jangled three times since he'd opened up at nine in the morning, and he'd taken a total of four and sixpence. He needed to be selling books, not wasting time on this nonsense.

He leapt to his feet when the door went again, or at least tried to. The cut on his foot still hurt, and his legs were stiff with kneeling. He cursed, stumbled, and straightened up fast as he heard the cascading thud of books hitting the floor.

Will headed rapidly round two sets of shelves, and came face to face with a giant. The man had to be a good six foot five, heavily bearded, and he was sweeping brawny armfuls of books off the shelves near him and hurling them on the floor.

"What the hell are you doing?" Will demanded.

The big man turned, made eye contact, and quite deliberately dropped another armful of books onto the pile at his feet. He pointed a sausagelike finger at Will. "Where's the information?"

"You're bloody joking. Who are you from?"

The giant took a step forward. Will stepped back involuntarily: the bastard was huge. "Where is it?"

"I don't know!"

The giant swung his other hand at a shelf, a careless gesture that sent books flying. "Oi!" Will shouted.

"Tell me!" The brute bunched a massive fist.

Will had left the Messer in the back room, hadn't thought he'd need it in broad daylight. He retreated a couple of steps. The giant strode forward menacingly, and Will pivoted to kick him on the kneecap as hard as he could.

The giant lurched and howled, but didn't go down. That was worrying. Will tried another kick, aiming to keep his distance since he'd be murdered at close quarters, and the big man caught his foot and twisted. Will threw himself into the movement rather than risking a broken ankle by resisting. He hit the floor, tried to roll away, and found a bookshelf in his face. He scrabbled backwards, trying to get away and up, but he couldn't kick himself free from the giant's grip.

The big man swung his foot with enough force to smash Will's jaw if he'd connected. Will lurched sideways, thrashing his leg to get free. The giant growled in a deep bass, got his balance, and raised his foot again, this time to stamp.

"Hoi!" someone shouted. "What's going on? Stop!"

The giant swung an arm behind him to bat away the intruder, and twisted over backwards with a yell, as if that arm had been seized. He also let Will's ankle go. *sexy n cool*

Will hadn't survived the war by missing God-given opportunities. He sprang to his feet, took a step back for run-up, and kicked the giant in the balls with all the strength he had. The impact made a satisfying thud.

The big man doubled over with a strangled noise. Behind him stood a slender, well-dressed man who appeared somewhat startled.

Will's instincts told him to follow up with a few solid boots to the giant's head. He forced that down, given the presence of a witness. "Watch out!" he said instead. "Man's a lunatic."

"I saw— Whoa!" The man recoiled as the giant lurched to his feet. It showed impressive stamina considering how hard Will had kicked him.

Will grabbed the table lamp off his desk, jerking the cord hard to pull the plug from its socket. It was an ungainly thing with a heavy metal four-cornered base that should do some damage applied to a skull. He brandished it meaningfully. The giant weighed up the situation, gave Will a glare of pure loathing, turned, and lumbered for the door, knocking the newcomer out of the way.

Sod that. Will went for him, but the other man moved at the same time and they collided with one another. Will attempted to get by without actually pushing his rescuer to the ground, but the other man was doing the same thing while moving the same way as Will, so they kept blocking each other. A jangle of bells indicated that the giant had pulled open the door.

"Hell!" Will shoved the newcomer out of the way as courteously as possible, and ran. The giant had picked up speed and was heading out of May's Buildings in the direction of Bedfordbury. Will sprinted a few steps, lamp in hand, before his thinking brain overtook his fighting one to enquire whether he really wanted to take on a man that size who might well feel quite ill-disposed to him by now.

He stopped. "Damn."

"Has he gone?" The newcomer had followed him outside.

"Seems so."

"A lunatic, you said? Was that an unprovoked attack? Shall I call the police?"

Will thought rapidly. "N-no. Best not."

"Are you sure? If you say so," the other man said dubiously, as Will turned back to the shop. "Oh, you're limping. Are you hurt?"

"No. Well, yes, but that was something else. I cut my foot."

"You've been in the wars. Can I get you a drink? Cup of tea, something stronger?"

Will stopped in the doorway to have a shufti at him. The newcomer was a fraction taller than himself, notably slimmer of build, and perhaps a little older, maybe close to thirty. The body that had collided with Will's had been firm enough, but if he was in training it was for long-distance rather than weights. He had dark hair under a fashionable sort of hat, and very dark eyes, the sort that appeared black in some lights, brown in others. Welsh colouring, Will thought. He sounded the epitome of upper-class English, and he looked upper-class too, of the nervy sort vaguely reminiscent of a greyhound, rather than the pink chinless kind. Not bad at all, if one liked the type.

"I beg your pardon, I haven't introduced myself," the man said, offering a well-kept hand. Will's were callused with heavy lifting, dusty with paper, sweaty from the fight. He wiped them on his trousers. The man didn't flinch as they shook. "My name's Secretan, Kim Secretan. Am I addressing a Darling, by any chance? You have a look of the late proprietor."

It constantly sounds like Will is being hit on lol

"Will Darling. He was my uncle."

"I'm sorry for your loss," Secretan said. "He was a marvellous bookman. Have you taken on the shop? I don't think I've seen you here before."

"He left it to me. I'm not a bookman myself, but I'm learning."

"When allowed to go about your business uninterrupted. Quite seriously, that must have been a horrible experience. At least sit down for a while and make sure you're not too upset."

"It's nothing."

"Being attacked is hardly nothing."

"I was in Flanders," Will pointed out with a smile.

"But this is England. You didn't expect to risk life and limb when you got up this morning."

Will wasn't sure if being fussed over like this was amusing or annoying. It might be both. "I'm fine. You've no need to concern yourself, I'm sure you have somewhere you need to be."

"My dear chap, this is a *bookshop*. There's never anywhere better to be. Good heavens, that fellow made a mess." Secretan contemplated the books on the floor with dismay. "These will all need reshelving. May I assist you?"

"There's nothing to assist with. They just go back on the shelves. There's no order to it."

Secretan grimaced. "There isn't, is there? Your uncle had the bibliophile's habit of mind, rather than the librarian's.

Which is to say, I'm sure he knew where everything was." He didn't sound sure of that at all.

"That's about the size of it. It's in no sort of order, there isn't an inventory, and I don't have a clue what I've got here." That came out sounding more like despair than a statement of fact. Will pulled himself together. "It'll be a task to sort out, but I'm jolly lucky to have it."

Secretan nodded. "The work would tax an experienced man, delightful though it is. Do you have someone who can help you go through it?"

That was as polite a way of saying 'you have no idea what you're doing, do you?' as Will could remember. "I wouldn't know who to ask. I don't know the trade. I didn't know my uncle until a couple of months ago and I only did a few weeks' work here before he died. I really am starting from scratch."

"Right," Secretan said. "Could I return to the subject of a drink? You look like you need one."

"I—" Will did want a drink, he realised. It was one thing to confront a burglar at night, quite another to be attacked in broad daylight by someone who could have broken him in half. That sort of alarm took a while to leave the body. In addition to which, Secretan appeared to be wealthy, friendly, and knowledgeable about the book trade. He'd be a fool to turn that connection down, or indeed a free drink. "All right. Thanks. Let me just ask the chap over the road to keep an eye out for giants."

They went to the Black Horse at the other end of May's Buildings, as the best of the three pubs on the little street. It was around two in the afternoon, so the lunchtime rush had gone. They took a table, and Secretan supplied a gin and tonic for himself and a bottle of Guinness for Will.

"To prosperity," he said, clinking glasses. "I've been

assuming you'll keep the place on, which is doubtless selfish desire. Is that your plan?"

"If I can. I don't really know what else to do. I'd just turned eighteen in the summer of '14, and joined up right at the start."

Secretan nodded. "And came out at the end to discover that employers are very grateful for your service, but unfortunately...?"

Everyone knew the situation: too many men, not enough jobs. You could hardly miss it while men with military bearing and rows of medals stood in the street with trays of matchboxes, one step up from begging. "That's the way of it," Will said. "A fit country for heroes to live in."

Secretan gave a wry smile. "They say you can't become a West End chorus boy without the Military Cross."

Will held the Military Cross, as it happened, and he'd have become a chorus boy like a shot if he'd had the build for it. "Exactly. And the shop's a going concern so I'd be a fool to give it up."

"It's certainly a marvellous opportunity. So bookselling isn't the family business?"

"Just my uncle. I don't have any other family." He expanded on that, in response to a quick, darting glance of concern. "My father died when I was very young. My mother got the Spanish 'flu."

"I'm sorry. That's hard lines. And you didn't know your uncle well, you said?"

"Not at all. He and my father fell out before I was born and Ma never got in touch, as far as I know, but when I wrote to him earlier this year, he welcomed me with open arms. I wish I'd mended matters before, but at least I was with him for the end."

"Yes, that's important. And he left you the shop?"

"He didn't have anyone else either. I'd like to keep it going, for his sake as well as mine. He loved the place."

"Here's to that." Secretan tipped his glass. His eyes were the colour of Will's Guinness, deep and dark. "I could recommend some very good men to help you assess what you have, if that would be useful."

Will had no idea what that might cost. "It might well, but probate won't be granted for a few months yet."

"Of course. Well, the offer's there should you need it, though I'm sure you'll find your feet."

"Thanks."

Will sipped his drink, staring into its depths because he felt somewhat awkward. He'd have very much liked to embrace the offer of help, but he didn't know how to ask, *Would these men work for a share of profits rather than cash up front?* Secretan didn't seem like he knew about not having cash up front, and the question might be embarrassingly naive. There probably wouldn't be profits worth splitting anyway.

Still, the man seemed friendly: he could ask. Will looked up from his pint to form a question, caught Secretan watching him, and instantly forgot what he'd been going to say.

Because Secretan was watching him. His absurdly dark eyes were dwelling on Will's face, and he didn't look away when Will met his gaze, so that their eyes locked and held for a couple of seconds too long before Secretan lowered long lashes and picked up his gin.

Well.

He wasn't sure what he thought about that. Secretan was decidedly attractive, and Will didn't have so many opportunities for recreation that he was eager to turn one down. It was just that he could have really used a knowledgeable friend right now, and he wasn't keen on offers of help that were contingent on getting his prick out.

When is it my turn?

He opened his mouth, but Secretan spoke first.

"You know, I hope you don't mind me saying so, but you really do seem worn out. And I can't help thinking that if I were randomly attacked by an oversized lunatic, I'd make a considerable amount of fuss, whereas you seemed quite unsurprised. Added to which, I did hear what he was shouting and he didn't sound like a lunatic. I'd have said he had a very clear purpose."

Will blinked, thrown by the unexpected words, and also by his own error. Had he misinterpreted that look as interest when it had been examination? That could have been catastrophic. He was clearly out of practice.

His face must have showed something because Secretan added, "I realise it's none of my business. It's just that there's clearly something up, I liked the little I knew of your uncle, and mostly I am insatiably curious. It's my besetting sin. So I will ask once more whether you're really all right, and if I can help at all." He raised his hands. "And if you say no, I'll drop the subject."

Will opened his mouth to say he was fine, and closed it again. He *wasn't* fine. He was in a mess, with no idea what was going on or how to proceed, and no allies except a milliner with a vivid imagination. He found himself saying, "I'm...not entirely all right. No."

"Do you want to talk about it?"

So Will did. He told him how the strange man with the tattoo had demanded information, about the burglary, and the visit from Ingoldsby who claimed to be from the War Office. Secretan stopped him there.

"Do you think he was a fake?"

"I've no idea. He didn't show me papers."

"I dare say he considered it beneath him to have to do any such thing. I see your concern. As it happens a pal of mine is in the WO. Would it be useful if I checked they had such a chap as this Ingoldsby on the books?"

"Lord, yes," Will said with his whole heart. "That would be marvellous. Would you mind?"

"Not at all. I can see you have enough problems without additional uncertainty. Carry on."

Secretan was an extremely intelligent listener, mostly silent except to request expansion or clarification. When Will had finished, he drew a breath. "You *have* been going it. Tell me something: if Ingoldsby proves to be the real thing, will you give him this paper?"

"I don't have it to give."

"No, of course not. Let him search for it, I should say, or hand it over if it turns up."

"I don't know. I don't like any of this. Suppose it's discreditable to someone? What if this Draven character had secret information he shouldn't have had?"

"Then wouldn't the WO be the best place for it?"

"I was in Flanders. I don't have the highest regard for the War Office." `What the fuck is Flanders?`

"Fair point."

"And suppose it's private matters? Suppose someone trusted my uncle with a secret that might be unlawful, perhaps, but isn't harming anyone else—"

Secretan was already nodding, without needing that spelled out further. "Yes, I follow you."

"For all I know, whatever it is might belong to the other chaps," Will said. "I can't assume the War Office has the right of it just because they're official. I'm not here to do Special Branch's job for them."

"You think this is a Special Branch matter?" Secretan's brows rose.

"War Office, talk of national security, several men working together on the other side, the tattoo—I know it sounds like the worst popular fiction, but I honestly wondered if they might be some sort of...well, gang. The man who confronted me didn't sound foreign, or Irish, but they could be anarchists or communists, I suppose."

"Would you sympathise if they were?"

Will shrugged. "I'll be voting Labour if this election comes about, and higher taxes and redistribution of wealth sound like good things to me. But I don't like bombs, or blowing up civilians."

"Moderate of you." *Witty* ♡

"Anyway, I'm probably wrong. For all I know, the information is a treasure map and they're all seeking the lost crown of the Anglo-Saxons."

Secretan grinned at that. He had a good smile, one that warmed his eyes and made the nervy expression disappear. It was the sort of smile you'd want a friend to have. "Good Lord, Darling." *IT SOUNDS SO FLIRTY!*

"I've been thinking about this too much."

"I can tell. Well, I doubt that's the answer, though it would be delightful, but I see your dilemma. You want to do the right thing by your uncle, by anyone to whom he might have made a commitment, and by your own standard of morality. Unfortunately, you don't know what that right thing *is*."

"That's about it."

"Then we should start by finding out," Secretan said. "I will ask about Ingoldsby, and I will also see if I can track down this Draven chappie. It's not a common name, is it? If it belongs to a known blackmailer or Bolshevik, we might have a better idea of what this is about."

Will sat back, startled. "Can you do that?"

"I can try. I know plenty of people who are awfully good at getting things done and can tell me how to go about it if I get stuck. I shall put enquiries in motion, as I believe the police say. And then—would you care for a hand sorting your uncle's papers, at all?"

"You don't want to do that."

"Oh, I *do*," Secretan said. "You can't tell me a story like this and not expect me to be fascinated. I'm desperate to know how this will turn out. If it earns me a seat in the front row, I shall search through papers till my eyes and fingers bleed."

Will couldn't help laughing. Secretan smiled back, and like blazes had Will been wrong, because if that wasn't an appreciative look, he was a Dutchman.

No matter. Secretan was extending a helping hand. If he was *also* appreciative—well, Will had hoped for a friend. A friend who wanted to fuck would be even better. *LOL*

"Thanks, Secretan," he said. "I'm grateful."

"Don't be. It's my pleasure. And—would you mind?—absolutely everybody calls me Kim. 'Secretan' always makes me expect a teacher to come looming over my shoulder." He shuddered delicately.

"All right then. And it's Will."

Kim raised his glass. Will clinked it. It seemed they had a deal.

THREE

The afternoon's work was a little less tedious on the back of two bottles of Guinness—they'd had just time for another before the pub shut at three—and the prospect of a bit of help. Will didn't let his mind linger on the other prospect, in case it didn't come off. He wasn't entirely sure how one went about these things in Civvy Street, at least when one knew the other fellow's name, but if Kim wanted to indulge, he'd doubtless say so. He was posh; he'd expect to have things for the asking.

That said, he wasn't a greatly forthcoming sort. They'd talked about this and that, and Kim had borne his fair share of the conversation in light and witty tones, but somehow Will hadn't come away knowing any more about his companion. Then again, he had given his own views fairly frankly, so it was possible Kim had decided to hold back the details of privilege to avoid awkwardness. He'd known a couple of officers like that, careful never to mention the things that set them apart from the common men, as if you couldn't tell.

Another night passed without disturbance. That was a relief, though Will didn't take it as a good sign. If he were the tattooed man, he'd let the interfering bookseller do the hard work and move in when the treasure turned up, rather than attempting to locate a needle in a haystack by torchlight.

The next day, he found a letter.

It was in a shoebox on top of a row of elderly Wisdens behind the desk, and contained mostly carriage notes and requests for this or that book. Will was putting those in a pile with the aim of taking the addresses for a list of possible customers, and he damn near put this one on it too before his mind shouted at his hand to stop. It was on plain cream notepaper, a tight angular hand in black ink, with no letter-head, address, or date.

I love this

My dear Darling,

> *You gave me grave words in your last and I have come to fear you are right. My work is only graves, and my gain accordingly.*
>
> *I have destroyed almost all, but I must preserve the fruit. Keep the enclosed safe for me. If you are asked to give it up, the word is Bluebell. Nobody must have it without that safeguard. I am sorry to burden you with this.*
>
> *Burn this letter. I dare say you will want to burn the other, but I know you too well.*
>
> *Yours ever,*
>
> *Draven*
>
> *I hope we will meet again, but I am afraid.*

Will read the letter several times, then sat back in his creaky chair to think.

My work is only graves. He didn't like that, and he didn't like any of the implications behind the need for a password, or the one Draven had used. He really didn't like the confirmation that his uncle had received the 'enclosed' without any hints as to what it was or where he might have put the damn thing. He hoped, strongly, that Kim would turn up this

Draven character safe and well. The last line did not fill him with optimism.

He considered for a moment, then found a pair of scissors in the desk, carefully snipped out *the word is Bluebell*, and burned the shred of paper in an ashtray before he could have second thoughts.

The bookshop didn't have a safe, and cashboxes were far too portable. Will was quite unable to decide what to do with the letter, and ended up sticking it in his pocket as the shop door opened.

Inevitably, he was faced with a busy day just when he could have used a dearth of customers. He sold a volume of Marlowe's plays, a cheap Bagehot, a full set of Trollope's Palliser novels, casebound, and two collections of poetry. He took in catalogues from three book dealers who stayed to offer condolences on his uncle's death, and cast a suspicious eye on everyone who came in to browse in case they started turfing books on the floor. Nothing out of the ordinary happened at all, unless you counted a good day's takings, and his nerves were strung up to fever pitch by five past five when the bell jangled *again*.

"We're closed!" he shouted across the shop, though admittedly his tone was rather more that of 'sod off'.

"I'm glad to hear it."

It was Kim's voice, giving Will a rush of relief. He swung round the bookshelf that obscured his view at the same time Kim did, just managing not to collide with him.

Kim gave a slightly startled smile. "In a hurry?"

He was wearing a different suit, something beautifully cut in a fawn sort of shade that suited his colouring, with a dark brown handkerchief protruding from his pocket. He was so spotless and elegant as to make Will aware that he wanted a wash.

"I've news," Will said.

so flirty

"So have I." Kim's eyes glinted.

"Let me lock up first. If you're all right to talk in here?"

"There is nowhere I would rather be," Kim assured him, and waited for him to secure the door.

"Back room?" Will suggested as he returned. "I'd rather not be observed."

Kim's eyebrow rose, just a little twitch, but enough to make Will redden. He jerked a thumb at the windows that ran along one wall.

"Quite so," Kim said. "Lead on. Good heavens, are these your quarters?"

The back room wasn't a bad space. It had the camp bed, a gas fire with an attachment for cooking, a sink with a tap, a dresser that could have held six times as many clothes as he currently owned. Kim had doubtless never lived like this: even during the war, most officers had done better for themselves. In the context of the housing crisis that had been going on for the last years, it was luxury. At least he didn't have to share the room with five others. "It does for me."

"Highly efficient," Kim said, tossing his hat on the dresser, next to the Messer. He couldn't have failed to notice the eight-inch blade but he didn't comment. "I suppose one uses the bed as a sofa? Comfortable *and* economical."

"I can bring in a chair if you like."

"Not on my account, dear fellow. I am big with news." He seated himself neatly at the end of the bed. Will took the other end, shifting his pillow out of the way rather self-consciously.

"Well," Kim said. "Who wants to go first?"

"You."

"All right. Firstly, I am disappointed to report that Captain Ingoldsby is indeed who he says he is, in that he's at the War Office and is considered highly conscientious if not likeable.

So if the official imprimatur sways your decision, you have it."

"Mph. If he's War Office, why couldn't he get a warrant to search the shop?"

"Good question," Kim said. "It may have to do with the second part of my news, which is that a man called Professor Edward Draven was found dead a fortnight ago. He seems to have taken cyanide."

"You're joking."

"I am not. Draven was a scientist who worked in his own well-equipped laboratory at home. There was surprisingly little information about his death in the newspapers, a mere sentence or two about the coroner's report."

Will whistled. "How did you find that out?"

"I started with Who's Who, which gave one sole Draven, in his early sixties, your uncle's age. He was a widower and left no dependents, according to the newspaper. His will, if he left one, might point us to somebody who can give more information, but it appears we have to wait for it to be lodged at Somerset House to have a squizz at it."

"I'm jolly glad you're in this with me," Will said. "I'd never have thought of that."

"I'm sure you would, but glad to be of service. So, to recap, the War Office is formally interested in information that was sent to your uncle by a scientist who was later found dead by his own hand. That's starting to sketch a rather worrying picture, to my mind."

"This might colour it in a bit." Will pulled out the letter and handed it over.

Kim read it, eyebrows moving steadily up. "Good Lord. Good *Lord*."

"I know."

"Were the censor's scissors yours?"

"Draven gave a code word, without which my uncle

wasn't supposed to hand anything over. That isn't much use if you let people see it, so I cut it out and burned it."

"A wise precaution, except—well, you do realise you've tied yourself irrevocably into this situation now?"

"I'm tied in it anyway. Listen. When the first chap turned up asking for the information, he said to me, 'the word is daffodil'. I thought he wanted a gardening book, but he must have meant Draven's code word."

"And that was 'daffodil'?"

"No, it wasn't, but it was a flower. A different one."

Kim's brows drew together. "That might be a very unlikely coincidence. Or it might suggest that someone had been putting pressure on Draven to hand over the information, and he gave them something sufficiently close to the truth that he could make it sound plausible—"

"Before he killed himself."

"Before he ingested cyanide, yes," Kim said. "I don't like that at all."

"Nor do I."

"This is gnarly stuff, Will. I understand that you are taking on your uncle's duty, but it sounds from this as though Mr. Draven imposed that duty on him without his agreement. He says that your uncle would have wanted to burn the enclosure."

"Then maybe I'll burn it. But I won't give it to anyone without knowing what I'm doing."

"It's moot in any case until we find the blasted thing." Kim turned the letter over and back. "It would be more useful if he'd specified exactly what he'd sent."

"Wouldn't it just."

"When next I send an acquaintance a mysterious letter, I'll write with posterity in mind. Why didn't your uncle destroy this as instructed, I wonder?"

"Maybe he was afraid he'd forget the word. Or he just put

the paper in a box out of habit. It's what he did with every other letter he received, after all," Will added sourly.

Kim grinned. "Long day?"

"If I never see paper again..."

"I can imagine. Hmph. *You gave me grave words*, he says, and *I dare say you will want to burn the other, but I know you too well.* We infer that your uncle knew about Mr. Draven's activities and disapproved, as well he might if Draven's *work is graves.* An ominous way to put it."

"It doesn't sound good, does it?"

Kim tapped the letter against his thigh. "Did your uncle take his obligations as seriously as you do? Might he have burned the enclosure after all?"

Will shrugged. "I didn't have time to get well acquainted with him, but he certainly took responsibility for me. I'd hope he or anyone would keep something safe if a friend asked him to, no matter his disapproval."

"Surely that depends. If it was a letter that was being used for purposes of blackmail, for example, and keeping something safe for a friend meant doing harm to the innocent, what would you do?"

"I'd burn the damn letter if it was blackmail, yes, but I wouldn't knowingly have a blackmailer as a friend," Will said. "And this doesn't sound like blackmail, does it? *I must preserve the fruit.* Sounds more like jam."

"If the War Office is in this because they want his recipe for bramble jelly—"

"Maybe the burglars were hired by the Women's Institute to eliminate a rival."

Kim laughed aloud at that. The bed shook a little beneath them. "Jam wars. If only. I think we have to assume that this refers to the fruit of his labours, which is to say something he's achieved, worked on. And he was a scientist."

"You think it's a discovery of some sort?"

"Discoveries are what scientists do. And the War Office wants it, and it looks like someone else forced a code word out of him to get it."

They were both silent. Will said, eventually, "Damn."

"Quite."

"Is there any way to find out what he was working on, do you think?"

"I suppose I can ask," Kim said. "If it was a patent lice medication, nobody will be trying to keep that secret. If everyone refuses to talk about it, that would also be suggestive. I suppose we're thinking about weapons, aren't we?"

"I suppose we are."

Kim made a face. "Then isn't the War Office the right place for this information?"

"You're joking," Will said. "If this is a scientific weapon, the War Office can go to hell."

Kim twisted to look at him. "Are you serious?"

"Were you ever gassed?"

"I wasn't at the Front."

"I was at Wipers in April '15, when Jerry brought out the chlorine gas."

"My God."

"I was well down the line, not in the thick of it, so I just had a whiff. Damned lucky. I saw men dead—a lot of men. More than a thousand in the first attack, they said, and it wasn't a good way to go. You breathe it in and it burns your lungs out from the inside. I know a fellow who trod in a pool of the liquid stuff, wearing boots, and he'll never walk without pain again. War is one thing, but gas is evil." He stopped there, because his throat hurt. The memory was blistering his lungs.

"I see your point," Kim said. "I truly do. But—and I don't say this lightly—is it not better that our government should have such a weapon if it exists? At least as a deterrent?"

if it already exists
its hard to say

"But it isn't a deterrent. When Jerry gassed us, we didn't surrender. We gassed him right back, with the same evil stuff, and he didn't stop once we took it up. It wasn't a deterrent to either side that the other one had gas, any more than that they had guns. They both had it so they both used it. I don't think the world needs new weapons."

"You've a fairly tidy one there, for a pacifist," Kim said, nodding over at the trench knife.

"Who says I'm a pacifist? I did my bit out there and I'd do it again, but I got my medals for hand to hand fighting. It's when you take the personal out of it—the barrage from miles away, the machine guns—that it becomes slaughter. And gas is worse than that. Gas is mass murder, and I'm not handing anyone the means to that. You talked about destroying a blackmail letter—well, I'd burn the formula for some new gas like a shot. Like a bloody shot."

Kim was watching him again, dark eyes locked on his face, expression intent. Will made a conscious effort to loosen his muscles and relax his shoulders. "Anyway. That's what I think."

"I hear you. Of course we don't know that it's a weapon."

"*My work is only graves.* What else could it be?"

Kim nodded reluctantly. "Certainly the priority has to be getting hold of it before your friend with the tattoo does. Because all this puts a rather different complexion on that business."

"Yes. Hell's teeth."

"Quite. If the tattoo man is, let us say, a German spy, or even a Russian one, a terrorist of one stamp or another—"

"We need to find this damn thing and make it safe."

"Are you sure you don't have any idea where it might be? Places your uncle put things? A safe deposit box?" Will shook his head. "I'm sure you've searched his desk."

"I emptied it after he died, and I had another look for

concealed drawers or whatnot yesterday, but there's nothing."

Kim sighed. "Then I dare say it will be somewhere in here, won't it? In a pile of papers, or perhaps he put it between the pages of a book, for safe keeping. Oh Lord, that's it, isn't it? If you really wanted to hide a paper in here…"

"Put it in a book, which might be on a shelf or in one of the piles upstairs, God help us," Will said hollowly. "Easy to find for you, infallibly hidden from everyone else."

Kim ran a hand over his sleek hair. "This puts you in a rather awkward situation, you realise. I'd feel happier knowing you could get this hot potato out of your hands."

"There's maybe forty thousand books in here. It would take an army to go through them all."

"Which is where the War Office would have an advantage," Kim pointed out. "If you want to be rid of it, and I would, there's your answer. If you're set on doing this yourself—well, I admire your stamina."

"I don't see I've a choice," Will said. "I'm trapped in here with several tons of dusty books to go through anyway: I might as well have a purpose. It'll add interest to the next six months of my life sorting all this out."

"I bet it will. Oh. I don't suppose you've been in the habit of shaking out books as they're bought, have you?"

"You mean, someone might already have walked off with it?" Will asked with a sinking sensation.

"It's possible, whether by accident or on purpose."

"Oh God. No. I'll start now, but if it's already gone, it's gone. I have to work on the basis it's still here, don't I?"

"I think so. We must assume, or hope, your uncle didn't put it in anything likely to fly off the shelves."

"On the bright side, I don't sell many books at the best of times."

Kim snorted with amusement. "That *is* a bright side. Well, I can't fault your attitude, so I shall try to imitate it. I have always wanted to go on a treasure hunt, after all. How much greater the achievement at the end if it takes six months' hard labour to discover it! What jolly fun this will be!"

Will grinned at that. Kim's face lit with an answering smile. "All right, maybe not, but it's a challenge."

"You like challenges?"

Kim's eyelids lowered a little. "Love them."

Will felt the prickle down his back that promised action. He wasn't sure if it was the puzzle or Kim or the combination of the two; he didn't care in the joy of his blood pumping again after years of civilian life, joblessness, poverty, and old books. He wanted to do *something*, and he had a pretty good idea what he could do right now.

"Me too," he said. "Don't know about you, but it's been a while since I enjoyed myself. I'm up for some fun."

He met Kim's eyes, saw them widen with recognition of the hint. Awareness crackled through him, of Kim's proximity and the curve of his mouth, and the length of time since he'd had a hand on his cock that wasn't his own.

Kim parted his lips, but no words came, just the tip of his tongue flickering over his lower lip. Nerves, invitation, both? The tingling moment held them, stretching out like warm toffee, neither moving.

The hell with it. Will shifted, moving a casual hand to brush his companion's leg, and Kim rose in a swift movement that jolted the bed. "I have to go."

"What?"

"Sorry. I forgot, I have to meet a friend. I'll be back tomorrow. Lost track of the time. Don't worry, I'll let myself out." He took up his hat and was gone, whisking out of the room without ceremony.

Will leaned back, banged his head gently against the wall,

and waited until the shop door chimed to release a grunt of frustration. He was, on the whole, grateful that Kim had made his excuses before Will done anything irrevocable, but it was a bit trying the man couldn't make up his mind what he wanted. Will was more used to the exigencies of wartime, where you didn't have the luxury of dancing around the subject.

"Back in the trenches we just got on with it," he said aloud in the tone of a crusty veteran, and laughed at himself as he rose to lock up.

Ah, well, never mind. Maybe Kim would, maybe he wouldn't: Will could wait and see. In the meantime, he still had his right hand and someone to think about, plus a sense of exciting possibilities that he hadn't felt in so long he'd almost forgotten what it was like. A fuck, a fight, a friendship: he'd take any or all.

"Thanks for the inheritance, Uncle," he said into the shadowy silence of the books. "It's a treat."

It took far longer than Will might have thought to shake out a shelf's worth of books. You had to riffle through each one, opening it wide to be sure you hadn't missed anything stuck inside, plus the time to check the surprising amount of paper that fell out, and to shake off dust and dead spiders. Allowing twenty seconds per book overall, if he worked eight hours a day to check forty thousand volumes…he got as far as pulling over a pen and paper, then decided that he'd rather not know.

He'd checked one whole bookcase by eleven the next day when Captain Ingoldsby turned up yet again. The pink-faced chap, Price, was with him this time.

"Mr. Darling," Ingoldsby said. "I understand you've had visitors."

"I've had a few customers," Will said. "One of them was very keen on this information you're after. Big chap, very threatening. Was he from you?"

"If I want to intimidate you, I'll do it myself. No, your large and disruptive guest was not from me."

"My— Are you having me watched?"

"Yes," Ingoldsby said without embarrassment. "You are in possession of information you refuse to hand over, despite being told its importance, and your shop has been visited by a number of extremely undesirable individuals. You want to consider the company you keep, Mr. Darling."

"I don't think it counts as company when they smash the place up," Will pointed out. "And I can't hand it over this blasted information when I don't know where it is. Moreover, you still don't have a warrant or you'd be waving it. I find that very interesting if this business is so important." He wondered whether he was obliged to show Ingoldsby the letter. The man didn't seem to have Kim's quick intelligence but he might reach the same conclusions, and Will wasn't sure he wanted that. "I'll say again: I might be more inclined to cooperate if you tell me what this about. I'm not buying a pig in a poke from you, the tattoo people, or anybody else."

"Aren't you?" Ingoldsby said. "You seem to have got very thick with Secretan."

"You do watch closely." Will's chest held a growing bubble of anger. "I wasn't aware Britain was a spy state. I thought we left that sort of thing to those Bolshevists you're so upset about. I'm a British citizen with nothing against my name and it's none of your damned business who I mix with."

"You're right that you've nothing against your name. In fact you have an excellent war record. The Military Cross with three bars, and two Mentions in Dispatches. Your employment since is less impressive, but these are difficult times."

"Have you been investigating me?" Will demanded, incredulous and enraged. "What the devil is this?"

"A warning," Ingoldsby said. "It would be a great shame if that record was besmirched now. We got off on the wrong foot, Mr. Darling. I take full responsibility for that—"

"Good of you."

Ingoldsby's jaw set but he kept his calm. "And I should like to amend it. You are clearly a man of strong principles; you served your country faithfully for four years. I'd like you to do that again. We have need of good men in this new world with which we find ourselves faced. Men who understand what loyalty is, and where it should lie. I'd like to count you as one of us."

Will leaned back against a bookshelf, folding his arms. "And does that extend to telling me what this is about?"

Ingoldsby opened his hands and said, "My hands are tied."

Will just looked at him. Ingoldsby scowled and put his hands behind his back. "That is, I cannot disclose classified matters of national security. Not yet. Prove to me that I'm right to trust you, Mr. Darling."

"I don't see you trusting me."

"I'd like to. I spoke to Major Chandos, who remembers you well. He had nothing but praise for you, told me I'd be fortunate to have you on my side. You aren't a man who should spend his life in a dusty heap of books; you need to be back in harness." He put a card on the desk. "Give it some thought. And then come and see me in Horse Guards Parade."

He nodded and turned on his heel. Price, hitherto silent, waited until the door bell had jangled, then gave Will a smile.

"He means it, you know. And he's a fine man to work with. I owe him a great deal."

"Nice for you," Will said absently. His mind was racing. Had Ingoldsby meant his offer, or was this a lure to get what he wanted?

"You can trust him, if that's what you're wondering," Price said. "He's absolutely reliable. It's more than I can say of Lord Arthur."

"Who?"

"Lord Arthur Secretan. He may have called himself Kim."

Will stared. Price nodded as if he'd spoken. "No, I didn't think he'd introduce himself truthfully. It's not his habit. Friendly warning, Mr. Darling: you might want to ask Lord Arthur what he did in the war before you decide to trust him."

"Conscientious objector? I've no problem with those."

"Nothing so honest, I'm afraid. No. The fact is, if Lord Arthur was the plain Mr. Secretan he likes to pretend, he'd have faced imprisonment in 1916. Not over matters of conscience, either."

Will thought he could guess what had got Kim in trouble with the law. He shrugged. "Well."

Price raised a brow. "That's a very relaxed attitude to what some might call treason."

"What?" The hair prickled unpleasantly on his neck. "Are you serious?"

"As I say, he was never tried. But he's still not widely received in good company, and that's a feat, given how keen people are to forget about the war." Restrained anger sharpened Price's voice. "Profiteers get knighthoods, heroes get the dole queue, and disloyalty to one's country is an upper-class peccadillo that gets brushed under the carpet. It disgusts me."

"What are you saying he did?"

* (British) unemployment

"Lord Arthur was a known and active Bolshevik who worked against his country and was lucky to escape gaol," Price said crisply. "Supposedly he is no longer a believer. Changed his ways when he thought better of it—or, you might think, when it became apparent his actions might have consequences for himself. If you place your trust in him, you'll be disappointed."

Will had absolutely no idea what to say to that. Price shrugged. "The past is the past, of course. Some people believe in repentance and reformation and letting bygones be bygones. I'm afraid I'm not so forgiving, and to my mind that gentleman is a very nasty piece of work, for all the charm. Watch your back, Darling. I'd be sorry to see a man with your record fooled by one with his."

FOUR

Will didn't do anything right away after Price left. He searched more books, dozens of them, including those few bought by customers, which got him some funny looks. It was mechanical work, which was useful because he needed to think. He hoped to God Kim didn't come round.

He shut up shop early and went to Lexington Street to wait for Maisie when she knocked off work. She came out with three other girls, all in very smart hats, who greeted Will with a chorus of giggles. Maisie bade them a firm farewell and linked her arm with his. "You're going to give me a reputation, turning up like this."

"I'm not, am I?"

She gave him a nudge. "Not while that Susie Allcott is going to a different club with a different fellow every night of the week."

"Should I be taking you dancing?"

"Not in those clothes. I've standards."

"You girls live it up."

He was trying for banter, but it clearly didn't ring true,

because Maisie shot him a frown. "What's up? Is it that business you talked about?"

"Sort of. It's all got a bit odd. Here, Maisie, you read the society papers. Have you heard of a chap called Secretan? Lord Arthur Secretan?"

"Secretan. That's the Marquess of Flitby's family name." Maisie consumed the gossips avidly, she claimed in order to see the fashions and keep abreast of her clientele. Will was fairly sure she just enjoyed them. "Oh yes, Lord Arthur. He's the second son, but he goes by another name."

"Do you have a picture?" Will blurted.

"I can find one at home, I expect. What's wrong? You look sick as a dog."

"I thought I had a handle on this business and it's all gone up in the air. I don't know what to do. And I need to know about Secretan."

"Come back to mine," Maisie said firmly. "I've biscuits."

Maisie's landlady was an artistic, Bohemian type who allowed male guests. Will hadn't been a frequent visitor in the hungry days because he hadn't wanted to scrounge, but sometimes Maisie had overruled his objections and he'd spent a few life-restoring evenings here, cocooned in care, before plunging back into the cold world outside. It was a useful reminder of what real friendship was.

He made the tea and put out the biscuits while Maisie delved into her stacks of *London Life* and *Smart Set*. "Here," she said at last, emerging with an expression of triumph and a flimsy magazine printed on already-yellowing paper. She handed it over and claimed her cup of tea with the air of a job well done, while Will stared at a slightly fuzzy photograph of Kim with a young lady on his arm.

Lord Arthur 'Kim' Secretan at the Cafe Royal with his fiancée, the Hon. Phoebe Stephens-Prince.

"Kim," Maisie said. "And how you get to that from Arthur, I've no idea."

Will didn't care. "Fiancée," he said aloud.

"For what that's worth."

"What do you mean?"

Maisie leaned forward conspiratorially. "No better than she should be, is what people say. Not in the magazines, of course, but in the shop—the ladies might as well be sucking lemons when they talk about her. She was a mannequin for the House of Worth one season, which upset lots of people. Well, it would, with her father a viscount."

"Is she one of, what do you call them, the Bright Young People?" *(Bright young things)young, Bohemian, aristocrats in 1920s*

"I think so. She's friends with Elizabeth Ponsonby and Bubby Fanshawe and that sort."

Will had no idea who they were, except that the newspapers treated them as people of interest. The interest seemed to lie in the fact that they frequently appeared in newspapers. "Is Secretan one of that lot?"

"You're supposed to call him Lord Arthur," Maisie said. "And when they get married, she'll be Lady Arthur, just imagine. No, I don't *think* so. He doesn't seem to draw attention to himself. Well, he wouldn't. I don't suppose anyone would talk to him if he wasn't Lord Flitby's son."

"Why not?"

"Do have a biscuit, they're awfully good," Maisie said, as if this didn't matter at all. "Oooh, now, let me get this right. I had it from our ladies in the shop when the engagement was announced. You'd be amazed what they talk about when they come in together, as though we're all deaf as posts. I could fill a gossip column, except that they couldn't print half of it. Anyway, what I remember is, he didn't go to the war."

"Conchie?"

"White feather. He was given enough to stuff a pillow,

apparently, after it happened. I'm getting to what," she added, at Will's protest. "Let a girl tell a story. Now, I'm not sure of the details—this is the problem, you have to pretend you can't hear the ladies, so you can't ask them to give you the background or spend more time on the good bits. But what I remember is, Lord Arthur was a Bolshevik, a proper Red. Didn't sign up, talked about the immorality of the war, spoke at meetings calling for revolution. You know the sort of thing. And of course with those people, the first son gets the title and the second one goes into the army and that's how it's always done. But Lord Arthur didn't, so his younger brother signed up as soon as he turned eighteen, and then he was killed in his first week out."

Will had seen a lot of new men killed. It had never seemed fair. Maisie nodded at his wince. "I *know*. And what they said was, Lord Arthur put on a black armband but kept on talking Bolshevism all the same—and going to parties too —and if you did *that* in Cardiff near the docks you'd have had a knock on the door, or the head, but I suppose a marquess's son can get away with more. Oh, they didn't like him at all, our ladies. Are you all right? You look a bit sick."

"I'm shocked, to be honest," Will said. "I met him. I thought he was a decent fellow. Helpful." He'd certainly inserted himself into Will's business very thoroughly and asked a lot of questions. He put down his half-eaten biscuit. "Is he still a Bolshevik?"

"I've no idea, love. They don't put that sort of thing in the magazines. If he is, he can't be a very good one, with the Honourable Phoebe on his arm. They got engaged this summer, that's why everyone was talking about them."

"Is he rich?"

"I suppose he must be," she said dubiously. "I don't hear about him running up bills like a lot of them, and she isn't an heiress." She contemplated the printed page. "I don't know if she's so pretty as all that, mannequin or not. What do you think?"

"I don't know how anyone tells anything from photographs. They never look like people to me."

"Is this like him?"

Will contemplated the printed Kim's bland smile. He wore evening dress much as Will had worn his uniform, and his striking eyes were reduced to a dot of black. "Not really. No."

"Well, there you are. All that said, some of our ladies are the most dreadful cats with never a good word about anyone, so it may not be true. And if it is, well, people change. It was a funny time back here while you were over there. A lot of people did odd things."

"People do change," Will agreed. "Not always for the better, though. Thanks, Maisie, that's been a big help."

"That's all right. Keeps me on my toes. I don't suppose you're going to tell me the real reason you're upset about this, are you?"

"I don't entirely know yet. I thought he was helping me, but it sounds like I've been played for a fool."

"Ooh." She made a face. "That's unkind, with everything you've had on your plate."

Will hoped it was only unkind. Kim had been very keen to interpolate himself into the whole business. If he'd had an ulterior motive, Will was going to have words. "It is a bit, but at least I have more of an idea now. I owe you one." Propelled by something he wasn't quite sure of, except that it included a lot of anger with Kim, he added, "Why don't we go dancing soon, when I've kitted myself out properly?"

Maisie gave him a long, examining gaze, then a decided little shake of the head, softened by an affectionate smile. "Buy me lunch when you know what's going on, and tell me all about it."

He didn't see Kim the next day. He didn't knowingly see anybody involved in the Draven business, in fact, though he had a suspicious number of browsers in the shop. That made him twitchy, and reluctant to riffle through books, since he didn't want to give anything away.

He had a number of conversations with Kim in his head, which he attempted to drive out with ferocious concentration on his book-dealing guide and making lists of customers to write to. At least he got some work done.

It was Saturday when Kim arrived, at lunchtime. He was wearing a sporting sort of check, a rakish hat, and a smile that made Will's skin prickle like nettle rash, because it was full of excitement and promise that were a bloody lie.

"Good morning, Will," he said cheerily. "Or even afternoon. Can I tempt you to a spot of lunch?"

"We're closing," Will announced to the two men who were browsing the shelves. "Sorry, no, I've to go out, don't have anyone to mind the shop. Another time, thank you very much, sir." He shut the door behind the disgruntled customer, flipped the Open sign to Closed, and shot the bolt.

"Firm of you," Kim said as Will brushed past him to return to his desk. "At least you didn't fling him out by the seat of his trousers. Would you like to know what I found out?"

"I'd like to know a lot of things." Will parked his arse against the edge of his desk and folded his arms.

Kim's brows drew together. "Is something wrong?"

"You tell me. Start with what you did in the war."

Kim was absolutely still for a few seconds, then he blinked once, a little too slowly. "I take it you've been listening to gossip."

"Not so much listening. I had the War Office round again,

accusing you of a lot of things. I went and asked someone to verify what I could. Now I'm asking you."

"So you are. I don't think I ever claimed to be a hero, did I?"

"I didn't ask for one. I met a lot of conchies out at the Front, mostly bloody brave men who did hard work and got kicks in return, and I don't suppose it was a picnic for the ones who went to gaol for their principles. Nobody had to be a hero, but I've no time for shirkers, let alone anyone who made our job out there harder."

"And you're the judge of the difference, are you?"

"There's a difference between people who did their bit and people who didn't!"

"Yes, the former supported the war," Kim said flatly. "If you did war work, you kept the war going. If you respect principles, you should applaud the ones who refused to do that."

"Principles, my arse. If you didn't go to the war or do the work *and* you didn't face any consequences for it, that's not principle, it's privilege. I was out there with a lot of men who didn't want anything to do with it, but they didn't have lawyers to keep them out of prison. Or a title to keep them out of trouble at home, Lord Arthur."

"My friends call me Kim."

"Dare say they do, Lord Arthur."

Kim gave a tight smile with no humour in it. "I see you've made your mind up. I'm a little surprised: I didn't have you down for the patriotism-or-death type."

"I'm not," Will snapped.

"Then why does my lack of war record distress you so much?"

"I could respect it if you'd gone to gaol. Not to parties."

"Life did go on back here, you know. Parties weren't illegal. Are you interested in my side of things at all?"

"Very," Will said. "Were you a Bolshevik?"

"I was," Kim said calmly. "I believed that they had the right of it."

Will clenched his fists. "While Russia was on our side?"

"Exactly so. I was against the war: why should I have demanded that the Russian people support it?"

"And now? Is that why you're interested in Draven's work?"

Kim looked entirely blank for a second, then he gave a crack of laughter. "Are you serious? You think I'm a Communist spy? For God's sake, is that what's being trotted out these days? I'll freely admit I mixed with some ugly customers for a while, but as to aiding the enemy, I can't imagine what help I could be, then or now." His lips twisted ironically. "I'm of very little account, you know. Just a younger son with a bit of money and no particular purpose. I did actually try to get myself gaoled as a prisoner of conscience, if that makes you feel better, but my father put paid to that. He's a marquess, as you have doubtless discovered, and privilege works wonders. I attempted to follow my principles without success, and made a damned fool of myself which I am in no danger of forgetting, but it's delightful to see people are still inflating it into *He was a Russian agent* or *He drank champagne while his brother died.*"

Will couldn't help a wince. Kim's expression was stark and ugly. "Yes, I'm not surprised you heard that. People do love to be appalled. If I told you— Well, it doesn't matter. I dare say I deserve the punishment, even if they're wrong about the crime. But I'd just ask yourself if you're quite sure you want to be divided from your allies like this."

"Allies? Not with you lying to me."

"I didn't."

"You didn't tell me the truth."

"Why should I have? Do you blurt out all your worst acts

and features on first acquaintance? I'm quite sure there's parts of your life you'd rather not reveal to me."

That was true, and thus intolerably unfair. Just as unfair was Will's sense that his anger, which he was quite sure had been justified, might be on shaky grounds. "I didn't ask you to trust me!"

"I didn't ask you to trust *me*. I offered you help, and I don't see I've let you down."

"You're engaged."

"Yes, I am."

He didn't follow that up, didn't ask why Will raised it, and that was as infuriating as anything. "Tell me this, would *you* trust a man with your record?"

Kim flinched, very slightly, but his voice was quite calm as he said, "I might. Honesty begins at home, and at least I admit what I've done. You should try it."

"What the hell do you mean by that?" Will demanded, his cheeks reddening. *Bullshit*

"I didn't mean anything in particular, but it obviously hit a nerve," Kim said, with a nasty edge to his voice and a slight tremor to his hand. He shoved it into a pocket, evidently aware of Will's scrutiny. "I'm going to go before anything else regrettable is said. Should you calm down, you can find me at the Junior Antinous, Pall Mall."

FIVE

Will could barely concentrate for the rest of the day. He wasn't sure if he'd been entirely right or entirely wrong or, worse, if there was no right or wrong, just a whole tangled mess of mistakes and human failings that needed picking over with care, but which he'd trampled over like some bellowing colour sergeant.

He went through another box of his uncle's letters at his desk, working mechanically, serving customers out of bloody-mindedness rather than enthusiasm. None of them seemed surprised by his attitude. Maybe he was getting the hang of bookselling.

Around quarter to five, he pulled a sheaf of invoices out of a thick-stuffed envelope, then sat there and stared at them.

The fact was, he couldn't do this on his own. Either he had to call Ingoldsby and tell the man to do as he pleased, or he had to take the job on himself, which meant recruiting help, and there was nobody else ready to help him. Kim obviously wasn't a Bolshevik: he'd tried from the start to persuade Will to give the War Office what they wanted. He

I dig this phrase [handwritten annotation]

had been fair, and Will had a nasty feeling that was more than he'd managed himself.

He propelled himself to his feet, shoving the papers back in the envelope. The bookshop wasn't on the telephone but the shop next door was. He strode out, only realising as he locked the door that he still clutched the invoices, and went next door, demanding, "Can I use your telephone?"

His neighbour, Norris, purveyor of umbrellas and walking sticks, waved an uninterested hand. Will picked up the receiver.

"What number please?" asked the operator.

Will had no idea. He hadn't decided who he was going to call, only that it had to be someone. The War Office, or Kim?

"Caller?" demanded the operator tinnily.

"Uh. The Junior Antinous please, on Pall Mall."

"One moment please."

Clicks and whirrs, then a deep and respectable male voice. "Good evening, this is the Junior Antinous."

"Good evening. I want to reach Lord Arthur Secretan. Kim Secretan."

"I regret Lord Arthur is not available."

Will wasn't sure if that was a relief. "Could you take a message please? Ask him to get in touch with Will. Will Darling."

"Mr. Darling," the voice repeated. "I'll give Lord Arthur the message. Thank you, sir."

Will put the phone down, and tuppence for the call, and returned to his shop with his envelope, wondering if he was doing the right thing. Sod it: he could always call Ingoldsby another day.

He didn't feel like going through more papers now. He put them all away and tidied up instead, sweeping the place as best he could. Kim wouldn't get the message for a while and there was every chance that, when he got it, he wouldn't be inclined to listen. Will hadn't listened to him, after all.

He made himself bread and cheese for supper, and a cup of tea to wet his dusty throat. What he actually wanted was a pint. Maybe he'd nip up to the Black Horse, get a game of darts or a chat about the football, something to distract himself. He glanced at the clock and was slightly surprised to see it was half past eight. That settled it: of course Kim wouldn't be coming back at this hour.

He put on his jacket and hat, made sure Draven's letter was safe in his pocket, and let himself out. It was pitch dark in May's Buildings since the close was unlit and the tall houses on both sides blocked out the ambient electric light from more important thoroughfares, so he had to lock the shop up by feel. He needed a couple of tries to get the key in the lock and was concentrating so hard on doing that, he didn't register the footsteps coming up behind him until it was almost too late.

He ducked violently to the side by pure instinct, and felt the swish of air against his cheek as something swung past, missing by an inch. *Cosh*, he realised, and flung himself violently at his attacker, sending him skipping back. Will barrelled into him, wishing he had his knife, and then pain exploded through the back of his head and he found he was face down on the cold, wet cobbles.

Ah. There were two of them.

He scrabbled to get purchase on the slippery stones and push himself up, but there was a knee in his spine, a hard hand twisting his arm up behind his back, and then the thin biting line of a blade at his throat. That last made him stop struggling.

"Get up," said a soft voice. "If you make a sound, I'll cut you."

Will got up, dizzy and sick. They marched him back into

the shop, which the other man had opened up again, and he was curtly ordered into his chair. The first man stood behind him with the knife pressed against his throat, point digging in, while the second, who wore a scarf tied over his face, fumbled to let down the blinds, sending a shower of dust and dead spiders over the newly swept floor. That done, he switched on Will's desk lamp, pulled out cord from his pocket, and lashed first Will's hands then his ankles to the chair.

The knife moved away from his throat, and the second man came round to stand in front of him.

It was the tattooed man, Will saw with no surprise at all. Libra, Ingoldsby had said, and now he thought about it, the tattoo might be a pair of scales. He'd seen a mark on the other man's wrist too as he dealt with the blinds.

Libra looked down at him. Will noted the healing cut on his face without surprise. "As you see, Mr. Darling, we've run out of patience. Where is it?"

"The information? I don't know."

Libra hit him hard, a backhander that smacked Will's head sideways and cut his cheek against his teeth. He shook his head to clear it. "Want to try that when I'm not tied up?"

"No," Libra said and hit him again, in the same place. It hurt. "I've had enough of this. Where is it?"

Will spat pink-tinged saliva at Libra's feet. "I don't know. I haven't found it."

"You found it today."

"What? Balls I did. What are you talking about?"

Libra leaned down, glaring into his face. "You found an envelope. You took it with you to telephone."

"That wasn't anything important, just a lot of old invoices. See for yourself, it's in the box over there."

He indicated the direction with a nod. The second man—he had blue eyes, Will saw above the scarf—went to search, as Libra demanded, "Then why did you take it to the telephone?"

"I didn't *take* it. I just forgot to put it down when I went out."

"Who were you telephoning?"

"A friend. I asked him to come round tonight."

Libra's scathing expression suggested the improvisation hadn't been a particular success. "No more games. You'd better know where it is, or it'll be the worse for you." He lifted the knife meaningfully, and traced a half-circle with the point under Will's eye, scraping the skin.

"Well, I don't!" Will strained against the rope, but it was strong, and had been well tied. "For God's sake. You can't do this!"

"I can do whatever I want, Mr. Darling. This is an unfrequented street and if anyone were passing, they couldn't see in. You have nobody expecting you to come home. With a gag in your mouth, no-one will hear you scream. I can spend all night working on you."

"But I don't have anything to tell you!"

"We'll be the judge of that."

Will stared up at him, mind racing. His bonds were well tied, the chair was too sturdy to smash apart if he went over backwards, and there were two of them anyway.

He could give them the letter, since it wouldn't do them any good. They'd demand he reveal the code word of course, and he could give them a false one—but would they believe it, would they even believe it if he gave them the true one? Would showing he knew anything simply make things worse? What could he do, with nothing meaningful to hand over, tied to a chair, with nobody at all to know what was happening to him?

He was in the middle of the biggest city in the world, and he was so alone it hurt.

"Listen," he said. "You know I only inherited this shop a few weeks ago. All I know about any of this is that whatever you're after, the War Office wants it too. If you kill me, they'll be in here going over the place with a fine-tooth comb, and I bet they have more manpower than you. Is that what you want?"

"There's nothing of any use in here," the second man said. He'd been searching through the box of papers all this time. Will saw him stand out of the corner of his eye. The movement seemed deliberate, and threatening.

"I've been through half a dozen boxes and found nothing but invoices and correspondence," he said. "You're welcome to try for yourselves. I cannot help you."

"Let's test that, shall we?" Libra moved closer, pressing the point of the knife hard against the bottom of Will's eye, pricking the skin and putting a sharp, sickening pressure on his eyeball. He couldn't breathe for fear of moving too much. Libra held the knife there for a second, then slid it down Will's cheek.

"I know you have it," he said softly. "You will give it to me."

Will strained against the rope, fingers flexing with the frustrated urge to hit. Libra looked down at his hands and smiled. He moved the knife-point to Will's right hand, trussed uselessly to the arm of the chair, and rested the point of the blade between the bones that led to his index and middle fingers.

His eyes were locked on Will's and there was a deep, dark pleasure in them. Will knew that expression. You didn't want men who wore it at your back on a raid, no matter how good they were: they enjoyed the work in the wrong way. "All I have to do is push down. Do you want me to do that?"

"I don't know where it is!"

Libra glanced up and nodded. A hand from behind seized

Will's nose; he clamped his mouth shut, knowing what was coming, but Libra slammed a fist into his gut and he couldn't help a gasp for breath. As soon as his mouth was open, a cloth was thrust into it. He thrashed uselessly, trying to spit it out again, rocking the chair violently so that Libra had to grab both arms, anything to stave this off—

There was a sharp papery thud and the second man cried out. Libra's head jerked up, his eyes widened, and he leapt away as the second man's cry became a scream. Will twisted desperately against his bonds, couldn't shift them, and wrenched his neck round to see.

The second man was crouched against the wall, right arm pressed against his chest as if it hurt, left up in urgent defence. Libra was in a fighting stance, knife out. Opposite him, in front of the open door to the back room, was Kim.

He was bareheaded but otherwise in evening dress— white shirt, white waistcoat, black tailcoat, smart as you like —and he had Will's trench knife in his left hand, the dull grey blade absurdly incongruous with the dinner clothes. It was a lot bigger than Libra's knife, but that wasn't going to help him if he didn't know how to use it, and the way he stood, feet placed and arms out like this was *fencing* for God's sake, made it quite clear he didn't.

Will urgently tried to force the cloth out of his mouth, shoving at it with his tongue. He needed to tell Kim not to be such a fucking fool, to run like hell, but he couldn't shift the cloth, and then it was too late.

Libra moved first, a swift, vicious attack. Kim's arm was held far too high, and Libra's lunge hissed under it in a single, lethal strike that went straight up into his ribcage.

Except somehow it didn't, because in that second Kim twisted his own long blade down, caught the attack to flick Libra's arm away, turned like a dancer, and swung the Messer back round and up in a snakelike strike that ripped through

Libra's clothing and only failed to open his belly because the man jumped away in time.

Libra found his feet and brought up his knife again, this time defensively. Kim adopted the fencing pose again. Somehow, it seemed a lot less amateur now.

Will's jaw had sagged. He took the opportunity to spit out the cloth and bellowed, at the top of his lungs, "Fire! Fire!"

Kim and Libra engaged again, blades scraping. "Fire!" Will yelled. The second man was edging around him, with blood running down his hand. Will tried to kick him even though his ankles were tied, out of pure desire to hurt. "Help! Fire!"

There was an answering cry from the street, and a rattle at the door. The second man turned urgently to Libra and his eyes widened. Will twisted back just in time to see Kim's knife slice into Libra's wrist. Blood flew, and Libra's knife hit the floor point first.

"Go on. Pick it up." Kim's teeth were bared in something close to, but not, a smile. "Fair fight, eh?"

Libra hesitated, as well he might, because if ever a man looked like he planned to kick his opponent while he was down, it was Kim. Will wouldn't have put a vulnerable spot within five yards of him at that moment, and Libra clearly reached the same conclusion because he backed away a step, then another. The door rattled again, and Will bellowed, "Help!"

The second man broke, and ran for the door. Libra snarled and followed on his heels. The bell jangled and Will heard a scuffle and shouting.

Kim was by him, slicing through the rope at his wrist with the Messer, a knife you didn't want near any blood vessels you were fond of. "Go after them!" Will snapped.

"Are you hurt?" Kim moved to do his other wrist.

"No. Go and get them!"

"What's going on, Mr. Darling? Where's the fire?" It was Norris from next door. "I heard shouts, and two men just barged past—Good God! Mr. Darling?"

Kim knelt to untie Will's ankles, somehow making the Messer with its eight-inch blade vanish in the movement. His face was a picture of shock as he stared up at Norris, hands shaking visibly. "Oh, thank goodness. There's been a burglary. Did you see them?"

"They pushed past me on the doorstep. What on earth is happening?"

"They tied him up," Kim said, sounding helplessly baffled. "It was daylight robbery—well, not daylight, obviously—they were going through the desk—"

"I'll get a policeman," Norris said.

"Have they gone, or might they attack other shops on this street?"

Norris's eyes widened at the thought his own shop could be visited. "They ran past me, but—"

"You'd better check," Kim said with great concern. "I'll get the police as soon as I've helped Mr. Darling free."

"Right. Yes." Norris hurried out.

Kim sat back on his heels. Will finished the job of untying his ankles, irritated that his fingers were so clumsy, then looked up and met Kim's dark eyes.

"Conscientious objector, my arse."

Kim grinned wolfishly. "Are you all right?"

"Fine. Aren't we going after them? Or getting a policeman?"

"No point. The fellow with the knife, was that your tattoo chap?"

"Libra."

Kim's face stilled. "Was that his name?"

"I don't know. Ingoldsby called him that, or at least said the word. But he had a set of scales tattooed on the underside of his wrist, and isn't that Libra, the scales? And I'll tell you what else, the other one had a tattoo in the same place."

Kim whistled soundlessly. "There's a thing. The same tattoo?"

"No, different. A head with horns, I think. A goat or a sheep, perhaps."

"How peculiar. Well."

He was still sitting on his knees. Will was still sitting on the chair. They stared at one another.

"How did you get here?" Will asked.

"I had your telephone message at the club. I popped round and arrived just in time to see you being bundled into the shop. It seemed a rather tough spot and I wasn't sure what to do, so I went round the alley that runs behind your yard, came over the back wall, and got in through the window."

Will blinked. "The window was fastened."

"It isn't now."

He couldn't argue with that. "Where did you learn knife fighting?"

Kim glanced to the door. "That sounds like your helpful neighbour coming back. Let's get rid of him, shall we?" He put his hands on the arms of the chair to stand, so his body trapped Will's for just a second, then headed to the door to do the talking.

SIX

Will let Kim deal with it. He didn't bother listening, just let the persuasive, mellifluous tone wash over him as he stretched and flexed his wrists. His blood was fizzing with unspent adrenalin and the need to act.

Kim shut the door behind Norris at last, and Will heard the bolt go. He came back through the shop to where Will stood, face unreadable, eyes watchful, incongruous and beautiful in his scuffed black-and-white finery.

Will stepped forward and shoved him against a bookcase.

Their mouths collided savagely. Will had him by the shoulders but Kim's grip on his hips was fierce, pulling him in, and he was almost biting at Will's mouth and tongue. Will kissed him back with equal wildness. The need was urgent, a physical desperation that howled through his nerves and skin. Kim wrapped his leg around Will's to bring their hips together, then grabbed his hair and tugged his head back to expose his throat, devouring the rough skin, open-mouthed and hungry.

Christ, it was good. Will shut his eyes to let sensation

overwhelm him, then had to open them again to flick a glance at the windows and make sure the blinds were down.

"We're behind the lamp," Kim said against the skin of his throat, voice vibrating. "No shadows."

"Shut up." Will pushed him back again, quashing a sudden mental image of the ranks of bookshelves going over like dominoes. He fumbled at Kim's waistband with one hand, holding him at the shoulder with the other. Kim's fingers came up to meet his, and Will grabbed his hand, feeling its warmth. A hand that could use a trench knife, pliant in his. He pushed Kim's arm back, interlacing their fingers, shoved clothing out of the way with his other hand, found the fierce stiffness of his cock.

Kim inhaled sharply. His pulse throbbed against Will's fingers. They stared at each other for a second, then their mouths met again, kissing with ferocity as Will worked him in fast, harsh movements. Kim panted into his mouth, little gasps that raised the hair on Will's arms with their increasing urgency, until at last he gave a muffled cry of release.

Will pulled his head away. They stood like that as Kim's eyes cleared, locked together in the moment. The blood pulsed in Will's cock.

Kim straightened up, then moved, that dancing fighter's twist again without releasing their locked hands, and Will found himself swung round. He stood with his back to the bookcase as Kim dropped to his knees.

"Oh Jesus." He let himself lean against the shelves, staring down. Kim let go his hand, leaving Will's exposed to the chilly air, dealt with his straining buttons, and took out Will's prick with delicate fingers. He paused there, as if examining it, mouth a little open, receptive, waiting to be filled.

There was no blood left in Will's brain. He could only watch as Kim leaned in and flicked him with a catlike tongue.

"Christ," he whispered.

Kim's lips curled. He ran both hands up Will's flanks, gripped his hips, and took him in his mouth.

Will had to hold on to the shelves. He'd only had this a few times in his life, and he'd been sloppy drunk for half of them. It was astounding. The sensation of Kim's lips forming a tight ring round him, the suction, the wet warmth—Kim wasn't even using his hands, just his mouth, and Will was afraid he might blow within seconds. He really didn't want to. This was masterly, and blissful. Lips, teeth, tongue, a blaze of sensation, his cock going far deeper into Kim's throat than he'd thought possible, plus Kim's hands on his hips, pulling Will forward.

Oh Christ, he wants me to fuck his mouth, he likes it in his mouth. The thought quivered through him. Will wanted to put a hand in his hair, to grab or caress, he wasn't sure. He wished he knew how to ask if Kim wanted him to thrust: he feared that might imply some demand or insult. Absurd to be self-conscious now. He could feel himself leaking.

Kim pulled back, his movement slowing to nothing but a touch. Will looked down and saw him looking up. His mouth was obscenely open, lips red with friction, and beautifully filled with Will's erection.

He made an embarrassingly desperate noise and felt Kim's smile curve round him before he started sucking again, harder and faster, till Will came helplessly with an airless groan, spilling deep into his throat.

He hung onto the bookshelves, arms outstretched as if crucified, head down. If he let go, he might well fall over.

After a moment he opened his eyes. Kim was sitting back on his knees again, wearing that oddly neutral expression of his, as if he wasn't sure what Will might do now.

Unfortunately, nor was Will. He had no idea what civilians, or civilised people, would say in these circumstances.

Thanks for that, old chap, much obliged, perhaps? Ought he apologise for coming in his mouth? Would this be a good moment to restart the conversation about where Kim had learned to use a knife?

Thank God they were British. He took a deep breath. "Cup of tea?" – *I love this book*

Kim went absolutely blank again. It was a trick he had, Will thought, as if the muscles of his face locked in position while his mind worked. Then his face cracked into an infectious wide smile. "Got anything stronger?"

"How about both?"

It was much easier to deal with the aftermath if you could occupy yourself. Will put the kettle on, poured them each a generous Scotch, and tried not to notice Kim seating himself on the camp bed while he got the mugs out.

Kim hadn't made a mess of the window in the back room at all. Will examined it while the kettle boiled. "How did you break in again?"

"I came through that little alley, the one to the side of the Black Horse. Up the back wall and over two other yards into yours because I miscalculated. I flipped the latch with a bit of metal I found lying about."

It was a sash window, and the latch wasn't precisely snug, but Will hadn't realised it was that loose. He made a mental note to fix it. "You came over the walls in those clothes?"

"Heartbreaking, isn't it?" Kim brushed at his knees, which were admittedly rather scruffy now Will noticed. "It's a good thing gentlemen aren't wearing trousers tight at the moment. That might have been difficult."

"All of it sounds difficult. I didn't hear you get in."

"I was trying to be quiet, for obvious reasons," Kim pointed out. "I'm sorry I took a while. I could see proceedings through the crack in the door, and I was waiting for a moment when I wouldn't startle that swine into stabbing you."

"Appreciated." Will took a mouthful of whisky. "And then you grabbed my knife and engaged a dangerous man in the sort of action I haven't seen since my last trip to Jerry's trenches."

"You were a trench raider?" Kim lifted a brow. "I did wonder why you had this pig-sticker lying around. Is it British army issue?"

"German. I picked it up in '15. Some people swore by trench clubs, with or without nails in them, but I don't think you can beat a Messer and a push dagger on a raid. How did you know how to use it?"

"I wouldn't claim I do. Did you buy it or was it, ah, a souvenir of a trip?"

Will declined that gambit with a look. "You don't answer many questions, do you?"

"Don't I?" Kim grinned at Will's expression. "Sorry. How I learned…ugh. I wasn't against the war because I'm a pacifist." *– HOt. Pacifists are lame*

"There's quite a divide between 'pacifist' and 'knife fighter'."

"You should go to some of the Anti-War League meetings, they get pretty heated. No. As I told you earlier, I mixed with bad company in my youth."

"Knife-fighting bad?"

"One was obliged to learn certain skills in anticipation of the revolution," Kim said. "It's not a period I like to dwell on."

"I'm sure it's not, but it saved my neck this evening. *You* saved my neck. I'd have been up a gum tree if you hadn't come back."

"Well, you called me. May I ask why?"

"I wanted to apologise. I don't think I had any right to go off at you like that earlier."

"You aren't the first to do so."

"That doesn't make it better." The kettle whistled. Will went over and poured water into the teapot. "I don't think I was fair and I'm sorry."

"Don't be," Kim said. "What you were told was essentially true. I mixed with—supported—a movement whose promise of a better future is not coming to pass, to say the least, and whose leaders were not the idealists I believed them to be. I didn't go to the war. My younger brother did, and died in my stead."

"I can't see that's your fault."

"Oh, it was. Noblesse oblige." Kim stared into his glass. "One of us had to go, for the family honour. When I refused, the burden went to him."

"The thing about that," Will said, and stopped himself.

"What? No, go on. I'd like to know."

Will took a mouthful of whisky to gather his thoughts, and perhaps his courage. "I was out there the whole time. Four years and change, not demobbed till late '19. I was at Ypres and Passchendaele. I did fourteen trench raids."

"Christ!" Kim said, sounding genuinely startled. "*Fourteen? Do you have a boxful of medals?*"

"Pawned them." _Their dynamic is great

"Sorry?"

"My grateful nation wasn't grateful enough to give me a job. I pawned my medals to keep a roof over my head and food in my belly, and I'll tell you what, the Military Cross doesn't fetch a great deal, no matter how many bars you have on it. The pawnbroker told me I should have tried for a Victoria Cross. That would be worth something, he said."

Kim's lips tightened. "Perhaps someone should have a word with him."

"It's a seller's market. Did you not read about the chap who marched down Whitehall with his pawn tickets pinned on his uniform where his medals should have been? Anyway, the point is, I know about doing your duty out there. And what you said about honour is balls." *Lol*

Kim raised his brows. Will pressed on. "Sitting around in the trenches, whittling and telling dirty jokes we'd all heard a dozen times. Going out with your mates knowing a load of them would die to win a hundred yards of ground that Jerry would get back next time, and then doing it over and over again. I got stuck in a shellhole with a sergeant once, under a barrage. We were there for hours, sat in freezing water if you could call it that, keeping our heads down, and once it got dark we crawled back through mud. Afterwards he said to me, 'When we started I was afraid I'd die out there. After an hour, I was terrified I wouldn't.' There was no honour or courage in any of that, just survival. Yes, I've got a boxful of medals. I won them for sneaking up on people and killing them from behind."

"Is that a fair way to put it?"

"It's what I did. And you know why I did it?"

"Orders?"

"I was good at it," Will said. "I *enjoyed* it. The danger and the challenge, mostly, but killing was part of the game too, and it was a lot better than sitting on my arse in a trench. I volunteered to go kill men who I'd have had a drink with if I'd met them in a pub, and that wasn't courage, just a twist in the head that went the other way round to shellshock. Calling it honour is putting ribbons on a pile of shit. It might look good, but it still stinks."

Kim was sitting still, his glass half way to his lips. Will realised he'd said rather more than he'd meant to. He went to pour the tea, an excuse to turn his face away. "Anyway. That's what I think."

Kim nodded slowly. "You seemed to feel strongly about those who didn't go, all the same."

"I do about the people who had their feet up while we did the work. People who thought they were entitled to stay out of it because their own lives were important and other people's weren't. And profiteers, they can rot. But I had my life saved by a conchie stretcher-bearer who went out under fire to get me back when I'd taken a bad one to the leg. *That* was courage, the real thing. And you came over a wall and through a window and took on a lunatic with a knife to help me out, so whatever you are, you're not a shirker. Milk and sugar?"

"Just milk. May I ask a question?"

Will didn't have a coffee table, and he needed to gather himself. He went to get the spare chair from the shop, put the mugs on it, and took up position on the bed, very aware of Kim's proximity. "Go on."

"Why did you not stay in the army?"

"I'm not officer class, and I don't like marching in step. I'm not good at obeying orders."

"You're good at trench raids. A talent you were obliged to develop over four years, and then to forget as inappropriate for civilian life."

"I've got a second-hand bookshop, though. Amounts to the same thing."

Kim choked. "Very true."

"Anyway. All I meant to say was, I'm sorry about your brother, but honour was the lie they told to get us out there. Nobody should have gone."

"Thank you, Will. That's kind of you."

Will shrugged, unsure how to respond. They sat in silence for a moment, then Kim said, "Meanwhile, do you have any idea what provoked tonight's excitement?"

"I think there's people watching me." Kim didn't seem at all surprised by this, which emboldened Will to go on. "No, I know they are. Ingoldsby and the baby-faced johnny knew you'd come here. And Libra said as much. He said I was seen finding papers in an envelope and taking them next door to telephone. That's why they came after me."

"What papers?"

"It was nothing, just invoices. I was thinking about something else, and I happened to hold on to them when I went to 'phone for you."

"Did Libra know who you'd called?"

"He said not."

"So you were seen but not heard. Someone in one of the shops across the street?" Kim tapped his fingers against the tumbler. "They had you watched, and when they thought you'd found the information, they attacked within a couple of hours. That's keen."

"Who *are* they?" Will asked. "The matching tattoos—are they a gang? A secret society?"

Kim didn't laugh at him, for which Will was grateful. "A secret society that uses identifying tattoos is making a schoolboy error, if you ask me. The chap with the ram's head was masked, wasn't he? I wasn't able to give him my full attention."

"He had a scarf round his head."

"But the other, Libra, didn't feel the need to hide his face. Of course you'd seen him before, but it still suggests an unpleasant degree of confidence. They're pretty nasty, these chaps."

"Very nasty."

"And there's a few of them. Which leads me to wonder whether it's a good idea for you to stay here alone."

"I don't have a great deal of choice. And if I leave this

place unoccupied, they could break in overnight and ransack it."

"They could do that anyway, cutting your throat as they pass," Kim pointed out. "I doubt they will, since that would invite the authorities, but they could certainly return to finish tonight's work. I don't much like that idea."

"I'm not very fond of it either." Will didn't want to say this next part, and made himself. "I can't afford a hotel, though, not till I get probate, and I'd struggle to find a cheap room at this hour."

"You're welcome to stay with me," Kim said matter-of-factly. "I've plenty of space and you need to get some sleep. Though, to be honest, I feel quite strongly you should reconsider letting the War Office in."

"You think that?"

"Yes, with my dreadful Bolshevik past, I do. I don't like this mob one bit, and I would prefer not to find you with your throat cut. I'm also going to hazard that the WO will find a way to lean on you sooner or later, and that won't be pleasant. I don't see this situation working out at all well for you unless you cooperate. I know you don't want to hear it, but I'd be dishonest not to say so." *Now he values honesty*

Will twisted round to examine his face. Kim opened his hands. "Sorry. But I can't guarantee to turn up with a knife next time."

"It's my knife, and next time I'll use it myself."

"And who'll run the bookshop when you're arrested for grievous bodily harm?" He raised a hand at Will's look. "All right, I hear you. You really are stubborn, aren't you?"

"I don't like to be pushed around."

"As I said. Well then. If you aren't happy leaving this place empty, I suggest I stay here overnight in case of further unwanted visitors, and tomorrow we search the blasted place from top to bottom. It's Sunday so you wouldn't be open anyway. Two men, twelve hours, partition it up: I think we have a fair chance. And if we don't find it, I vote we keep going next week until we do."

"Are you serious?" Will demanded.

"Why not?"

"I'm just wondering where you sprang from to make all my wishes come true."

He realised approximately a second later how unfortunate those words were. Kim opened his mouth, closed it, and then lifted a brow with a rueful smile that did something sharp and painful to Will's insides. "On which subject, we should discuss what happened earlier."

"Uh," Will managed. "Right."

"Or if you want to pretend that incident never took place, we can."

He sounded impossibly matter of fact. Will attempted to echo that. "Of course. If you want to, I mean."

"Do *you* want to?"

I'm not the one with a fiancée, Will thought, but didn't say. It was surely Kim's responsibility to take that into account.

He knew a sudden, wicked urge to ask if Kim had learned to suck cocks from the Bolsheviks as well. He was having quite a lot of trouble reconciling that expert performance with the earlier shyness, or this dancing about. But that wasn't fair. Kim was obviously torn in several directions, and making a fuss now would be an ungracious response to heroics that had saved Will a very nasty evening. "I...well, what do you want?"

Kim exhaled hard. "We appear to be locked in competition as to who has less of a spine."

That was embarrassingly accurate. Will tossed back the remains of his whisky, took Kim's tumbler from his unresisting hand, and put them both on the chair with the untouched mugs of tea. He shifted round as he sat back, and put his fingers to Kim's cheek: the soft skin, the faint hint of stubble, the angle of his jaw and the tension of the muscle over it. ~~They looked at each other for a moment, and then both leaned forward at once.~~

The kiss was a great deal gentler this time.

That's not talking dip-shits!

SEVEN

Will woke early the next morning, because it was bloody uncomfortable sharing a camp bed for one. It wasn't particularly spacious on his own; with another man sprawled across him it was positively cramped, and that with about a third of Will's body hanging precariously off the bed. The thought came to mind that he could get a bigger bed once he'd cleared an upstairs room for himself, and a less rickety one too, because he'd feared for its stability the night before. A bed you could fuck in, a bed you could share. — *Priorities*

Whoever he might share it with. Kim was Lord Arthur Secretan, with a fiancée and a gentleman's club and an upper-crust life doing whatever the upper crust did. He wasn't going to be here long. If and when Will got a bigger bed, he'd be buying it for himself.

They'd made it slow the second time. That was a rare treat for Will, being able to take his time. His encounters with men had mostly been in wartime, and the odd back alley at night since demobbing: all hurried, none safe. It had been good to explore at his leisure. Kim was lovely in his way, pale and lean, with a fair few thin white scars on his forearms to

one of my fav adjectives

suggest his lessons in knife-fighting had been practical ones. Will hadn't commented, in the hope he wouldn't have to field remarks about his own more numerous scars, including the ugly one on his thigh from a splinter of shell that had nearly done for him. Kim hadn't raised the topic either. He had touched the raised, jagged line on Will's belly very gently, but he didn't ask. *Men / ɔ MH*

They hadn't talked about anything, in fact, awkward or otherwise. They'd just touched and kissed, hands and mouths moving in silence but with building intensity, until Kim had pulled Will over him, directing him with fingers rather than words, and Will had fucked him between closed thighs, bewildered and joyous. *—cant picture that*

And now it was some time before six in the morning, with birds singing for the not-yet-broken dawn, Kim's arm was heavy across him in quiet-breathing slumber, and he was excruciatingly uncomfortable.

Bugger it. Will attempted to manoeuvre himself out of bed without falling on his arse, waking his companion, or knocking over the chair with its load of mugs and tumblers. He achieved precisely none of those goals.

"Christ," Kim said, muffled, as Will cursed and grabbed for a dishcloth to mop up the spillage. "Bit early for house removals?"

"Sorry." *LOVE this / word*

Kim kicked off the blanket and stretched, an uninhibited movement that Will couldn't help watching for the play of muscle under skin. It was hard to ignore that they both had a fair case of morning wood, but he did his best. "Tea?"

"Thanks. What appalling hour is it?"

"Five to six."

"Oh *God*."

Will put the kettle on and went about getting washed and

dressed. <u>Kim lay in bed, arm over his face, a picture of decadence.</u>

"I don't have much in for breakfast," Will remarked apologetically.

"There must be a cafe somewhere, Sunday or not. We should fortify ourselves for the day's work. And I need to fetch a change of clothes, too. Knife fights are one thing, but damned if I'm searching a bookshop when I'm dressed for the Savoy."

He was still intending to do it. That was all the fortification Will needed, though a large breakfast would undeniably help.

There was something he'd wanted to ask and forgotten about last night. In fact, there were a few of those, and in the light of day, driven neither by desire nor the aftershocks of fear and anger, they seemed rather more urgent. "There's a good cafe down the road. Why didn't you want to call the police last night?" *No. Directness all the way*

"<u>Good Lord, Will, at least give me tea before wrenching the subject around like that.</u> What?"

"You didn't want to call the police last night."

"Well, nor did you, or you would have done," Kim said unanswerably.

"But you said there was no point. Why not?"

"Ah, I see." Kim swung himself to sit up, casting a hopeful glance at the teapot. "To be honest, I didn't imagine it would be any use after what you said about reporting the first attack. I could have backed up your account of events, but I don't suppose my record would make me a terribly helpful witness. And, from a selfish point of view, I was a little concerned at the thought that only one person out of the four of us last night actually injured anyone, and that was me."

"You were defending me."

"Under highly implausible circumstances. And suppose we had been taken seriously? You'd have to say what you thought your attackers were up to, and then we'd have the Metropolitan Police tangled into this with the War Office, and I bet I know whose side they'd take and…ugh. The fact is, if you're determined not to cooperate with the War Office you can scarcely expect help from the other organs of the state."

"So you're for handling this ourselves."

"If you want to keep control, I don't see an alternative. If you want this to go away—well, I've told you what I think. It's your choice."

Will nodded. "Thanks."

"What, for supporting your pig-headedness against my better judgement?"

"Well. Yes."

"My pleasure," Kim said with a quick smile. "Is that tea brewed yet?"

Kim went home to change while Will nailed his back window shut, and returned to take him out for a slapping breakfast before they embarked on the search. He proved to be remarkably good at logistics, dividing up the bookshop into areas and allocating tasks. They worked together, Will going through the papers while Kim shook out books methodically and put a few aside if they were particularly interesting or valuable.

It was boring work, repetitive, dusty, and unrewarding, and it was the best day Will had had since Armistice.

He'd missed companionship more than he'd realised, being in harness with others and working together. Someone to talk to, someone who'd share your grumbles as you laboured to a common goal. He'd been bloody lonely since he'd come to London, at first because he barely knew anyone in the metropolis, then because the more your money dwindled, the harder it was to make and keep friends. You couldn't go out for a drink, you were ashamed of the shabby state of your clothes, you feared people might expect you to touch them for cash so you withdrew first rather than endure that additional humiliation on top of poverty's many other insults. Will's mother had kept the doorstep scrubbed even when she'd struggled to put food on the table, and he'd inherited that drive to put pride before all.

And here he was now in his own bookshop, well fed, usefully busy, and enjoyably partnered. It made the violent assault and threat of torture seem quite worthwhile.

Kim seemed to be in his element as well. He whistled intermittently and tonelessly—Will found it mildly satisfying that he couldn't carry a tune in a bucket—and seemed entirely satisfied to flick through book after book, with occasional little grunts of approval. They talked sporadically, not about anything that mattered much. Kim mostly commented on what he found in the books: cheques, shopping lists, newspaper clippings. He found a ten-pound note at one point, which Will took for the petty cash, and several letters, each of which caused them both to sit up with excitement before the inevitable letdown.

"Got something—no, Gertie thanks Claudia for the lovely Christmas card, damn her," Kim would announce as he pounced on them, or "This might be it—blast, it's a recipe."

"What sort of recipe looks like a secret weapon?" Will demanded.

"Stewed tripe and onions."

"Fair enough."

An hour after that Kim made an explosive noise. "Got something?" Will asked.

"Define 'something'."

He sounded odd. Will's ears pricked up. "What is it? What does it say?"

"I'm too embarrassed to tell you. And that's coming from a man who's sucked your prick."

Will choked. "What?"

Kim wordlessly presented a piece of notepaper covered in spidery handwriting redolent of forty years ago which reminded Will of his old schoolteacher's, at least until he started reading. It was a letter addressed to 'Snookums' from 'Booby', which recounted their last meeting in staggeringly explicit detail along with Booby's hopes for the next. The hopes in question appeared to involve every orifice both of the ladies possessed.

"Bloody hell," Will said, awestruck. "That'll teach me to underestimate the Victorians."

"Their ladies, at least. I stand in awe at Booby's turn of phrase." Kim's dark eyes brimmed with laughter. "I hope she had a highly successful career in some sapphic niche of the publishing trade, and that she satisfied all her desires with the delightful and accommodating Snookums. Except for the one in the last paragraph, because that's a bit much."

Will checked the last paragraph and winced theatrically. "No, I wouldn't if I was Snookums. That's got to sting. What did you find this in?"

Kim bit his lip, an absurdly boyish gesture, his eyes alight. "You won't believe me if I tell you."

"*Where?*"

"The Book of British Birds," he said, and doubled over as Will howled.

They stopped for ale and sandwiches at lunchtime, eaten companionably on the shop floor, and worked through the afternoon. It was profoundly soothing, even if it turned up no mysterious scientific discoveries.

Will called a halt around six. They'd got through a good

half of the shop floor and most of the boxes of paper in that time. It was dark, he was tired, and they were both saturated in paper dust. It was tickling Will's nose, clogging his fingers, drying his eyes. Kim's once-white shirt was tinted yellow-grey and his hair coated, like a stage performer trying to look old.

"I will be sneezing until 1940 at this rate." He blew his nose on what had long ceased to be a spotless handkerchief. "Well, that was a good start. Another two or three days should surely do it, assuming the information is in a book. If it isn't, I may weep."

"Same."

"I have also indulged myself as reward." Kim pointed to a small stack of books he'd put aside. "May I purchase those?"

"I think you can have them."

"Nonsense. List price. No, I absolutely insist," he said over Will's protestations. "Those are valuable, and I would have bought them otherwise."

"But you've done a solid day's work here, so—"

"Really, no," Kim said firmly. "If you are minded to reward me, could I have this?" He indicated Booby's letter.

"Of course. Er, why?"

"It will make the perfect Christmas present for a friend. She'll adore it."

Will picked up *The Book of British Birds*, slipped the letter inside, and handed it over. "It needs the packaging. And that's definitely with my compliments."

Kim calculated the cost of his purchases and paid up. His thumb left a smear of grime on one of the notes. "This must be what they mean by filthy lucre. You need an army of maids to clean this place, and I need a wash. I suppose there's no bathroom here?"

"Just the sink. There's a public bath a little way away."

Kim grimaced as if a public bath were an intolerably

tedious thing. "You'll need your clothes cleaned, as do I. Can I offer you my facilities? I live on Holborn, it's not too far."

Will hesitated, torn between a strong desire to say yes, concern about leaving the shop unattended, and a deep sense he'd taken as much help as he could reasonably accept. Kim evidently saw the debate on his face and gave a smile that fell somewhere between apologetic and hopeful. "Just a bath. Really, it would make life a lot more pleasant and I think we both deserve a *little* comfort."

If today had proved anything, it was that nobody was going to lay their hands on the information without a lot of time and effort. "All right."

Kim's smile twitched. "Jolly good."

Kim had a serviced flat on the north side of Holborn, on the second floor of a grand yellow-brick block called Gerrard Mansions. Will hadn't seen the inside of one of those before. It was very nice indeed.

"Comfortable," Kim said when he commented. "I've a man who lives downstairs, and there are housekeepers for all the cleaning and cooking. It's a great deal easier than keeping one's own staff."

"I'm sure it is," Will said drily.

That at least meant he didn't have to come into these clean, elegant rooms in his dirt and face the person who'd clean up after him. Kim went to run a bath, assuring Will the geyser would provide limitless hot water. Will took the chance to look around as best he could without leaving dusty fingerprints as evidence of his curiosity.

Kim had a good-sized sitting room with large windows giving a good view over the street. His furniture was all in the new style, with smooth modern lines and flourishes that seemed vaguely Egyptian to Will's eye. The many lamps had elaborate stained-glass shades. That was a little surprising: Will had assumed Lord Arthur Secretan the marquess's son would have piles of antiques. Possibly he was inclined to modernity, although the few paintings and pencil drawings on the wall were all pre-Raphaelite in style. In fact, as he looked closer, he saw they *were* pre-Raphaelites.

"This says Rossetti. Is that an original?" he demanded as Kim came back in his shirtsleeves. He'd washed his face, though his hair was still dusty.

"Yes, and that's a Burne-Jones." Kim indicated an exquisite little painting of a youthful medieval knight in yearning pose. "I know the style is terribly outmoded to modern sensibilities but I don't—whisper my shame—I don't *like* modern art. I prefer paintings to resemble the thing they depict, and I'd rather they depicted ideals and beauties than Dawn over an Industrial Graveyard or The Cost of War. I realise that my views are so naive as to be contemptible."

"Are they?"

"According to artistic friends. I mix with Bohemians, you understand, the cutting edge of Chelsea, and to be honest, most of them are dreadful. I buy their paintings as a friend must, but don't ask me to pollute my home with the things. If you want to give me your clothes, I'll have them cleaned as far as possible while you bathe."

He said that in quite a straightforward way, not at all like stripping bare was a prelude to more interesting activities. That reminded Will he wasn't clear why he'd been invited to this elegant flat. Just for the bath? For more? Did Kim quite know himself?

Well, he'd find out, and meanwhile his clothes were a disgrace. "Thanks. I will."

As a first step, he set to emptying his pockets, removing a handful of silver, a box of matches, an old bus-ticket, and a folded paper, which he realised was Draven's letter. "Better keep that safe."

Kim picked it up to read again as Will shed his coat. He felt remarkably self-conscious about such a normal act after last night, though not in a bad way. He was in favour of making the most of this opportunity, he decided. Maybe he should suggest Kim come and soap his back.

His companion didn't currently seem to have illicit intimacies in mind: his attention was all on the letter. Will knelt to unlace his shoes rather than applying his dusty backside to Kim's clean furniture.

"I must say, that was a damned good idea of Draven's," Kim remarked, as if they were continuing a conversation. "If I want to hide a paper where it will never be found, I shall definitely come to you. What do you think, another two days?"

"With luck, but it'll be harder upstairs where they're stacked rather than shelved. It's a devil of a job. I'm glad of your help."

"I just hope it amounts to something."

"Well, it has," Will said. "I've more or less conquered the papers, which is a load off my mind."

"That's something. I'm rather fretting that we have no way to know if your uncle destroyed the information, or indeed someone already bought it by accident. It's one thing to search for a needle in a haystack, another not to know if it's there at all. When would one decide to stop looking?"

Will put his shoes by the wall. He'd bought new ones as soon as his uncle had given him money, and they were decent; it was a shame his sock had a hole at the toe. "It would be tiresome never to know."

"Wouldn't it just."

"If it's not there to find, will the tattoo people and the War Office give up asking for it?"

"That's the problem, isn't it? Blast Draven—with all

respect to the dead, of course. I wonder if he secretly hoped your uncle would dispose of it. Finish the job as he couldn't bear to."

"He gave it to him to keep safe."

"Yes, but people are odd creatures. Maybe Draven hoped the decision would be taken out of his hands. Or perhaps he means exactly what he says. *I dare say you will want to burn the other, but I know you too well.* It does seem remarkable Draven could have relied on another man's sense of obligation to overrule his better judgement. Even if your uncle had your dogmatic principles— Oh, for God's sake!"

He yelped the last words, an expression of near-shock on his face. "What?" Will demanded.

"I've got it," Kim said. "Where does a wise man hide a pebble?"

"Eh?"

"On the beach. Have you not read the Father Brown stories? You hide a pebble on the beach and a leaf in a forest—"

"And a paper among papers." Will was a little disappointed. He'd expected a revelation. "I've been through all the papers."

"But Draven didn't send his 'enclosed' to a stationer's, he sent it to a bookshop. You hide a leaf in a forest, so in a bookshop you hide…?"

"A book? We've been searching the books."

"For hidden papers." He looked like he was about to shake Will for his incomprehension. "*Think.* What paper item would your uncle reliably refuse to destroy, no matter the provocation?"

"A book. Draven wrote it *in* a book, on the pages," Will said, skin tingling with understanding. "My God. Of course."

"On a flyleaf? No, even a bibliophile could tear out a flyleaf. On a page in the middle of a book. *That's* how you keep a secret. The odds of happening on a single book in that shop by chance are bad enough, but at least shaking out a book doesn't take long. Whereas if you had to check every single page of every volume—" The expression of triumph dropped away from Kim's face with almost comical speed. "Oh, my God. Oh, *no*."

"It's not a needle in a haystack," Will said hollowly. "It's a piece of bloody hay."

"I didn't look in any of them for writing. We'll have to start all over again."

"There's forty thousand books. Jesus, Mary, and Joseph."

"Seraphim, cherubim, thrones, and principalities." Kim rubbed his face. "Let's think about this, we can surely narrow it down. It would need to be something of no great interest to most readers or value to a book collector, so it's unlikely to be bought. Nothing rare or desirable, but also not so rubbishy that your uncle would find it possible to destroy it. Some tedious volume of a worthy philosopher, or a favourite poet, maybe. Do you know your uncle's favourite poet?"

"No idea."

"Is it worth asking his neighbours about his literary tastes?"

"They didn't come round much," Will said. "People have been pleasant enough, but I wouldn't call it friendly. Nobody drops in for a cup of tea. And Uncle seemed to have become very solitary as he got older."

"That happens. Men shut their doors against a setting sun." Kim said, and went absolutely still.

"Got something?" Will asked curiously.

"Got—? No, not as such." He shook himself and gave a quick smile. "I just had a horrific vision of my immediate future examining every book in your shop. At least this should cure me of bibliomania. I will never want to see a book again in my life."

"I'm getting there already," Will said. "I always liked books well enough, but a bookshop... It's like the difference between watching a bumblebee buzz around flowers, and realising you're caught in a swarm." *Gay*

Kim's face lit with delight. His attractiveness was in the movement of his face, far more than the features themselves, and that movement was startlingly expressive when he let it go. No wonder he had that trick of stilling his features: he must have betrayed himself frequently before acquiring it. He looked like a man who gave and took pleasure in that moment, and Will's chest tightened with anticipation and desire.

Surely they'd earned a bit of rest and recreation. He licked his lips. "So, that bath—"

"You should go and have it," Kim agreed, which was not what Will had been going to suggest at all. "Put your clothes outside the door and I'll get them seen to. Do take as long as you like. And afterwards..." He hesitated. "Well. Perhaps we can enjoy the evening."

"I'd like that."

"I could order dinner here." Kim reached out and brushed a dusty lock of hair back from Will's cheek with his thumb. "Make things a bit more comfortable than last night."

"Which part?"

"Well, the part where you were tied to a chair, certainly. I wouldn't do that to a guest." His voice sounded a little rough. "And the accommodations are somewhat less basic here. I aim to please."

"Very obliging of you." Will's voice was rather rasping too. It might have been the dust.

Kim's glance flickered down his body, a tiny movement but enough to make Will think of him going to his knees. "I've an obliging nature."

Will stepped closer. Kim was just a few inches away. He could reach out and touch. "Show me."

It came out sounding like a command. Kim's eyes met his, a swift, startled movement. They were so dark and his lips were a little parted. Will wanted to shove him up against a wall, to feel him give way, hear his gasps. *Make* him gasp. He'd shuddered with response last night, and Will wanted to make him do it again.

The desire sang between them. "I..." Kim began, then stepped back with a little shake of his head. "I shall. But, if I may, *after* a bath? We've all night and frankly, we're both a disgrace."

Cleanliness seemed highly overrated at this moment, but Will forced himself not to say so. Kim's immaculate rooms suggested a fastidious nature and he didn't want to behave like some vulgar lout. They did have all night, he reminded himself, willing his arousal down. He could wait. "I won't be long."

"No, take your time. I've a few things to do that I'd rather get out of the way, and your clothes will be a while, so you might as well enjoy yourself. I'll get you a gown."

EIGHT

The bathroom was pure luxury. Will hadn't used a private bath like this before: they'd hauled a tin bath in front of the fire at home. This was a whole room dedicated to plumbing, with a fixed tub and hot taps and space to stretch out, and even a hot-water radiator so the room didn't have that clammy feel you got when steam met cold air. It was like Buckingham Palace.

He caught a glimpse of himself in the mirror with some shock. His eyes were about the only part of him that weren't dust-coloured: no wonder Kim had insisted on bathing first. He washed his face and hands thoroughly at the sink rather than filling the bath with more dirt than he had to.

He got in, enjoying the outrageous luxury as hot water enclosed him, sinking into the pleasure. Remnants of a Puritan conscience nagged at him to scrub up and get out, but he dismissed it. He would take Kim at his word and enjoy both the bath and the anticipation of what was to come. Anyway, he could hear Kim's muffled voice from another room, obviously speaking on the telephone. He had things to do, and this was a pleasure to be relished, so Will let himself lie back and revel in the sensation of hot, clean water.

If this was how the other half lived, he wanted some of it. A private bath, a warm, clean, spacious flat, and he'd bet the bed was pretty good as well. He was looking forward to finding out.

Will ran a hand over himself as he lay in the bath, brushing his cock just a little, thinking of last night and the sounds Kim had made as Will drove between his thighs. Tiny pleading gasps, as though he'd been trying to hold himself back. If he had, he'd failed: he'd come hard against Will's chest, hips jerking with ecstatic agony, eyes black in the dim light.

God, that had been good. And Kim liked to oblige, he'd said. He'd certainly enjoyed having a cock in his mouth, a thought which gave Will a tiny electric shock of remembered arousal, because Kim's clear pleasure in performing the act had made it one of the most erotic experiences of his life. Perhaps he'd do it again. Did he kneel at the altar? It seemed possible, the way Kim had wanted him thrusting between his legs. Would he bend over for Will? What might that be like to do with time and care and a comfortable bed? He let his mind wander over that for a while, and had to rein back his imagination before he got carried away.

He needed not to put too much on this thing—arrangement, affair, whatever it was. Kim was an odd fish and difficult to interpret, to put it mildly, between his obvious experience and pleasure in the act and his reluctance to get on with it. Will's own experience with men didn't compass anything that had lasted longer than about half an hour, or repeated encounters with anyone since Alfie Greenaway, with whom he'd had a week of stolen moments in Flanders before a sniper's bullet had stolen Alfie. Neither of them seemed to know precisely what they were doing, certainly not with each other, and they didn't have any commonality of class or background or occupation to get them through awkwardness. They had a job to do together, and once that ended, so would their reason to associate. As it had to because, of course, Kim was engaged to be married.

Well, that was the way of things. Will would take whatever Kim might want to give, and vice versa, while it lasted. Sooner or later that would be nothing, so he'd make sure he accepted dismissal with grace, and in the meantime he'd enjoy whatever pleasure was available.

He bent his knees on that thought, slid underwater to submerge his head, and worked on scrubbing the dust out of his hair.

By the time he was done and out, the bathwater was cool and grey and he feared he'd overstayed his welcome despite Kim's assurances. The water was filthy, too, and Kim probably never washed in other people's grimy water. Maybe he'd run a whole clean bath.

He contemplated himself in the mirror. His hair was sticking up at all angles, and even more strawlike than usual, and his skin was rather pink from the heat, but at least he was clean. Ready to get dirty in a more enjoyable way.

After a moment's consideration as to the possible benefits of walking out naked—after all, Kim had made himself clear enough—he decided he didn't have the nerve. He put on the red bathrobe Kim had hung up for him, went through the little corridor, and came into the living room, where an elegant blonde sat on the sofa, reading a magazine.

Will stopped dead. She glanced up and her eyes widened. "Oh!"

He recoiled, appallingly aware of his undress. "I beg your pardon!"

"No, no, not at all! Not at all." Her voice was crystalline upper-class, moving almost instantly from shock to assurance, and she examined him with interest and no obvious reserve, up and down. "You did startle me, but I dare say I startled you too. You must be Will. Kim left you a note— terribly bad of me to have read it, but I assumed it was for me and by the time I realised it wasn't, it was too late. On the table." She indicated a paper, which Will picked up. It was a few lines, indicating that Kim had had to go out briefly but would be back in a jiffy, and would Will please run him a clean bath. It didn't say anything about other visitors or, thank God, about private matters.

"Of course, Kim's idea of a jiffy is not ours," the woman said, proving that she'd made herself mistress of the letter's contents. "If you'd like to get dressed, don't let me stop you. Unless you don't want to. I'm dreadfully modern, you know, and quite unshockable."

"I can't," Will said. His face was still red from the heat of the bath, which saved time. "He's taken my clothes. To be cleaned, I mean. We were doing a rather grimy job today."

"I've seen Kim do dirty work but rarely literally," she observed. "How keen of him. And how terribly awkward for you, and of me, turning up like this. I'm Phoebe Stephens-Prince." She unfolded a pair of extremely nice legs—her skirts barely reached mid-calf—and stood, holding out a hand.

Will took it with deep reluctance. "Will Darling."

"Delighted to meet you. Any friend of Kim's, of course. *Any* friend of Kim's." With that elliptical remark, she sat down again and took out a cigarette case and holder. "Smoke?"

"I don't, thanks."

"Really?"

"Gas," Will said briefly. His lungs hadn't taken bad damage and a cigarette wouldn't send him into a coughing fit: he simply couldn't bear the sensation of inhaling smoke.

It gave him an irrational fear that his chest would start to burn again.

Her hands stopped moving. "I'm so sorry. Would you prefer I didn't?"

"No, go ahead."

She fitted a cigarette into an ebony holder with deft movements. Her lips were painted red in a Cupid's bow, her dark golden hair fashionably bobbed and waved. She was strikingly pretty, with large grey-blue eyes; she seemed decidedly smart to his inexpert eye. She was Kim's fiancée.

"Are you waiting for me to give you permission to sit? Darling, please do. Oh, how absurd of me: *Mr.* Darling, darling, do. But that's no better, is it? It sounds like a popular song. Daisy, daisy." She lit her cigarette herself, which was a relief as Will had been wondering if he was supposed to do it for her. "So tell me, how do you know Kim?"

Will cursed him mentally. "I have a bookshop—"

"Oh, you're the book chap! Darling, how exciting! I really must stop doing that," she added. "I suppose it's a terrible nuisance to you. One would go out for a cocktail and think one was being continually summoned from all sides. Do go on."

"Uh," Will said. "Did Kim tell you about my shop?"

"He said there was all sorts up, and I wasn't to worry if he came home with a black eye. I won't, you know."

"Home? Do you live here?" Will demanded, and could have kicked himself at her raised brow, even if it came with a quiver of amusement. She was a fiancée, not a mistress. "In the flats, I meant."

"Of course you did, darling. No, Grosvenor Square, too tedious. Imagine Kim coming home there with a black eye. *Quite* unthinkable. Mother would never tolerate such a thing, but those Victorian relics are so dismally dictatorial about behaviour, aren't they, though I expect they were as bad as everyone else once upon a time, just in private. Anyway, tell me *all* about the bookshop."

"It was my uncle's. He died recently, and he left something important in the shop. Kim was helping me search for it today." He sounded horribly wooden; he couldn't make himself speak with ease.

"You'll be all right then. Kim's marvellous at puzzles," Miss Stephens-Prince said with authority. "And terribly good about helping one with things, too."

"He's been very kind."

"He is, isn't he? Or, rather, no, he isn't. *Kind.*" She appeared to consider the word. "He does things when he thinks they ought to be done, but I don't know if that's kindness or just rightness. Do you know what I mean? Kim says, *Well, that needs to be dealt with,* and he deals with it, and then you'll be sorry. Whereas most people say, *Oh, how dreadful, you poor dear,* and they don't do anything at all. Or they don't say anything nice *and* they blame the person in trouble, so maybe Kim *is* kind by comparison even if he isn't sympathetic in the slightest. Yes, that's it. I'm so glad you see that because so few people do and it's not fair. It makes me really quite cross." She screwed her face up as an illustration of crossness. "People are *vile* to him because of that dreadful brute Chingford and they've no idea at all."

Will was hopelessly lost by now, and somewhat baffled, since Kim seemed pretty sympathetic to him. "Uh—"

"Chingford. Kim's brother, have you met him? No? Well, you haven't missed much, he's utterly ghastly. Though it's partly Kim's fault, of course, sometimes I think he positively enjoys martyrdom. I suppose we all enjoy having a bad reputation, don't we, because the kind of people one has to please in order to have a *good* reputation are so very dreadful that one positively delights in appalling them, but you see *I* can have a bad reputation merely by going to night-clubs and driving too fast, whereas Kim...well. And I don't think he *does* enjoy it, actually. It's all self...what do you call it? Not self-flattery, though really it might as well be if you think about it, though the other way around. Like a hair shirt. What am I thinking of?"

Will couldn't begin to answer that. She mused. "Self, self...like monks, you know. Anyway, that's Kim. I'm quite sure Dr. Freud would have things to say about that, but *will* he submit to analysis? Of course not. Well, I wouldn't either, but I'm not complicated so it would be a terrible waste of money. Self-flagellation! That's it." She blew a perfect smoke ring. "Anyway, if he's got your case you're in luck, because he's awfully clever. Heavens, listen to the Devoted Fiancée. I'll be darning his socks next." She struck a coy pose that belonged on a Victorian sentimental print, her eyes sparkling with laughter. "Now, would you be a dar—a *dear* and make me a drink? The cocktail things are over there. You see, I feel quite entitled to order you about. If you're on borrowed-dressing-gown terms with Kim, we shall unquestionably be friends." She smiled at him. She had a very wide and endearing smile.

"What would you like?" he managed. Kim's 'cocktail things' proved to be a cabinet with a lot of different bottles, multiple glasses of various shapes, and several silver containers which held slices of lemon and even ice cubes. You could run a night-club in here. Will had no idea what to do with any of it.

"Do you know how to make a sidecar?"

He stared at the range of bottles. One of them held blue liquid and another green. Who drank this stuff? "I'm afraid not."

"Oh, well, never mind. Gin and tonic, please, with a slice of lemon. I shall treat it as a health cure. Thanks awfully. And that's another good thing about Kim. Other men might come home to find their fiancée having cocktails with a strange man wearing his dressing gown and take it amiss. I can't bear that sort of thing, can you?"

"What sort of thing?" Will was forced to ask as he poured what he hoped was a ladylike measure of gin. He wondered what path this could possibly go down.

"Jealousy, darling. Possessiveness. It gives me the horrors. People who think they can tell one what to do and who to see as if they own one, or that they have the right to sit in judgement on one's behaviour. There's a great deal too much of *that* about." She gave her cigarette a darkling look, as though blaming it, and stubbed it out. "What *I* say is, one can be as moral as one likes but one should have the courtesy to do it in private, like any other bad habit. Goodness me, I didn't ask, how rude. Did you have any joy from your labours today?"

"No. No, we didn't find anything." He handed her the drink.

"What a shame. To better fortune soon." She raised the glass in a toast. "Do make yourself something, won't you? Is it madly interesting, owning a bookshop?"

"It's pretty challenging at the moment," Will said, with some understatement. "I haven't done it long."

"Kim loves books. I quite like reading—novels, at least—but he likes books as *things*. I suppose that why he wanted to work with you, he'll be in his element. Like a fish in a very dusty leatherbound sea. He's secretly quite old-fashioned, of course. He's got the most appalling taste in art, don't you think? So dreadfully conventional." The words might have been damning, but the smile with which she said them held such deep affection that Will's chest constricted.

"I should run that bath," he said, knowing it was abrupt and ungracious but needing to get out of this room, away from her. "Excuse me."

He lurked determinedly in the bathroom, draining the bath, rinsing the grime off its sides and refilling it slowly, and didn't emerge when it was done. After about five minutes sitting on the lavatory cursing Kim and himself, he heard a door open elsewhere in the flat.

"Kim, at last!" Miss Stephens-Prince called. "Where *have* you been?"

"Phoebe? What the blazes are you doing here?" Kim didn't sound pleased.

"Seeking refuge from Mother, of course. I met your new friend."

"Oh God. Where is he?"

"I don't know why you say it like that." Miss Stephens-Prince sounded a little hurt. "I haven't thrown him out."

"I should hope not. I was more afraid you'd you eaten him alive." Kim's tone was rather more conciliatory this time.

"Well, I wouldn't say no, darling, he has divine calves. I do like a good calf. He's hiding in the bathroom."

"I'm not surprised," Kim muttered as his footsteps approached the bathroom. "Will? I've your clothes."

Will opened the door a crack, no more, and stuck out a hand to take the pile extended to him. He didn't want to see Kim; he couldn't look him in the eye. He hadn't been able to look at himself in the mirror either.

It was very easy to disregard a fiancée who was no more than a name and a blurry black and white image in a magazine. He couldn't ignore the vibrant Miss Stephens-Prince who quite clearly adored Kim, who spoke to and of him with laughing fondness, who shared jokes with him and was going to marry him and had no idea she'd been talking to a man he'd betrayed her with, twice.

You shit, Will thought. *You utter shit, Kim. If that was my girl...*

No wonder Kim had blown hot and cold with Will. He was doubtless ashamed of himself, and he bloody ought to be. Will was ashamed of the pair of them, and the fact that he hadn't previously thought of Miss Stephens-Prince as a person rather than a concept, a fiancée in the abstract, was no excuse. If Kim didn't realise she deserved better, he was a fool, and if he did, he was a knave. Will didn't think he was a fool. And everything he'd done, Will had aided and abetted. Initiated, even.

It's not my job to keep him up to the mark, he thought fiercely. It did absolutely nothing to assuage his guilt.

He got dressed with some relief. Whoever had cleaned his clothes had done a good job. They'd been beaten, sponged and pressed, and he looked a great deal more decent than he felt when he emerged from the bathroom to brave the sitting-room.

Miss Stephens-Prince was still there, smoking another cigarette with a rather mulish expression. She'd finished her gin in short order; Kim was at the cocktail cabinet mixing something complicated.

He glanced round as Will entered. His face wasn't precisely frozen but it was entirely impassive. "Will. I understand you've met Phoebe."

Miss Stephens-Prince beamed, the sulky expression vanishing. "Yes, we had a delightful talk. Well, it was more that I talked and he listened, but he was awfully nice about it. Darling, do make Mr.—no, really, I'm simply not going to do this. May I call you Will? And I'm Phoebe, of course. We're all first names these days, you know, and much better it is for everyone. Sweeping away the barriers of class and sex in the what-do-you-call-it of modern thought, and I'm sure *that* will be easier with trousers on. Now, let Kim make you a cocktail, Will, he's quite the mixologist, and come and talk to me properly. Darling, make Will a sidecar. I feel quite sure you'll like it."

"I don't—"

"Brandy, Cointreau, lemon juice," Kim said. "Or would you prefer whisky?"

"I'm sorry, I really must go." Will didn't think he could bear another minute of this. He wanted to punch something, preferably Kim.

"Oh, no, please don't!" Phoebe sounded dismayed. "Not on my account. You had things to do, I'm sure. If I'm intruding—" She started to rise.

"Not at all," Will said firmly. "I only came to borrow the bathroom because my shop is in a bit of a state. I'll leave you to your evening."

"I wish you wouldn't." Kim sounded light, but as he gave Phoebe her drink and turned, his eyes met Will's, making a quick, direct connection. "Phoebe just dropped in for a chat on her way to meet a friend for dinner. She isn't staying."

Will didn't know much about women's fashions, but he was damned sure Phoebe wasn't dressed for dinner, and she hadn't said anything about meeting someone else. He was not going to stand here and watch Kim throw her out. "Then you'll be dining alone because I'm going home."

Kim's eyes narrowed slightly. "For heaven's sake, have a drink first. We did a solid day's work, and you deserve one. I need one, I can tell you."

"I won't, thanks, but carry on." He scooped his things into his pocket. "I'll be off."

Kim exhaled through his nose. "If you insist, but give me a moment first, will you? I want to talk about tomorrow. We still have a lot of work to do and I think we need a quick chat about that. In private, if you don't mind, Fee."

"No need," Will said. "I'll see you as and when."

He almost enjoyed the frustrated expression on Kim's face. *Almost* because he'd have liked to see hurt there. Kim deserved to be hurt. Will was hurt, far more than he should have been because he'd brought this on himself and had no reason to expect better. Phoebe would certainly be hurt one day, and badly. The least Kim deserved was a bit of discomfort when he got trapped in the hole he'd dug for himself between two lives.

"Miss Stephens-Prince," Will said, with a nod of farewell, and strode out. Kim said, "Will, wait!" sharply behind him. He didn't stop or look round, but headed down the stairs of the mansion block at some speed. By the time he got out, he was almost running.

Damn Kim. Damn him and damn himself, too, for a fool. It wasn't as though he hadn't been warned about Kim. Cowardly, vacillating, treacherous, no moral fibre, *engaged*: he'd been told it all and he'd still let himself believe there might be something between them, that the physical pull and the instinctive liking and the companionship added up to anything worth having.

Not at this price. Not at the price of betraying someone to whom Kim had made promises, who'd opened her heart to him, and even, instantly, to Will as his friend. If you couldn't have a thing without hurting someone who didn't deserve it, you shouldn't have it.

Will had seen wedding rings on a couple of partners in Flanders, but that had been different. The urgency of wartime and the possibility of there not being another chance ever; the distance from home; the fact that nobody ever promised more than snatched moments. It wasn't like spending a night and a day in companionship. It wasn't the same as inviting a man into your home, your bed, and smiling into his eyes and making it seem like you had more to offer than a quick fuck.

He wouldn't have minded being Kim's quick fuck. He objected violently to being part of a betrayal.

He strode on, propelled by anger at himself as much as Kim, then saw a tram slowing for a stop up ahead and sprinted for it. He was still in the habit of saving pennies, but there was an unpleasant light drizzle in the cold air and his hair was a little damp yet from his bath. He'd treat himself to a swift journey home and a good solid meal, and then do another hour or two in the shop, alone again.

He hated Kim for making him feel more alone than he had before.

The tram took him all the way to St. Martin's Lane. He briefly considered going straight to the warm, inviting cafe over the road, but it didn't have a licence, and he was in a foul mood. He would go home first, he decided: have a drink by himself, pick up a book to read with his dinner, and calm down.

So he turned into May's Buildings, and saw men coming out of his shop.

He stood and stared, hardly believing his eyes. They must surely be emerging from the shop next door—but they weren't, it was *his* front door, bold as brass.

"Hoi!" He set off for them at a run, bellowing threats at the top of his voice. There were two of them, wearing pinstriped suits like office workers, with his door standing open behind them. They glanced round in alarm as he approached but they didn't run, and as he skidded to a threatening halt, a third man emerged from the shop door.

"Ingoldsby!" Will roared. "What the bloody hell do you think you're doing?"

Captain Ingoldsby drew himself up. "Mr. Darling—"

"Do you have a warrant? *Do* you? Do you have my permission to enter my private property in my absence? How dare you break into my shop!"

"Please calm down."

"Breaking and entering!" One of his neighbours had

emerged to find out what the noise was. Will swung round to him. "Call the police! These men broke into my shop. I'm pressing charges."

"That would be extremely ill-advised," Ingoldsby said.

"Don't you tell me about ill-advised." Will was fizzing with rage. "Police! Hey, police!— You show me your warrant to search my premises and I'll stop making a fuss. No? Well, then. Police!"

To his delight, a constable appeared round the corner, a man Will had met and chatted to as he went round on his beat. Captain Ingoldsby made an exasperated noise in his throat as he proceeded over.

"Trouble, Mr. Darling? What's going on here?"

"These men broke into my shop," Will said over Ingoldsby's reply. "I just got back and look at him, he's standing there on my doorstep! I want to press charges for breaking and entering."

The constable did look at Ingoldsby in his smart suit, and the two rather red-faced men hanging around him. One of them was Price, Will realised, who had tried to warn him about Kim. Fucker. He shot him a resentful glare.

The constable cleared his throat. "Anything to say for yourselves?"

Ingoldsby flicked out a card. "My name is Captain Charles Ingoldsby and I work for the War Office. This is official business, constable."

The policeman's eyes went wide. He glanced at Will, who snapped, "I don't care what he does. It doesn't give him any right to break into my premises!"

"No, indeed. Mr. Darling. *Did* you break in, sir?"

"I did not," Ingoldsby said smartly. "I have a key." He stepped out, locked the door behind him in a demonstrative way, turned, and held out the key between finger and thumb.

Will snatched it before the policeman could. "What the devil— How did you get this?"

Ingoldsby's eyes met his, a cold, hard glare. "I suppose you are at Vine Street station, constable? If Mr. Darling chooses to press charges, please ask Superintendent Waddleston to contact me at the War Office. I think that should suffice."

The constable was clearly out of his depth. "Mr. Darling, if there's no break-in—?"

"They were trespassing on my premises. You saw them. And I didn't give him that key!"

"No? Then who did?" Ingoldsby enquired, and let that hang a moment. "I think that will do. Good evening."

"Wait a moment," Will said harshly. "I want to be sure they haven't walked off with my books, since they were trespassing on my property. I suppose I can insist on that much?"

Ingoldsby opened his coat and turned out his pockets with an expression of profound sarcasm. His men did the same, then the three turned and left without further ado. Will stared after them, humiliated, enraged, and with a growing sense of nausea.

"Well, now," the policeman said, in a tone that clearly meant *Now what?*

Will toyed with the idea of asking him to have a look at the shop, but he didn't have the strength. The place was a mess anyway, and if they had found anything, he wouldn't be able to tell.

"I don't know," he said, suddenly exhausted. "Could you —I don't know—could you just keep an eye? There's been a lot of funny business here. You know I reported a break-in last week? If whoever's on the beat could poke their heads round now and again, I'd be grateful. I'm going inside."

He locked the door behind him. It was pitch dark inside, in part because Ingoldsby and his men had pulled down the blinds to go about their work, a little domestic touch that made him quite furiously angry all over again. He turned on the lights, and went to check the top drawer of his desk. As he'd expected, the spare that lived there was missing. Because, of course, he held it in his hand. He put it back and shut the drawer.

They hadn't made a mess. There was no sign of anything disturbed on the desk or in the back room. Even his knife was still there. He thought a moment, then walked up and down the rows of shelves.

He'd dusted thoroughly the other day, but his and Kim's work today had raised a vast amount of dust. It lay in a thick layer on the edges of the bookshelves, a fine powder clearly visible in the electric light, and even more so once he'd fetched an electric torch. He beamed that on each shelf in turn.

There was a drag mark through the dust in front of an edition of the complete works of Shakespeare. It was neatly lined up with the books on either side, but it had unquestionably been moved. Will pulled it out to mark the place. A few books along was a second drag mark, also Shakespeare, and he found a third on the next set of shelves. He went over the rest of the bookshelves methodically, but saw nothing else.

He took the three volumes to the desk, poured himself a large whisky, and sat down to make himself face the facts.

Kim had had his inspiration about the secret being written in a book. He'd packed Will off to the bath, told him to take a long time, even removed his clothes to keep him in the flat. They'd had that conversation with the promise of *all night*. Then he'd made a telephone call and gone out, and when his fiancée had appeared unexpectedly, he'd tried his hardest to detain Will instead of getting rid of him like any sensible adulterer.

But Will had left, which had been no part of Kim's plan, and got home as fast as was humanly possible, and he'd just caught Ingoldsby and his men heading out of his shop. If he'd walked, or waited two minutes for the next tram, they would have had time to raise the blinds and lock up, and Will would never have known they'd been there.

The conclusion was inescapable. Kim had taken the spare key at some point today. He'd had some sort of brainwave about which book the secret was hidden in, and set out to keep Will busy thereafter. He'd contacted Ingoldsby to tell him to search the shop while Will was in the bath, and gone out to give him the key. And once Will had left, he must have telephoned someone to warn Ingoldsby he was on his way back and tell him to clear off. Doubtless that 'someone' was one of Will's neighbours. He was being watched, after all, and it seemed there was no limit to betrayal.

Will knocked back about half his drink in a swallow. What had Phoebe said of Kim? *If he's got your case, you're in luck.* He'd thought it was a figure of speech, just as he'd thought that Kim had turned up by chance in the first place. It seemed he'd been wrong.

He tried to make himself consider this calmly. Did the War Office want the information badly enough to put an undercover man on the job? Perhaps they did: Libra had wanted it badly enough to threaten torture.

But Ingoldsby was War Office and he hadn't tried to make Will trust Kim. He, or his sidekick Price, had said those unpleasant things about Kim, tried to put Will off him...and the net result had been to make Will trust him more. Of course it had. On another man the same tactic might have worked the opposite way, made him feel that Ingoldsby was the honest one, but Will had always been stubborn in the face of authority.

He'd been played like a fish. No, it was far worse than

that, he realised, with a plunging sensation. He'd been hooked, netted and put on a slab, and he hadn't even seen it coming.

Kim had trapped him so neatly. And carefully, too, with those lingering looks that never took it too far, ensuring Will made the first move. He couldn't possibly call it entrapment. And Will had made that move, and now there was a small matter of two years or so for gross indecency to be used against him at any time. Doubtless Kim would disappear from the charge sheet, or maybe they simply knew that Will couldn't risk it getting that far.

Did Ingoldsby know? He'd dared Will to ask who'd given him the key. Had Kim told him how he planned to keep Will occupied?

Will wanted to be sick. He wanted to strip the sheets off the bed he'd shared with Kim last night and burn the damned things. He wanted to burn down the entire fucking bookshop, in fact, just to make sure that piece of shit never got what he was after. If the tattoo people came back, he'd give them free range over the place.

He finished his whisky and poured another, aware of his empty stomach but with no desire to put food in it.

It all fit together too well for any other explanation. Kim was Intelligence of some sort, had been from the start. That was how he knew how to fight, not any nonsense about Bolsheviks. He'd been sent to ingratiate himself with Will. In fact, odds were he'd supplied the big thug himself as a way in and to give Will a reason to trust him. The giant hadn't had any tattoos on his wrists, had he?

And come to that, after Libra and his pal had attacked, Will had spoken of the second man's tattoo as a sheep's head, but Kim had said ram's head. He knew who they were. He'd known everything all along.

"Christ, Darling, you're thick," Will said aloud into the

empty shop.

He wanted to break things, important things, just like Kim had. He wanted, violently, to go back to the flat in Holborn and pound Kim's face to jelly, the treacherous bastard. Or, he supposed, the dedicated patriot. He knew that attitude bitterly well. No action was too dastardly and no damage too great if one acted in the service of one's country.

Balls to that. Kim was a treacherous lying shit, Ingoldsby was a housebreaker and would-be thief, and if that was what it took to defend your country then your country could rot. Fuck the lot of them. He wasn't standing for this.

He made himself a couple of large sandwiches with the last of the bread and cheese, and a pot of strong tea, then he settled down to work. He checked the three Shakespeares first, page by tissue-thin page, a job so lengthy and boring that his resentment of Kim doubled for making him do it. He found no missing pages, no writing.

Fine. He'd just find every other edition of Shakespeare, single plays or collected works, that his uncle had accumulated over the last forty-odd years.

It was two o'clock in the morning before he was reasonably confident that he had them all. By this time he was dusty again—good, he didn't want Kim's cleanliness—and had learned to hate publishers who didn't stamp the name of volumes clearly on the spine, but his haul included twelve complete Shakespeares, ranging from relatively cheap card bindings to an extremely nice leather-bound 1822 edition, and some fifty copies of individual plays.

He checked the flyleaves on every single damn book, because "Ex Libris Dr. Draven" would have been a useful thing to see at this point, then he ferried the lot into the back room, stacked them under his bed, and settled down for the night with his knife under the pillow.

The bedsheets smelled of Kim.

NINE

W ill kept the blinds down and the Closed sign up the next morning. Quite a few people knocked on the door; he ignored them all. He didn't delude himself that he could do so forever—he'd have to leave the shop for food at some point, and anyway night would come, and with it threats. He couldn't live under siege, and even were that possible, he couldn't afford to keep the place shut indefinitely. But for now, he needed the breathing space.

He went through each Shakespeare methodically, page by page by thousands of pages, and found the secret in the fifth copy. It was an 1895 print of the Globe edition, cover faded, good condition, but nothing particular to attract a buyer. The writing, a spidery mass of black ink down both gutters of a spread, came in the middle of *Timon of Athens*, a play he'd never heard of. Will couldn't make head or tail of it—it was all abbreviations and chemical symbols, plus some cryptic notes on production techniques.

What he did find was the lines that must have given Kim the clue. That was what a posh education got you.

What is amiss plague and infection mend!

Graves only be men's works and death their gain!

"My work is only graves," Draven had written. Same thing. Not a good thing.

"Cheerful," Will muttered aloud, but irony wasn't any sort of shield from the cold feeling in his head. Plague and infection, it said, next to a scientific procedure that people burgled and tortured and whored themselves to get hold of.

This was very, very bad. Should he just tear out the pages and burn them? That might be best all over, but it wouldn't get rid of the War Office or the tattoo people. If he told them he'd burned the information, he doubted he'd be believed, and if he was believed, he'd probably face retaliation. Libra hadn't seemed a man to take defeat with grace. If he didn't burn it he'd have a bargaining chip, but not one he wanted to use, and there was always the risk they might find it.

He couldn't see any way to square that circle without damning himself. Could he pass the black spot to somebody else, as Draven had to his uncle? No: that was unfair, and he didn't know anyone he could trust. In books, the hero usually had an uncle or family friend who worked for an unspecified intelligence agency and could be relied on to get one out of a tight corner. Will was fresh out of uncles, and his only friend who worked for an unspecified intelligence agency was bloody Kim.

Fine. He'd do it himself.

"I didn't live through Flanders to get killed in Charing Cross," he said aloud, and took the books' silence for agreement.

By eleven he had a plan of sorts. He went out through his back yard and over the walls to carry out his scheme and made a trip of it, eating a large lunch at a nearby Lyons. He also bought food for a couple of days. When he got back to the shop with his bags, Price was waiting on his doorstep.

"I wouldn't if I were you," Will told him. "I'm not in the mood."

"You were warned," Price said. "I've a message from Captain Ingoldsby."

"If he wants to give me a message he can deliver it in person. I've a few things to tell him myself."

"Will you hear the message?"

Will indicated that he would not, and added his opinion of proceedings to date, using verbal skills honed over four years in the trenches. Price's ears went extremely red, and he retreated in short order. Will let himself in to the shop, flipped the sign to Open, and set about raising the blinds.

Two men came in about a minute and a half later. "Afternoon, gentlemen," Will called, without looking up. "Can I help you?"

"Just browsing," came the reply from behind a shelf.

"That's fine. If you're after Shakespeare, it's at the front."

There was a short but expressive silence, then a man appeared round the shelves. He was a nondescript sort of fellow, not one Will had seen before. "What was that?"

"If you're after Shakespeare, it's all here." Will indicated the small set of rolling shelves he'd set up next to his desk, with four Collected Works and all the single-play copies. "Browse away. Or let me know if there's a particular play you're after." He swung his feet back on to his desk and carried on reading *War of the Worlds*, a copy of which he'd found between *Measure for Measure* and a battered volume of Mrs. Beeton.

The man hovered a moment. Will looked up again with the put-upon expression of a bookseller expected to sell books. "Anything I can do for you, sir?"

The man tensed. Will pulled open the drawer to his right, where he'd put his knife. "Whenever you like."

Their eyes locked, then the man turned and walked away. Will heard extremely quiet whispering from behind the shelf. He got silently to his feet, the Messer behind his back, and cat-walked to the end of the aisle.

He wasn't at all surprised to see the second man was Libra.

"Hello, there," Will said. "I asked your pal if I could help you."

"You're playing games," Libra said. "That's a bad idea."

"I am now," Will agreed. "Everyone's been playing with me, and the name of the game is silly buggers. I've had enough of it."

"Then let's not play. You have the information. Mr. Darling. You've found it. Now you need to hand it over."

"I told you before. Draven made conditions on who it should go to, and set a password. If you have that word, I'll give you what you want."

Libra took a step forward. Will did too, settling the knife hilt in his hand. "No funny business. I'm not in the mood, and I'm not a fool. The information isn't on the premises any more."

"I expect you could lay your hands on it easily enough."

Will grinned mirthlessly. "That wouldn't be very clever of me, would it?"

Libra scanned his face, then stepped back. "You're a shop-keeper, Mr. Darling. I suggest we make a deal."

"You're offering to buy it?"

"It's valuable information. I'm happy to pay. I can be more generous than any other buyer, just as I can be more implacable than any other enemy."

"Don't threaten me," Will said. "I don't take it well. As you say, I'm a shopkeeper so I need to consider my price.

Come back to me—in three days' time, say, at four in the afternoon, no earlier. And no funny business before then or the information goes direct to the War Office. That stunt you pulled the other night won't do any more. I've got the whip hand now and I'm taking precautions."

Libra didn't move, but Will could see the tension in his stillness. He shifted his weight slightly, letting his knife hand come to his side. Libra's eyes flicked down then met his.

"I wonder if you're a brave man, or a stupid one."

"Mostly I'm annoyed," Will said. "Clear off. I've work to do."

The next arrival of note was Ingoldsby, an hour or so later. He stormed down the street past the window, threw the door open with a wild jangle, and stamped to the desk. Will kept his feet up. If he was going to be a member of the awkward squad, and he was, he might as well play the game to the full.

"Ah, Captain. Pull up a chair."

Ingoldsby glanced around, realised there wasn't a chair, and gave him a fulminating glower. "Well, Mr. Darling?"

"Well, what?"

"You informed my colleague you wished to talk to me."

"No, I told him you should deliver your messages in person. I expect you'll start with an apology for trespassing."

"That isn't my intention," Ingoldsby said through his teeth. "Make no mistake, you would be well advised to co-operate, starting now."

"If you threaten me, I will throw you out of here by the scruff of your neck," Will said. "Be quiet and listen. I found your information."

"Where is it?" Ingoldsby snapped.

"Where you knew it was. Written in the margins of *Timon of Athens*."

"*Where?*"

"All the copies of Shakespeare I have are on that shelf." Will indicated it with a lazy hand.

Ingoldsby took two steps to the bookshelf, glowered at it, and swung back. "What are you playing at?"

"Is there a problem?"

"There was at least one other copy, a different edition, that's not here."

"Well observed," Will said. "Actually, there's quite a few others gone as well. I spent some time this morning distributing them outside this shop. But I expect you already knew that because you were having me watched."

"Enough tomfoolery. Where is the information?" The cords of Ingoldsby's neck were standing out.

"Where you won't find it. If you want my cooperation, you'll need to persuade me I ought to cooperate, and I mean persuade, not threaten. I've already told that to your friend Libra and his gang."

"Libra," Ingoldsby repeated.

"Also round here this afternoon, looking for Shakespeare—"

"Are you certain of that?" It was almost a bark.

"Ask your watchers if you don't trust me. I intend to give this thing only to someone who can give me Draven's password, or who can persuade me that their right to have it outweighs my uncle's obligation to keep it safe. So what I want from you is frankness. Not orders, not trespassing, and if I get one more threat from you you'll never see it at all. I mean that. I will burn the damned thing if you menace me again." He let that sink in. "But if you give me an honest explanation, and have a reasonable case, I'll be reasonable too. By the way, I'm sure you know this Libra chap knocked me on the head and tied me up and so on. If you want to have him arrested for his efforts in this business, I'd be very happy to cooperate in that. As a starting point, he'll be back here in three days to offer me money for the papers—which, for the record, I have no intention of selling to him or anyone. I thought you might be able to use that."

Will had planned what he was going to say and thought it was pretty good overall—sensible, suggesting a possible way forward without giving in, and offering something useful. Ingoldsby didn't react as he had hoped. He simply stared in a silence that lasted a worryingly long time. Finally, and in a much calmer tone than before, he said, "You really have no idea what you're doing, do you?"

"That's because nobody will tell me anything. Feel free to start."

The man breathed very deeply, in a commendable effort at self-control. "I will need to discuss this. In the meantime— and this is not a threat but a warning—I strongly suggest you stop playing with fire. You are swimming in deep waters, Mr. Darling."

"Wouldn't that put the fire out?"

Ingoldsby snarled, and left. Will grinned to himself and returned to HG Wells while he awaited further developments.

TEN

F urther developments duly came the next day, just before closing time, in the form of Kim.

Will had the warning from the bell. He heard the jangle, then footsteps, then the scrape of the bolt as someone locked the door. He sat up, reaching for the knife, and didn't hurry to put it down when Kim appeared around the shelf.

He seemed different, harder-faced, or perhaps that was Will's imagination, but he sounded quite normal as he said, "Good afternoon."

Will looked at him, looked at the knife, considered his options, and went for, "Go fuck yourself."

"I take it that means there's nobody else here?" Kim enquired, and waited for Will's nod. "Good. I realise I'm not welcome."

"No, you aren't," Will said. "You set me up, lied to me for days, and stole my key. You worked out the answer in front of my face, and sent your War Office pals to rummage around my shop instead of telling me. You got me to trust you and abused my trust, and that's not the half of it. You betrayed me, you lied— I'd call you a whore but you're nothing so honest. Were you really going to let yourself get fucked all night just so your War Office pals could search my shop? I don't even know a word for that."

Kim didn't respond. His face was impassive.

"And apart from what you did to me, you also dragged me into the shitty way you treat your fiancée. You were trying to throw her out so you could—with me, for the sake of the fucking War Office— I hope to God she finds a better man than you. It shouldn't be hard."

"You might think so. Is there any chance you'd listen to me?"

"I listened to you last time. Didn't do me much good."

"Indeed not. Nevertheless, I don't want to see you suffer over this."

Will took a long, slow breath and let it out silently, the way he'd been trained. "If you've come here to blackmail me—"

"I suppose I deserved that," Kim said tightly. "No, I have not."

"I don't know why you're getting on your high horse. Does it not count as blackmail if you supply the evidence and let someone else do the extortion? You sold me to Ingoldsby, you shit!"

"Christ, Will. I am not here to threaten you."

"You'd better not be, or I'll break you in half."

"You're the one who's going to get hurt here," Kim said, with unsettling certainty. "I understand you found the information. Was it *Timon of Athens*?"

His tone was so matter-of-fact that Will found himself responding, "How did you know?"

"That letter had been nagging at me since I read it. *My work is graves.* Couldn't place it. Then I quoted a line to you —*Men shut their doors against a setting sun*—which also happens to be *Timon*, and it clicked."

"So you ran off to give your boss my key and tell him to raid my shop."

"Ingoldsby's not my boss," Kim said. "But yes, I did. You weren't supposed to come back in time to find out."

"No, you were going to keep me busy, weren't you? An evening on your knees for king and country. Pity your fiancée showed up, really. I was planning to enjoy myself." He saw the red bloom over Kim's cheekbones with bitter satisfaction. "Was it a relief she arrived when she did, rather than when I had you over your bed? Or do you enjoy your government work?"

The red spots spread. "Will—"

"I'm sure you've got a justification. I dare say you can explain how very important this information is and why it was all worth it. Don't bother."

"It is important." Kim's voice was steady, even if his skin was treacherous. "I'm told you wanted answers. I have them."

"Are you saying Ingoldsby sent *you* to tell me what's going on? You? To me? Christ, you people have a nerve."

"There's nobody else, for reasons I can explain if you'll listen. Or you could not listen and carry on, but I wouldn't put money on your chances of living to Christmas that way. That's not a threat, incidentally. It's a prediction."

Will gave it a moment longer, then he swung his feet up onto the desk again. "Go on."

Kim contemplated him, then strolled into the back room, returning with the other chair, which he set down by the desk and sat on. "Let's start with Professor Edward Draven. He was a scientist, a very bright man, and a lone wolf. He had an independent income, and his own laboratory. He became very interested in what the Germans were trying to do with anthrax and glanders in the war. And a few months ago, he claimed to have developed a new sort of weapon."

"A new sort of weapon," Will repeated. "Gas?"

"Not exactly. It would be spread from canisters in a similar way, but the essence of it isn't gas. It's disease."

Will stared at him. Kim met his eyes and spoke levelly. "Imagine the Spanish 'flu again, but this time on purpose."

"*How?*"

"I don't know. He said he'd found a way to create plague in a test tube. Invisible, deadly, and highly contagious. A terror weapon of monstrous power, because once people knew others carried it, they'd shut their doors against survivors of an attack, or just shoot them. Drop a few canisters on a capital city and watch the people turn on one another in fear of their lives. So he said."

Will's breathing had gone shallow. He could smell the pineapple-pepper scent of gas, feel the acrid tang in his mouth. "Go on."

"I don't know if he fully appreciated what he was doing in human terms, at least at the time," Kim said. "He was interested in the science, not the slaughter. It's all theory if you sit sufficiently far away, isn't it? Anyway, he came up with this little flower of genius, and contacted the War Office wondering if they might be interested."

"Christ."

"And this was when things got tricky because, shortly afterwards, Draven was contacted by a group who had heard about his research and wished to have it for themselves. They are, or they say they are, anarchists. They want to destroy the capitalist power structures and, by means of radical disruption, usher in a new era of equality and jam for all. They are called Zodiac."

"Libra," Will said.

"And Aries, who you also met, and the rest. They run on a system of anonymity like all the best secret societies. The important thing here is, to borrow your favourite phrase, a new era of equality my arse." He gave Will a mirthless smile. "Zodiac have true believers—useful catspaws—but the ones at the top are out for nobody but themselves. They would happily burn down the world in order to sift the ashes for gold. Of that I am quite sure."

"Who are they?"

"I believe rich men, plutocrats and aristocrats. People who already have power and wealth and don't feel like sharing; who see things like universal suffrage and the labour movement and higher taxation as an attack on their divine right to sit at the top. They don't like the way things are going, and they'll do anything to their own benefit, in service of which they leave a trail of ruined and ended lives. Blackmail, destroyed businesses, murder."

"Why isn't something done about this?"

"We're trying," Kim said shortly. "Zodiac are rich, secretive, and powerful. They're clever, too, using people they despise as cover for their own schemes. If someone gets caught, the blame goes to Bolshevists or anarchists. And they are ruthless. They are driven by staggering greed at the top and fanatic idealism below, and between greed and fanaticism people can justify anything. If they got hold of this monstrosity of Draven's, they'd... I don't know what they'd do. Hold it over the heads of governments, perhaps, ransom entire cities. Wipe out the London and New York stock exchanges, and make a killing in the resulting chaos. They intend to entrench their power and wealth at other people's expense, one way or another, and they *must not* get their hands on this weapon to help them do so."

"No," Will said. His chest hurt. "I see that. If you're telling me the truth, of course."

"Could you please assume I am for long enough to hear me out? I'm not enjoying this meeting any more than you are. I'm here because this matters."

Will tried to read his face, failed. He had no idea what a truthful Kim might look like. The man sounded sincere, but he'd sounded sincere when he was advertising his obliging nature.

What the hell. "Go on."

"Thank you. So this now brings me to the current problem. You told Ingoldsby that Libra had been here, and that he was searching for Shakespeare."

"Yes," Will said slowly. "He was, and he knew I'd found it, too. But how—"

"How did Zodiac know?" Kim asked for him. "How did they know about a revelation I'd had literally the night before and communicated only to the War Office? Good question. Right up there next to the question of how they found out about Draven's invention in the first place."

"You've got a leak. You fucking useless bastards have a leak."

"Don't be so generous. What they have is a traitor," Kim said flatly. "Someone in the War Office is owned by Zodiac. Hence my involvement now: they are locking down the flow of information since they don't know the point at which it's being tapped. I'm sure this will strike you as an extremely good reason not to hand over Draven's work to the aforesaid useless bastards, but unfortunately there is really no choice. The WO have plans in place to keep the invention safe—yes, quite," he added at Will's snort, "but if worse comes to worst, at least we'll *also* have it as a deterrent, and our scientists can perhaps find a counter or antidote. What we can't risk is for Zodiac to have the weapon and not us."

"How about neither?"

"If one could rely on neither, it would be marvellous, but we can't. Don't delude yourself you've a choice, Will. You can't just burn the pages. Or, rather, you can, but you've been sufficiently obstreperous that nobody's going to take your

word for it that you did. Zodiac will kill for it, and the War
Office isn't going to take the risk of you quietly selling it.
You're up a gum tree, and I don't see how you get down
short of handing over the information to the WO and hoping
Zodiac turn their attention away from you."

That was more or less exactly what Will had concluded.
He swung his feet back to the floor so he could put his
elbows on the desk and his head in his hands. "Shit."

"Quite."

"It kills entire cities." Will could picture it. London still
and silent. Bodies lining streets and Tube platforms, driver-
less trains full of corpses rattling on towards their terminus.
He imagined an apple spilled from an abandoned straw shopping basket with extraordinary vividness; it took him a
moment to realise that was a memory from Flanders.

"That's what Draven claimed." Kim tipped his head back.
"It may not work, of course. I've lain awake at night trying to
tell myself he was a fantasist."

"Do you think he was?"

"We can't risk it. We have to take this seriously."

"What happened to him?"

Kim shrugged. "He destroyed his laboratory—notes,
samples, equipment. Burned it all, except for the aide-
memoire he sent to your uncle. Then he contacted a chap in
the War Office to say that Zodiac were making intolerable
threats to him and others and that the information was with
his old friend William Darling, and took cyanide the same
night. He didn't give them a code-word; possibly he simply
forgot to. God knows what was going through his mind, the
poor swine."

"I've seen gas go through people's lungs. I hope he burns
in hell."

"Also a viewpoint. Anyway, that's your truth, Will, that's
what it's all about. I don't blame you if you aren't impressed

by Draven, or Ingoldsby, who is perhaps the worst man to have handled this, or by me. I'm not greatly impressed by myself." He shrugged. "Needs must."

Will had an unpleasant crawling sensation all the way up and down his back. Something had changed in the way Kim spoke, a tone altered or a pose dropped. Before there had been a likeable air about him; now it was gone as if it had never been, and those dark brown eyes weren't warm any more. He remembered Phoebe's chatter. *Kim says, 'Well, that needs to be dealt with,' and he deals with it, and then you'll be sorry.* He had to make an effort not to reach for his knife, just to have the comforting sensation of a weapon.

They sat in silence for a few minutes. "I don't know," Will said at last. "I need to think."

"You need to act, because you've made rather a tangle of things and we have limited time and capacity to unpick it. What did you do this morning? Everyone is terribly confused."

Will shrugged. "I dug out all the Shakespeares in the shop—"

"How did *you* know it was Shakespeare, by the way?"

Will explained briefly about the dust tracks. Kim's mouth twitched. "Very nice. Sloppy from Ingoldsby, though. Tut."

"I dare say he was in a hurry. I looked through them this morning and found the copy with Draven's work in it."

"So it unquestionably exists?"

"Well, there's a lot of writing, very small, with chemical symbols."

Kim sighed. "I had held out a little hope for, 'Ha ha, fooled you all'. Never mind. Go on."

"I'm not telling you what I did with it. But I took eight of the other Shakespeares over the back way, and hid them in bookshops up and down the Charing Cross Road."

"So I am told. Several agents are cursing your name. Why?"

"I thought all the people watching me could have fun playing Find the Book in the Bookshop too, since you and I enjoyed it so much."

"This isn't a game, Will."

"Then why is everyone toying with me?" Will demanded. "Why couldn't you be honest with me from the start?"

"I've been honest now. Has it changed your mind about handing over the information?"

"No."

"Well, then."

That left Will briefly speechless. "You didn't have to lie! You didn't have to— Christ, man!"

You slept with me, he wanted to say. *You kissed me and sucked me off and whimpered when I fucked you. You came, twice. Did you enjoy it? Tolerate it? Hate every touch?* He wasn't even sure if he'd been the abused or the abuser; the thought made him sick. "Was that—what we did—were you acting under orders all that time?"

Kim's face was statue-like, remote and unmoving, saying everything with its silence. Will was almost glad not to have an answer in words. It was too shameful to bear. "And what about Phoebe?" he demanded. "Your fiancée?"

"Don't worry about her."

"Don't *worry*?" Will said, latching on to something he could be uncomplicatedly angry about. "You made me a party to adultery, or near as dammit! Don't tell me not to worry!"

"Oh, come off it. You knew I was engaged. You chose your course."

"I hadn't met her then!" Will shouted, knowing as he spoke it was paper-thin. Kim might have pointed that out but instead his composure cracked unexpectedly, a little smile tweaking his lips.

"Yes, I know what you mean. She's wonderful, isn't she? A wonderful tissue of nonsense from head to foot. Her welcome to you was quite real, you know, and she will be bitterly disappointed to learn you've joined the ranks of people who will never speak to me again."

Will sat back in his chair. "You don't deserve her."

"No, I don't."

"Doesn't that bother you?"

"You assume she's an idiot," Kim said. "She's not, and her affairs are none of your business."

"You made them my business."

"You did that too. I didn't assault you."

"No, you took damned good care to let me make the first move, didn't you? And did you report back to your masters at the War Office afterwards? Blow by blow account, was it? I assume the plan is to threaten me with prosecution for gross indecency if I don't hand over the information."

Kim's face was unmoving, but you could no longer say it gave nothing away, because Will could see the tension of the muscles keeping it still. "That is not my plan."

"It's Ingoldsby's."

"Did he say that?"

Will had to stop and think back. "He implied a threat. He didn't specify it, but he wouldn't have to."

"Not if you have a guilty conscience."

Will nodded. "Proud of yourself, are you?"

"Not really."

"I wouldn't be, either. Go to hell."

Kim smiled mirthlessly. "I have no doubt I will oblige you, but you're still evading the point. You are in trouble, Will. Two years for gross indecency is trivial compared to what Zodiac might intend for you. Just hand over the information. Please."

"No."

"You will get yourself killed through bloody-mindedness. You cannot handle this alone."

"I know. That was why I wanted your help," Will said. "Shame how it worked out. What's the thing the chap says in *Timon of Athens*? 'I wonder men dare trust themselves with men.' I read that yesterday. Stuck with me, for some reason."

"'Oh, happy they that never saw the court, nor ever knew great men but by report'," Kim retorted. "A bit late when the bodies are piling up. I suggest you concentrate on getting out of the situation you're in now."

"Tell me something," Will said. "You didn't, still don't, strike me as being without shame. You've betrayed me, and your fiancée, and every decent impulse. I assumed that was because you thought it was the right thing to do. Am I wrong? Did you just do it for the money? For fun?"

"It was—is—the right thing to do," Kim said levelly. "We need this information."

"You'll do the right thing by your lights, no matter the unpleasant consequences. Fine. I don't know why you're assuming I'm more cowardly than you."

Kim examined him, face unmoving, for a long moment, then quite suddenly shoved both hands into his hair. "Will..."

"No."

"Please. If you won't give me, or Ingoldsby, the papers, give them to *someone*. The Prime Minister. Anyone."

"No."

"Then at least let me help."

"If you're going to ask me to trust you, don't," Will said. "It would just embarrass us both."

Kim's head dropped back. "Yes, I suppose it would."

"What you can do is remind your master of what I said to Libra and get him to organise whatever he's going to do."

"What you said," Kim repeated. "What, precisely, was that?"

"He wanted to buy the information. I told him to come back with an offer in three days. Ingoldsby can arrest him."

"…what?"

"You can arrest him on whatever charges. I'll gladly cooperate with that."

"In the course of which, you have agreed to sell Libra Draven's work?"

"I told him to make an offer. Why not? I'm not going to do it."

"God almighty." Kim put a hand over his face, massaging his temples. "You bloody fool. You idiot. It's not illegal to offer to buy a private citizen's papers from another private citizen in lawful possession of them."

"It was illegal for him to tie me up and threaten me!"

"And? This is not going to be played out in the courts, Will. What do you think would happen if we arrested Libra?"

"Maybe you could get some information out of him!"

"We already know who he is. Worthless stuff: he's a true believer, not of the real inner circle. Give me Capricorn and we might have a bargain." Kim exhaled hard. "And even if Ingoldsby wanted to set up some sort of trap, may I remind you that Zodiac would probably find out all about it in advance? There's nothing for him to gain here so he won't do a thing except, possibly, wait for them to wring the papers out of you and then see if he can swoop in."

"So he won't help. Fine. What's your problem?"

"My problem is that Libra will turn up here with a suitcase of money, expecting victory, and when he doesn't get it, his masters will be *very disappointed*. And Zodiac do not have a positive history with disappointment. I'd expect Libra to do a great deal to avoid that. Most of it to you."

"But—"

"No, Ingoldsby won't help," Kim said flatly. "Or, rather, he will if you give him the papers. Not otherwise. It will be his view that you put your head in this noose, and I'm not sure he's wrong."

Will stared at him. Kim's mouth was set. "I wish this were a threat, Will, but it's not. I have no power to order protection for you and I really do promise you Ingoldsby won't. He's there to protect the British state, not its inconvenient and unhelpful citizens who bring trouble on themselves. Is the information somewhere safe, and can you get at it?"

"Yes, and not easily."

"Improve on that one way or the other. If your priority is to live, you'll want it to hand so you can give it to them to make them stop hurting you. If your aim is to keep the thing safe, you ought not be able to get hold of it at all, because keeping quiet under torture is not usually possible, no matter how brave you think you are. Would you like my advice?"

"No."

"Give us the information and go. Vanish. Disappear off to Ireland or the north, but not Northamptonshire because we all know where you came from. Change your name, grow a moustache, and pretend this never happened, though keep a weather eye out for strangers anyway. If you can't stomach handing over the papers, burn them and go anyway."

"Go?" Will repeated. "You do realise it's not that easy? I've been unemployed since the war! My entire income is the bookshop. What am I supposed to do in Ireland?"

"You said your uncle left you money. The solicitors will give you an advance while you wait for probate."

"And how long will that last? Is that the best advice you've got?"

"No: my best advice is to hand over the information. I can't help you if you won't listen." Kim rose. "You know where to find me. My telephone number." He put a card on the table with a precise little click. "I will help if you let me."

"By which you mean, if I do what you want."

Kim gave a tiny shrug. "I hope you make a sensible decision. And I hope you don't leave it too late."

He turned on his heel. Will watched him go, not caring that he'd got the last word. He was too tired to argue any more, sick and sad to the bone. He'd thought Kim to be an out and out villain, and what he'd just seen had been far worse: a decent man debased. Debasing himself, compromising everything in the service of a sordid aim and an untrustworthy master.

Will wasn't doing it. He would stick to his guns whatever came along. He didn't, at this stage, have much choice.

ELEVEN

W ill expected trouble that night, or at least feared it. He didn't drink, put his knife under his pillow, nailed a board across the back window, and checked all the locks were fast. It gave him no great security but a mildly comforting illusion of control. He slept lightly, waking at the slightest sound from the city and the creaks of the shop, and by six in the morning had reached the conclusion that he really did need to move to a hotel or some such. If only he could afford one.

He'd go and see the lawyers, he decided, asking for an update on the process of probate and, while he was at it, for a further advance of a hundred pounds against the estate. Cash in hand would be vital if he had to disappear in a hurry. That sent his mind back down the pathway Kim had set it on, not for the first time.

He couldn't just disappear without money. He'd tried life with no friends to call on, no meaningful experience, and nothing but the clothes he stood up in, and he'd all but starved. Work was simply too hard to find these days. If he could sell the bookshop it would be different, but he couldn't do that until probate was granted, and he was fairly sure international criminal gangs worked faster than lawyers. He'd have to find someone trustworthy to administer his affairs, who would send him the money without disclosing his whereabouts. It could doubtless be done. It would have to be done, because he couldn't stick around here to be shot at.

He rather regretted that. Bookselling hadn't been the career of his choice, but now he saw its charm more strongly. He liked the old shop, he was getting used to the smell and the slow pace. He'd have enjoyed mastering the trade and taking time to read. He could have made a life here.

He didn't care about leaving London as such, but he would miss Maisie badly, and for all Kim's talk of disappearing, to leave her without a word of thanks or farewell would be villainous. She was a good friend, a real one. If things had gone down a different track, they might have made a couple. Thank God they hadn't, because the only thing that could make his situation worse at the moment would be if he had a fiancée for Zodiac or the War Office to bully.

Well, not quite the only thing. Kim could make it worse.

Will didn't want to think more about that. He cleaned up and swept the shop, made it to the lawyers' office at nine-thirty on the dot, and charmed his way into five minutes with Mr. Deakin, his uncle's solicitor. That was about as far as his luck ran.

"I understand your predicament, Mr. Darling," Deakin assured him. "And I do appreciate that the law seems to laymen to drag its feet more than is reasonable. However, let me assure you that matters are proceeding as swiftly and smoothly as possible."

"I don't doubt it, sir, but even if probate is granted next month—"

"That is, I think, a *leetle* optimistic."

"—I need funds now," Will pressed on. "There's no doubt

about my claim, is there? I'm William Darling, the money's there, it's coming to me, right? Well, I'm in a sticky situation and I need it now."

"I shall happily write you a letter to assure any creditors that the funds will be available."

"I need ready cash," Will said. He could feel himself going red. "An advance against the estate."

"Now, I do understand your situation," Mr. Deakin said in a soothing voice that Will was beginning to find extremely irritating. "But I'm sure you realise that we have already been as obliging as possible, and as your uncle's solicitors, while we are concerned to assist you as best we can..."

Will stopped listening. He knew this tone well: it was the tone of *Of course we're very sorry* and *It must be awful for you* and *Something should be done* which made it very clear that the speaker wasn't going to do anything at all. Advances on legacies were obviously for people who had money already.

He managed to wring twenty pounds out of the man as a sop, and headed home. It seemed running wasn't an option, so he'd stand and fight. He'd have a word with the constable on the beat, and Norris next door, say he was being bothered by thugs and ask them to watch out for trouble. He'd cope somehow. He'd done worse.

He had quite a few customers that morning, plus a dealer with a catalogue, and two lurkers. He tried not to let the latter bother him.

Maisie arrived around half past noon. He wasn't expecting her at all, still less the large basket of silk flowers which she manoeuvred past the shelves and shoppers.

"Hello, Will," she said cheerily. "Flower?"

"Eh?"

"Flower. I'm selling them to raise funds for the Equal Citizenship Society. There's to be another big push for the voting age. So..." She angled the basket invitingly. It held a variety of artificial flowers: some of them crocuses or irises in suffragette purple, white, and green; others in more usual shades. "You'd pay a lot more than I'm asking now for these on a bonnet, I'll have you know."

"Not sure a bonnet would suit me."

"Then have one for your buttonhole." Maisie nipped a red flower that Will tentatively identified as a peony from the colourful mass, threaded it into his buttonhole with a nimble movement, and secured it with a pin. "Very smart. Two shillings."

"Do I have a choice?"

"No."

"Then do you have one that's a bit less…bright?"

Maisie narrowed her eyes. "You need brightening up. I worked hard on that one, so take care of it."

Will fished out the required levy as a customer approached. He sold the man a copy of *Lady Audley's Secret* while Maisie stowed the money in the collecting-box that hung round her neck. "How are you, anyway? I haven't seen you in ages."

"I'm…all right." He was appallingly conscious of the lurkers. "You know. Been a bit busy."

"Haven't we all. This is my first time off in I don't know how long."

"And you're spending it raising funds? Good for you."

She made a face. "I'm putting an hour in before I go to visit my auntie in Watford. She's been taken poorly again. But my group leader has a way of being disappointed at us if we don't do our bit."

That reminded Will too strongly of Zodiac. He forced a smile and looked up, a little relieved, as the door bell jangled. "Well, I hope you do all right. I'm not sure I'd come to a street of bookshops, though. Were my neighbours generous?"

"Not to speak of," Maisie said with a sniff. "Talking of neighbours—" She broke off. That, Will realised too late, was because he'd stopped paying attention to her. He was staring at the new arrival who'd come up behind her.

It was Phoebe.

She was wearing something in a shimmery blue-grey that, in the way of female clothing magic, made her eyes astounding, and she smiled blindingly at him and then at Maisie, who had turned to see. "I beg your pardon for intruding, do you mind? Will, darling, I wanted— Oh, what glorious flowers! Suffragette violets! That is absolutely adorable, may I see? My goodness, these are perfect—and that peony, too divine! Did you make these? You must have the cleverest fingers. Darling, do introduce me."

"Yes, do, *darling*," Maisie said, sounding just a little sharp.

"This is Maisie Jones," Will said. "Maisie's a milliner at Villette, on Lexington Street, if you know it? Maisie, this is the Honourable Phoebe Stephens-Prince."

Maisie and Phoebe both gave him the sort of look that said he'd got something wrong. "You just say 'Miss'," Maisie informed him.

"And I *told* you it's Phoebe, darling," Phoebe added with a little reproach.

"And I'm quite sure Miss Stephens-Prince doesn't shop on Lexington Street."

"But perhaps I should start because these are lovely," Phoebe countered. "Did you make that charming hat too?"

Maisie touched her hat, as though checking by feel. "I did, yes."

"It's perfect for you," Phoebe said, tilting her head to examine Maisie with a surprisingly professional expression. "Quite *quite* for the shape of your features, and the colour is exactly right. That is very clever. Villette, did you say? I shall pay a visit. In the meantime, may I buy a suffragette bouquet? These are irresistibly lovely. I shall hand them out to my relatives next time I go to tea."

She bought seven flowers, which Maisie tied up in a twist of green ribbon, to the accompaniment of Phoebe's coos of delight. This somehow led to an animated five-minute discussion of hat trimming techniques during which Phoebe's hat was removed, thoroughly analysed, tweaked in arcane ways, and replaced. Will, who had never thought about hats beyond putting them on his head, was lost in the professional mysteries, but he could tell from the way Maisie's expression changed from stiff wariness to animation that Phoebe knew what she was talking about.

"Well," Phoebe said at last. "I must borrow Will now, Miss Jones, but I shall come very soon to see your work. It was a great pleasure to meet you. Goodbye." She put out her hand. Maisie, obviously charmed and equally obviously dismissed, did a sort of half bob, half touch of the hand, said, "See you, Will," and left in some confusion.

"What a delightful young lady," Phoebe said when she'd left. "Is she *your* young lady?"

"Maisie? No, nothing like. We're friends. I used to work at her old place for a while."

"She's very good." Phoebe examined her artificial bouquet. "I do like a woman with clever fingers. Now, Will, I came to ask a favour, and I hope you won't refuse me."

You were meant to say, "Anything" in response to that sort of remark from a beautiful woman, but this was Kim's fiancée. Will said, warily, "If I can help…"

Phoebe beamed. "Good. Take me to lunch?"

"Sorry?"

"I'm simply starved, and I can't possibly eat alone. I'm sure you know some nice little places."

"Not the sort of nice little places you go," Will said with certainty.

"Nonsense, darling. I told you I'm awfully modern. I should love to go somewhere Bohemian and—and ordinary."

Will contemplated the cafe where he'd breakfasted with Kim. No. "I don't know anywhere Bohemian." She gazed at him with big-eyed reproach and he heard himself say, "But there's a French restaurant round the corner."

"Perfect. Shall we go? I really am terribly hungry."

He gave in. "Just let me get ready, then, please."

It was an insane extravagance in the circumstances, but he had a strong urge to know what was going on, and there was the ten-pound note Kim had found in the book the other day. He might as well enjoy himself while he could. He took a moment to wash his hands, regret having shaved in such a perfunctory way this morning, and comb his hair. Then he headed out to escort the Honourable Phoebe to luncheon.

The French restaurant round the corner had red awnings and plants outside, and cosy dark wood booths. It was exactly what a French restaurant ought to be, and Phoebe seemed perfectly satisfied as she sat. Will examined the menu with the dreamlike sensation of a man with only a very vague idea what was happening, though he still checked the prices carefully. It was more reasonable than he'd feared.

"I expect the onion soup is marvellous," Phoebe said. "I shall have the chicken livers and the roulade. Are you ready?" She waved at the waiter as she spoke.

Will made a hasty decision to have onion soup and the beefsteak and added a carafe of red wine to the order, feeling very cosmopolitan indeed with his fashionable companion. He listened to Phoebe chirrup about the weather, the shocking news from abroad, and the doings of a set of people he'd never heard of while they waited for the wine and then the first courses to arrive. Once he had his bowl of onion soup—impossibly savoury, redolent of melted cheese and toasted bread—he let himself enjoy the first spoonful, and said, "Did Kim ask you to do this?"

"Kim?" Phoebe's blue eyes opened wide. "No, darling, why?"

"Either you wanted to talk to me or you wanted to get me out of my shop. I wondered which." That was rather blunter than he'd have preferred, but he didn't feel up to verbal fencing or games.

"Or I might have wanted to pursue your acquaintance," Phoebe remarked. "Or possibly I was hungry."

She'd eaten one corner of her chicken liver on toast. "Hungry," Will said. "And just happened to be passing my shop by pure chance? Are you often in May's Buildings?"

"Always," Phoebe said with great firmness, then her expression dissolved into a wide and mischievous grin. "Well, perhaps not. Of course I wanted to speak to you, darling, and I shall, but there are niceties to be observed in these situations."

"What situation is this?"

"A Kim situation." Phoebe met his eyes with meaning, cut off another tiny corner of toast, and ate it with great attention. Two could play at that game, so Will went back to his soup.

"It's impossible to eat onion soup with dignity, so please don't try," she remarked, which was embarrassing because he hadn't been trying. "What were we saying? Kim. No, he did not ask me to speak to you."

"Didn't he?"

"I do have ideas of my own, darling. That didn't change when I put a ring on."

"When are you getting married?"

"Next winter." Her eyes were a little distant. "I'm awfully fond of Kim."

"I'm sure you are."

"No." She sounded, suddenly, quite serious. "You don't understand. Kim is my best friend. He's twice stepped in to save my neck when I was in the worst trouble of my life. I trust him more than anyone, I adore him, and I want him to have anything that would make him happy. And goodness knows *that's* a challenge because sometimes he's determined to put himself on a rack or an iron maiden or whatever those ghastly medieval things were called. But I should do anything for him, just as he would for me."

Oh God, Will thought, *is she here to warn me off?* The thought was like a frozen plunge-bath. Surely she couldn't mean to have that conversation with a man, in public? Had Kim been that careless about his affairs? Had he done this before?

"It sounds like you'll be very happy together." His voice sounded appallingly wooden. He tried to put a bit more warmth into it, to say *Message received.* "I hope so. I wish you both well."

Phoebe made an exasperated noise and leaned forward, lowering her voice a little. "You aren't listening, darling. Kim and I got engaged because it was convenient for both of us, just as marriage will be convenient for both of us. Neither of us would wish the other one to be unhappy, before or after the wedding. I want Kim to have what he wants, and he wants me to have what I want. Which is why I am talking to you. Do you follow me now?"

Will was holding his spoon half way between the bowl and his mouth, strings of cheese making spiderwebs to the murky soup. He put it down carefully so as not to splash. "Uh. I don't know if I do."

"I'm quite sure you do, darling," Phoebe assured him. "You have awfully expressive eyes. Hazel, although that's such a vague word, isn't it? People use it to mean absolutely anything. Yours are quite golden in some lights. You should wear yellow more. Deep ambers or golds, with browns, that would bring them out awfully well."

"Maisie said that," Will said numbly.

"Of course she did, she clearly has a wonderful eye for colour. Was that a Welsh accent?"

"Cardiff, yes."

"And you and she aren't walking out?"

"No."

"I'm delighted to hear it. That is, I'm sure you'd be very happy if you were, but since you're *not*— And you aren't seeing anyone else?"

"No..."

"Quite," Phoebe said. "So there's no reason you oughtn't pursue other interests, is there? I know you and Kim hit it off, and now you know how *I* feel about that, so we all know where we stand. Which means we—you and I—can be friends. Can't we?"

It was not possible to eat onion soup while having this conversation. Will pushed the bowl away and asked the least impossible question. "You want to be friends?"

Phoebe smiled at him. It seemed like a real smile, not a society one. "Kim doesn't like many people. If he likes you, I expect you're rather special. And I could see you felt dreadfully awkward meeting me, which I truly do appreciate in principle, it's madly considerate and gentlemanly and so on, but I can't have you labouring under a misapprehension because honestly I've no desire to—what's the word—interpolate. Not interpolate. Intercept? Get in the way."

Will groped for words. "You're going to marry him!"

"Red tape," Phoebe said. "We won't have the part about forsaking all others in the vows."

"Then why are you getting married?" Will demanded, before his brain could remind him that this was none of his business.

She didn't answer for a few seconds, and when she spoke there was no humour at all in her tone. "That's another story and, if you'll forgive me, not one I want to tell you at the moment. Suffice to say I love Kim dearly, but 'love' means an awful lot of things. I think more people should understand that."

Will had no idea what to say. Phoebe gave him an elegant little shrug. "Conventions are ghastly and bourgeois, and life can be so much better when one discards them, but there's also the risk that things get awfully tangled, especially if one's dealing with people who *haven't* discarded them. Being at the vanguard of social upheaval is dreadfully confusing sometimes. Vanguard *is* the front, isn't it? It always sounds like the back to me, like the guard's carriage on a train. Anyway, I think it's far better if we all talk to each other, and then everyone can decide what they want and how to go about it without getting tied up in knots about things that might not matter at all. So now you know that Kim and I assert no claim over one another, which means you aren't a... a claim-jumper. Oh, that's good, isn't it? Like in the Westerns. I must tell him that."

"Does he know you're discussing this with me?" Will asked faintly.

"Good God, no." Phoebe smiled at the waiter as he removed their barely touched plates, and took out her cigarette case and holder. "Do you mind? Sure?"

Will shook his head and watched her light up. He wished he wanted to smoke, and had a fairly powerful urge to knock back his entire glass of wine in one, come to that.

What she was saying seemed clear enough. Startling, because he hadn't expected a noble young lady to have quite such a louche approach to relationships, but there you go, that was Bright Young People for you. Maisie had said she was no better than she should be. *Define 'better'*, Will thought.

But she was labouring under a misapprehension. She clearly had no idea what Kim had done, if she even knew what he did, and in conscience Will ought to tell her that her blessing wasn't required because the only thing he planned to do to Kim in the future was kick him downstairs.

"Does he know you're here?" he said instead.

Phoebe blew out a stream of smoke, angling it away from Will's face. "Do you think he should? Or are you worried I'm lying? No, I didn't tell him I was going to do this. It seemed clear that you were worried about claim-jumping; I thought that would be a shame; I've told you there's no such thing; now you can do as you please. I don't know why men make everything so complicated."

"Kim didn't mention anything about your, uh, arrangement."

"Ask him why not," Phoebe suggested. "And that's quite enough of serious things. You and I have come here to enjoy a delicious lunch—I'm sure it will be delicious when we concentrate on the food—so let's enjoy ourselves and talk about something else. Yes?"

Will searched her face. She smiled at him, merry-eyed. "What, darling?"

"I think you're rather lovely," he said, startling himself.

"I know I am," Phoebe assured him. "But it's always nice to be told so."

It was remarkably easy to talk to her, Will found, Honourable or not. He wouldn't have imagined he'd be able to spend an hour chatting with an upper-class woman at all, infinitely less one who knew that he'd fucked her fiancé. He should have shrivelled up like a salted slug with shame, and the fact that he didn't was entirely down to his companion.

It was impossible to be embarrassed in the company of someone who so evidently didn't feel he'd done anything wrong, and who was so open-heartedly pleased to be talking to him. Phoebe had an endless supply of chatter but somehow Will also talked far more than he'd expected to. Perhaps it was because she was cheerfully ready to fill in the gaps while he gathered his thoughts; more likely it was that she seemed to find everything interesting. By the time they were sipping appallingly strong and tiny cups of coffee, Will had explained how the new football pools worked, and learned about the manufacture and utility of artificial silk stockings. They'd discussed the likelihood of any women being returned to Parliament at the forthcoming election, and were well into what one might put in one's sealed tomb if one were an Egyptian pharaoh. Will was strongly in favour of cursing his tomb to safeguard his riches. Phoebe gurgled with laughter and pointed out it was only fair to share, especially if one were dead.

She smiled at the waiter as he came with the bill, then raised her brows comically at Will. "Now, do listen, darling. We're friends, and you haven't got your lovely legal thingie yet. Like healthy food, which of course is right because one can hardly live without money, can one?"

"Probate," Will said confidently. He was getting the hang of this.

"Exactly. So suppose you let me pay for this meal as a what-do-you-call it against probate—I'm sure there's a way lawyers would say it, so imagine I did—and then you take me somewhere absolutely marvellous once your affairs are in order?"

It was as well phrased to soothe male pride as it could possibly be, but Will had that ten-pound note, so he shook his head. "That's very thoughtful of you but I wouldn't dream of it. No, really. And, Phoebe, listen." He wasn't sure how to say this, and knew very well he should have corrected the misapprehension before, but the truth was he'd been enjoying his escape from reality far too much and this was going to throw a bucket of cold water over everything. "What you said earlier. About, um, claim-jumping. It was a very kind thing for you to say but it's not, uh, relevant."

Phoebe gazed at him steadily. Will felt himself redden. He didn't want to lie to her, even by implication, but he had no desire at all to go into detail either. Perhaps he was bourgeois and conventional, but in his world encounters between men were a secretive thing, not a subject for lunchtime conversation. He ploughed on. "I've fallen out with Kim very badly, and that's entirely down to something he did—a work matter. He didn't behave well. I don't imagine I'll encounter him again and to be honest, I don't want to."

Phoebe considered him for another moment, then her face crumpled quite suddenly, like a child's. "Oh, no. Really? But Will—oh, ugh. Did he do something awful? You needn't worry about hurting my feelings."

"He did, yes." Will took an odd relief in saying the words out loud. "Really awful."

"He *would*," she said viciously. "Honestly, he'd be his own worst enemy if he wasn't so busy making other people be that for him. It's too maddening. I *am* sorry, Will. I shan't argue, or give you a list of his good qualities, because that's irrelevant when someone's been dreadful even if it's true and it sounds very much the sort of thing women say about men who hit them, doesn't it? 'Oh, he's not like that really, you don't understand.' Well, he is. I love him, but he is." She took a long, soothing drag on her post-prandial cigarette. "I'm terribly disappointed. He doesn't make friends lightly, and he liked you very much."

"I don't think he can have, in the circumstances."

"I know him better than you do." There was the tiniest flash of steel in her voice there, glinting like the blue streak of a jay's wing as it flew. "Which is why I came trampling in on this, when clearly I should have left bad alone. No wonder you were startled."

"I should have told you right away," Will said. "Sorry. I was enjoying our lunch too much."

Phoebe gave him a sudden, brilliant smile. "Oh, well, that's something, isn't it? And I've had a wonderful time too, so we shall be friends and never mind Kim. Thank you, darling. I shall make you take me to lunch again."

If he'd absolutely had to blunder into the minefield of the unconventional upper classes, Will wished to hell he'd met Phoebe first. She was lovely and vibrant and fun and, unlike Kim, *not* a treacherous shit who used you with cold, deliberate intent. Will had no illusions that he'd have stood a chance with an Honourable, of course, even a Bohemian one, but she'd have let him take her dancing, he was sure, which would have been a lot more fun than the prospect of the dock. If he hadn't already bedded her fiancé, he'd have chanced his arm and suggested dancing now.

And if he didn't have the War Office and a criminal gang to think about when he left this charmed interlude, of course.

"Lunch would be marvellous," he said, and gave her the best smile he could.

TWELVE

Will woke up the next morning feeling very worried indeed. Libra would be coming today to offer him money for the secret. Will would refuse—he had to, if he believed a tenth of what Kim had told him—but then what?

He'd say he'd burned the pages. He had no other choice. If he claimed he'd given them to the War Office Zodiac would find out quick enough that he was lying, what with having a spy in their department. He wished he found that harder to believe.

Libra arrived at four o'clock that afternoon with a Gladstone bag. Will didn't even want to know what he had in it. There was nobody else in the shop, so he stood behind the desk, knife once again in an open drawer, close to hand.

"All right, Mr. Darling. I think you'll find we've been more than generous," Libra said. "I can offer you two thousand pounds—"

"How much?!"

"Two thousand. One thousand now, the other to be paid into your bank the moment you hand over the information."

Will remembered to breathe. "That is extremely generous.

But I'm afraid I've changed my mind."

Libra looked at him levelly. "I advise you to change it back."

"I can't," Will said. "I burned the information. The War Office told me what it was about and I didn't think they or anyone else should have it, so I burned it. I'm sorry for your wasted trip."

Libra's face didn't change except the colour. He was going decidedly red. "I don't believe you."

"I can't help that. It's gone."

"I hope for your sake you're lying." He took a step forward. "You owe us that information. You will deliver it or face the consequences."

"I owe you nothing."

"You made a deal. Don't try to back out of it."

"The paper's burned, and don't ask me to remember what it said, because I didn't understand a word. It's over. You won't have it, and nor will the War Office, so nobody loses. Or maybe you both lose, I don't care. You can all find someone else to bully."

"It doesn't work like that," Libra said. "You made a serious mistake when you refused to hand over our property the first time, and you're making it a great deal worse now. Give me the information now, and I'll give you the contents of this bag. Defy me once more and you'll soon be begging me to take it."

"Go to hell. I told you not to threaten me. You'll have nothing from me now or ever, so get out of it. And if you come any closer, I'll carve you like a Christmas goose," he added, as Libra began to move.

Libra glanced down at the Messer in Will's hand and seemed to decide that discretion was the better part of valour. "You're a fool," he said, voice not quite level. "That was your last chance and you'll regret wasting it."

"Oh, sod off."

Will let out a long breath as Libra left. That had gone badly, but at least it was over for now. He wondered if Zodiac might believe him, and if they would bother with revenge. Maybe they'd just write the whole thing off and move on. It would be nice, he thought, and didn't believe it for a second.

The next day was a Sunday. Will had gone to the pictures with Maisie of a Sunday a few times in the past months, and absently wondered if she might accompany him before remembering she was visiting her auntie, not to mention that he shouldn't endanger her by being seen in her company. Damn it. He'd have liked to be with someone today. He felt oddly isolated from the city's bustle around him: a marked man, targeted, cut away from the herd.

He briefly imagined inviting Phoebe to the cinema, which she'd probably pronounce 'kinema'. He could find the Stephens-Prince household in Grosvenor Square, saunter up what were doubtless polished marble steps, ask the butler if she was in. That was laughably improbable, but all the same he'd bet she'd come if he asked her, and laugh and squeal at the screen with as much glee as any shopgirl.

He didn't want to think about going to the pictures with Kim because that was plausible, which made it painful. He meant the false Kim, of course, the one he'd spent a night and day with, and liked, and thought he knew. He could have imagined going to see a Western or a mystery with that man. Sitting together to laugh and gasp, maybe a hand sliding up his leg in the dark of the cinema. Certainly a drink at the pub afterwards, before the night really began…

But that man didn't exist, so he wasn't going to the bloody pictures with Will, was he?

He had a powerful urge to go alone. Lose himself in an adventure story, forget about the chaos he'd fallen into. And why not? Someone could break into the shop in his absence with his goodwill, since the information wasn't there, and if they wanted to set fire to the bloody place as vengeance, it was insured. He might as well enjoy himself while he could.

That was what he did. He shaved, slicked back his hair, made sure the bright silk flower was firmly fixed in his buttonhole to gussy up his appearance, and stepped out. He sauntered round Trafalgar Square like any day-tripper, and dropped in to St. Martin's-in-the-Fields to listen to the singing—he wasn't a religious man but church music was a comforting reminder of home. He treated himself to a fine lunch, and then watched *Smilin' Through*, the latest Norma Talmadge picture, admiring her beauty and Harrison Ford's good looks rather more than the plot. It was quite hard to follow the story with his mind jumping spasmodically back to his own predicament every now and then but he managed to lose himself in the tale for the last half-hour all the same.

This was playacting at a carefree existence, but he needed a breathing space without unwelcome anticipation crushing his chest. He needed some time not thinking about threats, or money, or mistakes he shouldn't have made.

He saw another feature after *Smilin' Through* ended, this one with the implausibly handsome Ivor Novello, had a bite to eat, and reluctantly returned to the bookshop around seven-thirty. Night had fallen, and May's Buildings was very dark and unwelcoming. His heart thudded unpleasantly as he approached his door, and he checked over his shoulder three times as he put the key in the lock.

The key turned, so the lock hadn't been forced in his absence. He flicked the switch and knew a moment's relief when the lights came on, driving the shadows to the edge of the shop. He secured the door behind him and went up and

down the stacks, then thoroughly checked the back room—
under the bed, door and window—and even ascended to the
upstairs rooms, before sitting on his bed and accepting that
there was nobody in here.

He couldn't live like this, waiting for attack. It was intolerable and, worse, unsustainable. You couldn't stay at this
pitch of alertness. Either he'd get used to it and then he'd be
sloppy, or he wouldn't and he'd exhaust himself jumping at
shadows.

The electric light was yellowy-dim and it mostly made
him conscious of how many dark corners the shop had. He
didn't want to be here alone in the silence of the books. He
didn't want to be alone at all.

Shouldn't have been so bloody obstinate, should you?

He consigned the voice in his head to the devil, and
leaned back against the wall, wondering what to do. If he'd
had a telephone to hand, he might have been very tempted to
call Kim. Now he thought of it, there was one of those new
public telephone boxes on Charing Cross.

And if he 'phoned, what would he say?

He didn't try to answer that. He sat alone in his empty
bookshop for a while, with paper slowly turning to dust
around him, watching spindle-legged harvestmen weave
webs to replace the ones he'd swept away. Then he got up,
and put his coat on.

There was no queue at the telephone box. He read the
number off the card to the operator, who said, "One moment,
please," and waited for an answer. He'd just decided he
should hang up when Kim came on the line.

"Secretan here."

"It's Will." He didn't know what else to say.

"Are you all right?" Kim asked sharply.

"Yes. Fine."

A tiny pause. "Is someone there with you?"

"I'm not being forced at gunpoint to call you, if that's what you mean."

"Glad to hear it." Another pause. "Is there something wrong? Can I help?"

"I—" He didn't know what to say. "Nothing. It's nothing." He couldn't think of what to say. He ought to hang up, except that the voice on the end of the telephone was a glimmer of light in a very dark place.

"Long day?" Kim asked.

"Bit of one."

"Will you come over?"

Will stared at the wooden telephone mount. The varnish was already starting to crack and peel. "All right."

He took the tram, watching huddled people out of the foggy window and the pools of yellow light from the lampposts grow and fade as they passed. There was a persistent drizzle in the air by the time he got out, not quite rain, leaving a film of droplets over his clothing and hat. He shook himself like a dog as he went into Kim's building.

The doorman had clearly been given his name because he let Will go up with a nod. Will knocked on the door. Kim answered.

His rooms were warm, and well lit, with half a dozen lamps giving the place a domestic glow. He was wearing a velvet smoking jacket in a deep purple shade, and matching velvet slippers. Will stood in the sitting room, wet and cold and entirely out of place.

"Sorry," he said. "You look like you were having a night in."

"I still am," Kim pointed out, hanging up the damp hat and coat. "Would you like a drink?"

"I…" He wasn't sure if he wanted to drink, to sit on a sofa and make awkward conversation.

"Have you eaten?"

"Yes. Thanks," he added a bit too late.

"Are you here to give me the information?"

"No."

"Has something terrible happened that I ought to know about?"

Will managed a smile. "Not yet."

"Well, that's all the other options," Kim said, and stepped close.

Will didn't move. Kim examined his face, eyes searching. He moved his hand up slowly—not tentative, simply giving Will time to push it away or step back. He didn't.

Kim's fingers brushed his cheek, then slid down, over his jacket front. "That's a dramatic flower."

"My friend made it."

"Phoebe told me. She gave me a suffragette orchid. Did you have a pleasant lunch?" His hands closed on Will's lapels, gently lifting the jacket as if to slide it off his shoulders.

"I—" He wasn't going to stutter all night, damn it. "Very pleasant. Can we not talk about that?"

"We might have had enough lying for the moment," Kim said. "Phoebe knows who I am. So do you now."

"I bloody doubt that," Will said, and reached for him.

Their mouths met hard, lips crushing together. Will had Kim's face in his hands, cupping the fine structure, the high cheekbones. Kim's hands moved down to Will's waist, under his jacket, pressing hot against his shirt. They kissed in bites and gulps, like starving men. Kim pulled himself close to press his hips against Will's, and Will snarled in his mouth and grabbed for his arse to grind him closer still. Kim bent against him, pliant, and Will could feel the need pounding in his groin.

"Are we going to be interrupted?" he demanded, lifting his mouth away.

"Not if I lock the door." Kim clamped both hands over Will's arse, a very deliberate gesture, gave it a second, and stepped back. "Which I shall now do." He did so, turned, and stood rather than coming back, eyes on Will in the lamplight.

Will took the scrutiny for a few seconds. "Well?"

Kim's mouth twitched in that little almost-smile he did when things weren't really that funny. "I'd just like to be sure you want this."

Will ran a hand over his trouser front, deliberately vulgar. "Find out."

"It would be my pleasure." Kim's eyes were very dark.

"You said you liked to be obliging."

"And you told me to show you."

Their eyes were locked. It felt like a battle. Will wasn't sure if they were on opposite sides or the same one.

"Go on, then," he said.

Kim came over, walking with a lot of grace for a man in purple slippers, especially one sporting a solid cockstand. He hooked his thumbs into Will's waistband, bringing them very close together, face to face, mouths a whisper apart.

"I like to please," he said, voice low. "I like sucking pricks. Does that bother you?"

Will wanted to make some sarcastic rejoinder, but whatever part of his brain was still functioning sent up an alert. Kim hadn't sounded provocative so much as defensive, even defiant, and there was a wary look in his eyes.

"Why would it bother me? Means a good time for everyone."

"You'd be amazed." Kim sounded a little waspish, but the tension in his face relaxed. "Well, since you say so..." He took Will's lapels again, and this time Will let him push the jacket off. Kim tossed it out of the way onto a chair, and slid Will's braces off his shoulders, then tugged him round and urged him backwards, towards the sofa where Phoebe had sat before. Will took the seat, watching, as Kim dragged the coffee table out of the way with a soft scrape of metal on carpet. He nudged Will's calf gently with a foot, urging his legs apart. Will spread them wide and leaned back, sprawling like a lout in this beautiful setting, vulgar and transgressive. He wondered if that was what Kim wanted.

It seemed that way, because his mouth was a little open, his arousal visible despite his clothing, and Will could hear him breathing.

"Go on," he said roughly. "Suck me."

Kim dropped to his knees, between Will's spread thighs. He put his hands on Will's knees, ran them lightly up and in. Will inhaled more sharply than he'd meant.

They stayed like that for a moment, Will seated, Kim's palms warm on his inner thighs, then Kim reached for the buttons at his waistband. Will lifted his hips a little to help Kim ease his stand out. It seemed to him the business would be more efficient done standing, but it was pretty clear which one of them was the expert here. And there was unquestionably something about this, about lounging while Kim knelt to serve him, and knowing Kim was just as aroused. He could get used to this.

Kim had his prick, holding it with three light fingertips, examining it as if he was going to find a clue there. Will watched his face, and after a moment Kim's dark eyes flicked up. He gave a little half smile, leaned in, and took Will in his mouth.

"Christ." Will sagged back a little more, resting his head against the wall, and gave himself over to sensation.

Once again Kim didn't use his hands, just lips and tongue

and teeth, the lightest scrape, and he took his time. He switched from tantalising touches to taking Will deep, sucking hard then pulling away for long caressing licks as Will's pleasure mounted. It was ecstatic, obliterating everything in Will's brain but the pleasure of that clever mouth and his own spiralling need. He groaned as he reached the brink, and gave a grunt of agony as Kim lifted his mouth off.

"I want to keep you here a little." Kim sounded raw. His lips were red. "Can I?"

"Christ." It was about the only word he could remember. Kim mouthed his cock from the side, not enough to bring Will to the peak, worked his way slowly around, flicked his tongue over the head as if he liked the taste of Will leaking. Lips sliding up and down, fingers tense, mouth shamelessly wet. Will found he was running out of breath. His toes were curling, his balls painfully tight.

"Please," he gasped. "Please, now."

Kim's mouth was light and taunting but his fingers dug hard into Will's spread thighs. He took Will down again, lips just barely touching the spit-soaked length, and slid back up. "Do you want to come in my mouth?"

"So much. Jesus. Kim!" He stared down at the dark head as Kim bent over him, sucking in earnest now, bringing him off with such deliberate power it was more like being forced than pleasured. Will didn't stand a chance. He came as hard as he could remember in his life, so hard that his balls hurt, his vision blurred, and he cracked his head hard against the wall as he threw it back. He didn't even care.

"Oh Christ," he mumbled when he regained the power of speech. "God."

Kim was still bent right over him, Will's prick pressed against the back of his throat. He wondered for a fraction of a second if he'd somehow asphyxiated the man, and had just time to envisage explaining *that* to the police before Kim lifted his head away. Swollen lips, reddened skin, mouth wet with saliva. He'd never looked better.

"You," Will said, and added, "That," when he had a bit more breath back. "Jesus."

"It's nice to be appreciated."

Kim didn't move from his position, kneeling there with his hands on Will's thighs. Will took a couple of moments to let the blood stop roaring in his ears, then sat up. His slackened prick was still hanging out. It seemed appropriate.

He eased himself forward and slid down off the edge of the sofa, so he was straddling Kim's bent legs. Kim met his eyes dark and unreadable, and Will leaned in and kissed him. His mouth was wet and tasted of—well. Himself. Couldn't complain.

Kim responded open-mouthed, bending backward. Will urged him further back still, kissing him all the way, until they were lying on the ground, Kim supine, Will over him and fumbling for his prick. It wasn't difficult to find.

"You do like pleasing people." He took a grip of the length, and started moving his hand, feeling Kim strain up into his fist. "Are you this hard from sucking me off?"

Kim's eyes snapped to his and his hips stilled. Will grinned savagely at him. "Because I've got to tell you, that makes me fucking horny."

"Does it." Kim sounded breathless but he started moving again.

"If you were getting this worked up…" He didn't even know why the idea was so arousing, except he'd always assumed the act was a one-way street, one man giving pleasure and the other taking it. "I wish I'd known. That's hot stuff."

He worked the prick he held steadily. Kim's breath was already coming fast. "Glad—you think so," he managed jerkily.

"Do you like to rub yourself off while you do it?"

"However you want."

Kim was so close. Will could feel it. "I want you on your knees, with your mouth round my cock. I want to watch you loving it. And I want you right now thinking about sucking me off and how you're going to do it again—"

Kim's back arched, and he came hard, pulsing in Will's hand, face twisted as if the climax hurt. Will stroked him through it, not letting go until he sagged slowly back on to the floor.

They stayed there in silence. Will didn't want to move, or let go. Kim was warm and willing and alive under him, and he didn't want this to be over, to go back into the dark.

At last Kim said, "I suppose it's too much to hope that my smoking jacket escaped unscathed." His eyes were still shut.

"Uh?"

"Not that it matters in the great scheme of things, but it's hell to get jism out of velvet."

The garment had fallen open but Will checked the purple cloth anyway. "No, I think you're all right."

"Thank God for small mercies." Kim opened his eyes and gave Will a rueful grin. "Well."

"Well."

"I'm not going to press you." He sat up as he spoke, forcing Will to move away. "Your choice. But I don't suppose you came here lightly so...will you stay tonight?" He touched a finger very lightly to the corner of Will's eye. "Just one night. You're tired. And—well, the door's still locked."

Will knew what that meant. When Kim unlocked the door, he'd go back to working for the War Office and Will would go back to the bookshop and everything else that waited for him. He didn't want to think about any of that now.

"I'll stay."

THIRTEEN

They moved to the bedroom. If you sat in a sitting-room with a drink, you had to talk, and he doubted either of them wanted that. So Kim brought a cut glass decanter of very good single malt Scotch and two crystal tumblers, Will kicked off his shoes, and they both lay on the huge double bed. It was lit by more elegant lamps and adorned with pillows in crisply ironed purple linen cases. Kim's quilt was purple as well. It was a very comfortable room indeed, except for the elephant in it.

Will had no intention of mentioning Draven's monstrous creation, or Kim's betrayals, or his obvious wariness about his preferences. The former two would unlock the door and let the world in; the last of them was far too much like saying he cared.

"Thanks for taking me in," he said instead.

Kim gestured with his glass. "Who would turn away a lost waif on a cold night?"

"Waif?"

"Metaphorically speaking." He looked like he was about to say something else, but stopped himself.

Will answered anyway, since the question was obvious. "The bookshop was a bit lonely tonight. Lot of dark corners."

"And easily broken windows, and easily forced doors."

"That as well."

"Hard to get a good night's sleep under the circumstances. I see that."

"You don't have many dark corners here. Your electric bill must be something."

"Lighting is an essential part of the design of a modern home," Kim informed him in lofty tones.

That sounded like Phoebe. Will sipped his Scotch. "I don't think Phoebe should come and see me any more."

"I'm not her keeper."

"I don't mean as matter of feeling. I'm not sure it's safe for her. I was thinking today that it's a good thing I don't have any family, or a girl, right now."

Kim gave one of those backwards whistles, inhaling rather than exhaling. "That bad?"

"I might just be nervy."

"You are a terribly delicate flower."

"It's the waiting," Will said. "At least in the trenches, when they tapped you for a raid, you know it was happening and you got on with it."

"Scheduled mayhem is more convenient? I suppose you can put it in your diary. Work around it."

"'Sorry, I've no time for a knife fight in the street on Thursday, could you make it Friday?'"

Kim spluttered into his whisky. Will couldn't help grinning. That had been the first lesson in surviving Flanders: it was always easier when you laughed.

"Have you been in the shop all day?" Kim asked after another, slightly more comfortable silence.

"I went out. Had lunch, saw a couple of pictures. *Smilin' Through* and the latest Ivor Novello thing."

"Any good?"

"Not sure I was in the best of moods for them. But, you know. Trying to keep myself occupied."

Kim twisted round so he was on his side, facing Will, propped up by an elbow. "Do you know, if you asked me what I thought would be the best thing for you to do at this time, going to the pictures would not have been in my top five suggestions."

"I thought we weren't talking about this stuff."

"That's why I'm not going to give you one to three inclusive," Kim said. "Suggestions four and five, on the other hand, would be well within the evening's terms and conditions."

Will shifted round as well at the note in his voice. "And better than the pictures, you reckon?"

"Well, you get colour and sound. It probably won't last as long as a two-reeler, but one can't have everything."

"I hope you're not casting aspersions on my manhood," Will said. "What's number four, then?"

Kim gave him a long, glinting look, under lowered eyelids. It was the sort of look a seducer might give a girl in the pictures. Will was no girl, didn't need seducing, and still felt a pulse of something a little bit like nerves. "Do you like to fuck?"

"Er, yes? Oh. You mean all the way?"

"Absolutely all."

Will had to lick his lips. "Me doing you?"

"Ideally with a better verb but yes. If you'd like. Is that appealing?"

In theory, absolutely. Practice might be different. "Thing is I've only done that once and it wasn't marvellous for anyone. You know. Flanders."

Kim paused. "Do you mean Flanders as in 'it was

wartime', or is there a Belgian buggery problem I should know of?"

Will almost spilt his drink with the force of his bark of laughter. Kim was obviously amused by his own joke, eyes warm, face light and lit. "Arse. Wartime. Everything in a hurry, military police, no privacy all that. The point is, I wouldn't know what I was doing, and I wouldn't want to hurt you."

Kim's eyes flicked to his, then away. "You didn't have a good first experience, then?"

"The other bloke didn't seem to, and that's not my idea of fun."

"It can be good. But it's entirely up to you."

Will examined his face. "Do you want that? I mean, is it something you like to do?"

Kim didn't answer for a few seconds. When he spoke it was deliberately, but not with the earlier defiance. "I like getting fucked, yes. I realise one isn't supposed to, but there we are. Does that matter?"

Will's previous partner had initiated the experience as well, for all that was worth. "Of course it does. I don't want to do anything you don't want. That's no way to go about things."

"You said something along those lines before. That it made you, ah, horny to think I liked sucking you off." Kim sounded as though he'd never used the word before in his upper-class life. It was oddly endearing.

"It does."

"Why?"

"I don't know. *Because* you like it, that's all. I want you to want it, and to tell me so." He saw the velvet darkness growing in Kim's eyes and went on, deliberately. "I like knowing that you want me to fuck you, even if you aren't supposed to want it. Especially that, maybe."

"One really oughtn't, of course." Kim spoke softly, almost purring. "And yet I just can't help myself. The sheer pleasure of getting fucked—the feel of a man in my mouth, or bending me over a bed—"

"Oh God." He couldn't believe Kim was admitting this; it was killing him, tightening his gut and constricting his ribcage with desire. He wanted to give him what he asked for, make him gasp and beg and spend. "Do you—uh—"

"Spit it out. As it were."

"The first time, when I was standing up. I wondered if you wanted me to move. To fuck your mouth for you."

"Interesting you should say that," Kim said. "It's suggestion five. I rather thought at the time that you might like to."

"I didn't want to be rude."

"Manners maketh man." He ran a finger along Will's cheek. "How do you want me, Will? Would you like to find out just how hard it would make me to take your cock?"

"Jesus. Yes. You'll have to talk me through it, though."

Kim plucked the whisky glass out of his hand and put both tumblers on the bedside table. "My pleasure."

It was the sounds that Will remembered most, later. Other things too. Kim's long, pale body by lamplight, and the feel of his elegant hands. His low voice, so matter of fact, turning what Will had found a physical implausibility into something almost easy. The strangeness of working his way in, well lubricated with Vaseline—someone deserved a medal for inventing that—and the feel of Kim's body impossibly tight round his prick, and the astonishing moment when he worked a hand under Kim's belly as he thrust and found him standing as hard as promised. That had nearly sent Will off there and then, just the thought that he was fucking Kim Secretan, and Kim was loving it.

It was mostly the sounds, though, because it turned out that Kim whimpered when you took him, desperate breathy noises that sounded as if he couldn't help but make them. Will never wanted to forget those. It was a sweaty, earthy business, all damp skin, hard movements, harsh breath, but those little helpless gasps were so soft, so needy and vulnerable that Will found himself pushing harder to wring more of them out. He held his own climax off by sheer willpower, biting his lip hard enough to bruise, and telling Kim straight out he wanted him to come first, please, do it now with Will inside him. He wanted to feel it. And Kim had, convulsing under Will, thrusting into his hand, and tipping him over into the second hardest orgasm of the night, and also his life.

He stayed awake just long enough to have a wash, fell back into the bed, and was asleep before he could say good night.

And then it was Monday morning and the world started once more.

Kim was already awake and dressed, sitting at the kitchen table with a cup of tea, when Will made his somewhat bleary and cautious way out of the bedroom in a borrowed bathrobe. He looked up with a smile that was a bit too polite for the circumstances. "Good morning. Sleep well?"

"Is that tea?"

Kim was already pouring him a cup—an actual cup, china, with saucer. Naturally he wouldn't have anything as plebeian as a mug. "Here you go."

"Thanks. What time is it?"

"Half past nine."

"It's what?"

"I let you sleep," Kim said. "I thought you needed it."

"Don't you need to go to work?"

"No. And I assumed your employer would be under-standing."

Will rubbed at his hair, which felt vaguely sticky, unless that was his hand. "I expect he'll sack me for not turning up."

"I never liked him. Breakfast?"

"I should get dressed first."

"Not on my account. It's already cooked. Chafing dishes are all very well, but I find bacon can become leathery if one leaves it too long."

"Did you say bacon?"

They ate in the kitchen, a small space that didn't seem as though it got much use. The heated silver dish held bacon, sausages, and grilled tomatoes for two, evidently not cooked in here. Kim provided hot toast with competence.

"So you just order breakfast?" Will asked. "And people bring it up?"

"Well, not usually. I generally have toast." He had taken just two strips of bacon from the plentiful selection. Will went for the fourth sausage without compunction. "But that's how it works, yes. It's a serviced flat."

"That's right, you said. More convenient than servants. I mean, that's fair. I don't have 'em in the house myself."

It was a joke, mostly. Kim didn't smile. "I grew up with servants. I was born in a stately home. We had a staff of forty or so. Fewer now, I believe."

Will waited to find out where that was going. Apparently it was nowhere, because Kim didn't add anything. "You believe? Don't you keep count?"

"I'm sure somebody does, but I haven't been welcome in my father's house for six years."

"Right." Will had no idea how to cope with a statement like that. He took a mouthful of tea. "That... That's pretty horrible."

"I brought it on myself."

"Come off it."

"Oh, I did," Kim said. "Ask Phoebe."

"She said you'd be your own worst enemy if you didn't make sure other people did that for you."

Kim smiled properly then, a sudden grin that illuminated his face like dawn. It was—no, it was good that mention of Phoebe could make him smile like that. Definitely good. "Did she? Of course she did, the wench."

Will had a sudden, violent urge to push. "She told me this was all right with her. You and me."

"Yes. I'm a little surprised by that, even for Phoebe. Not surprised that she feels it, but that she sought you out to tell you so."

"I said, why didn't you tell me yourself, and she said to ask you."

"Which you haven't done." Kim stood, clearing away his plate. He'd left half the bacon untouched. "Wisely. Nothing's going to change, Will, no matter how much anyone might wish it would. When you walk out of my front door, you'll still be in possession of information affecting national security, and I'll still be the shit who lied to you and deceived you and betrayed you in an effort to get it. I can't change sides now."

"I didn't ask you to."

"You don't ask much." He leaned on the kitchen counter, his back to Will. "If you don't hand over the information, nobody's going to help you."

"I burned it. I told Libra that, and you can tell the War Office."

"I'm sure everyone will take your word for it," Kim said politely.

Will pushed his plate away. "When I go home, will I find my shop's been searched?"

He didn't know if that shot went home. Kim's voice sounded quite normal as he replied, "Possibly, but it won't be my doing. I haven't lied to you in, oh, a good twelve hours."

"Amazing. Did it hurt much?"

Kim turned then. "You came here, remember? Not my idea. It was a good idea as far as it went, but it was all yours."

That was true enough. "So now what? How does this work? I leave and you report in to Ingoldsby on how we spent the night?"

"Don't be a shit," Kim said, and the worst part of that was he sounded entirely resigned, as though he expected Will to be a shit. "I'm not that bad, and you're not that stupid."

"Sorry."

"Christ, don't apologise. You have every right to expect the worst and I dare say you should. Just not in this case."

"Then what now?" Will said again. "I leave here, go back to the shop, we forget this ever happened?"

"What else is there?"

He sounded almost like he was expecting an answer, or hoping for one. Will didn't have anything to offer. Kim's life had collided with his for the worst possible reasons. There was no point where they fit together except behind a closed door, and what could he say about that? *I could come round to fuck now and again, when you aren't working for the Government or taking your fiancée to parties.* No.

Kim shrugged, as if Will's silence had been agreement. "Quite. After all, you've got more important things on your plate."

"And you've got Phoebe."

"Don't remind me. And for God's sake don't tell her you've been round or I will never hear the last of it."

"What? I thought—"

"She won't be angry, you fool, she'll be *optimistic*." He said that with despairing resignation. "Phoebe is ever hopeful that

I will meet a nice man. Don't ask me what I'm supposed to do with one."

"You two really are strange," Will said. "Why in God's name are you getting married?"

"Because her life is not the sunny bubbling stream of joy she makes it appear, and I can at least be of some use this way," Kim said with a bite in his voice. "Mariage blanc is convenient for both parties, and hardly unusual."

"I don't know what that is."

"Unconsummated. Marriage for the look of the thing."

"I was taught it was a sacrament," Will said. "Vows. Something to take seriously, not to play with. And never mind you finding a nice man, how about giving her the chance to? What's she going to do if she falls in love with someone and she's married to you already?"

"Are you under the impression we haven't thought about the consequences?" Kim enquired icily. "It really is not, with the greatest respect, your business."

That was pretty final. "I dare say not. Well." Will stood. "I'll get dressed and go."

"Yes."

Will headed out through the sitting room where Kim had sucked him off with such abandoned pleasure last night. He wished he'd got dressed before: he needed to be gone from here. From Kim.

He was in the bedroom and starting to remove the borrowed gown when Kim spoke from the doorway. "Will."

Will pulled the sides of the gown together before he turned. "What?"

"I apologise for that. I intended to handle this morning a lot more graciously, but—well, I failed. I realise we can't stay on good terms but I'd like to part on them. May I try again?"

Will nodded. Kim offered him a smile that seemed real, if tentative. "What I wanted to say, should have said, was that it was a good night. More than good, it was a privilege. Thank you for being so generous with your pleasure. And thank you for trusting me enough to come here at all: I doubt I'd have done so in your shoes."

"It was good for me as well," Will said, wholly inadequately. He wished he could find words a fraction as eloquent as Kim's. He wished he knew what he'd say if he had them. "Thanks for breakfast. And I'm not going to hope you find a nice man when you have a perfectly lovely woman, but the next arsehole who insults you for enjoying yourself when you fuck, bring him round to my place and I'll teach him some manners."

Kim winced. "That obvious?"

"Afraid so."

"I will bear that offer in mind. Actually, I'll take you up on it. Thank you."

He sounded sincere. He looked smart and well groomed and rich, and his eyes were as raw and lonely and full of wishes as Will felt.

Fuck it. "You don't have to go to work?"

"No."

"Front door's still locked."

"Yes..."

"Suggestion five, then?" Will said. "Since we're here."

They crashed onto the bed in a tangle of limbs, kissing frantically. At least Will didn't have to shed anything but the dressing gown this time. He didn't undress Kim, just got his trousers open, and worked him with his hand till his prick was leaking and he was gasping.

"Will. Going to—"

"Not yet." Will let go. Kim made a strangled noise that sounded like actual pain, and added several surprisingly vulgar words.

"You did worse to me last night," Will pointed out.

"I did not. Is this vengeance?"

"I want—I really want you to come while I fuck your mouth," Will said. "Can we do that?"

"It might be difficult not to." Kim spoke with feeling. "I… Christ. You want that?"

Will had a fair idea of what he needed to hear. He put a bit of gravel in his voice. "I want to hear the sounds you make while I'm doing it. I want you to know how hard it makes me, knowing you love it. I want us both to remember that."

Kim's mouth opened silently. Will dipped his head and dragged his tongue over Kim's lips. "That's right. Open wide."

Kim did as bid. He didn't make a sound as Will straddled his chest, but as Will leaned over, he said, "Hold my wrists."

His arms were above his head. *Helpless* came into Will's mind again. "You can't touch yourself if I'm holding your wrists."

"Please." Just the one word.

Will nodded, then another thought came. "Hang on. If it's too much or I'm hurting you, how will I know?"

"I'll bite."

"What?"

"I'll shake my head, you idiot."

Will put his work-hard hands over the slim wrists, pressing down. Kim inhaled, a quick little noise that went straight to Will's groin. He positioned himself over Kim's open mouth with a second's uncertainty, and eased himself down. Kim's lips closed around his length, and Will thrust, first gently, then a little harder.

Kim moaned. It could have sounded like distress but there was nothing of alarm in his dark eyes, fixed on Will. Will thrust again, and again, gaining confidence, putting his weight forward so he was pressing Kim into the bed with his arms. Kim was moving under him, twisting with frustrated arousal, and the way his mouth looked around Will's cock was almost unbearably wrong and filthy and perfect.

"Jesus," he said aloud. "I know you want this. I love how you want this. More?" Kim made a desperate noise. Will was slightly fearful of choking him, but he leaned in, going a little deeper, rubbing against the roof of Kim's mouth. And Kim's whole body was pushing up under him, thrumming with tension, and the sounds he was making were too much, wet and explosive and desperate.

Kim tugged frantically sideways with his left hand. Will let go, bowed his head, and thrust deep into Kim's throat, feeling his lover's arm move as he worked himself. Kim cried out, the sound vibrating in Will's length, and they were both coming at once, thrashing against one another, Kim's spend spattering Will's bare back, Will gripping the wrist he held savagely as he came with ball-aching force that left him dizzy.

He lurched sideways and rolled over to thump down onto the bed. Kim lay beside him, breathing harshly.

"All right?" he said after a while.

Kim coughed, sounding a bit phlegmy, and cleared his throat. "Very much so."

Will gave it a moment, until he was fairly sure he wouldn't pass out if he sat up too fast, then a few minutes more because he was in no hurry. He really didn't want to go, to return to the bloody bookshop and the mess of his life. He liked in here with the version of Kim who wanted to make sure he got enough sleep, and told him the truth, and made him feel like a god when they fucked.

But there was no choice, so he rolled onto his side. "This isn't a bad place to leave things, so I'm going to go now. Thanks for having me. And vice versa, I suppose." Kim's lips curved, almost reluctantly. "So—well. See you."

He got dressed in silence, aware of Kim watching him, as

debauched as a man could look while mostly clothed on a rumpled bed. Neither of them spoke; there wasn't anything useful to say. He found his shoes, hat, coat. As he headed for the door, he glanced around. Kim was standing at the other end of the room, watching him.

"Bye," he said.

Kim opened his mouth and hesitated. Expressions flickered across his face, too fast to read, then he gave Will a little smile. "Goodbye."

FOURTEEN

The bookshop had indeed been raided in his absence. That was irritating. The bolted door had been jemmied, splintering the wood and destroying the lock, and Will was pretty sure he'd need to replace the frame as well.

Whoever had done it hadn't bothered with subtlety. All the papers he'd spent hours sorting lay in drifts over the floorboards; books had been carelessly tossed into splayed and crumpled heaps. His desk drawers were all open and, Will quickly saw, the petty cash had gone.

The War Office wouldn't have taken the petty cash, he thought, so he probably believed that Kim hadn't tipped them off. Unless someone else had taken advantage of the open door, of course. He *wanted* to believe Kim, and wished he didn't have to think about it.

There was no post on the mat either. He wondered if that was a sneak thief hoping for postal orders—good luck with that—or Zodiac keeping an eye on his letters for something that wasn't books or bills.

Will spent the rest of the morning cleaning up. It was dirty, backbreaking work and he resented it, but there wasn't a lot of choice. If he couldn't sell books, he would struggle to make it to whatever distant date the lawyers got on and declared probate. It was quite hard to keep that thought in his mind simultaneously with *The people who did this might come after me any day now.* That had been another thing that was easier in the war. You took it a day at a time and you never thought about the future at all because of the odds that would be a waste of energy. It made life a lot simpler.

He nailed the front door shut, and went out over the back walls to find a locksmith, who promised to come over the next day. He found the Messer under the bed, and kept it in his belt while he worked that afternoon.

Late on, there was a tapping on the window. He glanced up, and saw Phoebe, exceedingly lovely in a close-fitting cloche hat, golden hair curling from under the brim. She smiled as she caught his eye, and pointed at the door with an exaggerated expression of puzzlement.

God damn it. He'd told Kim to tell her to stay away. He didn't want to lie to her now; he didn't want any more to do with Kim Secretan and his honourable fiancée and whatever peculiar dance they were treading out. He had work to do.

But she was there. "Two minutes," he mimed through the glass. He rinsed his dusty hands and face, took the knife from his belt, threw on his jacket, still adorned with the silk peony, and went out to scale the back wall yet again.

Phoebe was waiting in the street when he jogged up. "Hello, there. Is your door broken?"

"And nailed shut. Burglars. I had to come round the back."

"You've been burgled? Will, I am so sorry. How awful."

"Yes. Phoebe, I don't think you should come to see me any more."

Her eyes widened with hurt. Clearly Kim hadn't had a conversation with her yet. "But I thought—"

"It's not you," Will said, keeping his voice low. "Or anything else we talked about. It's—look, there's some very unpleasant people with a grudge against me right now. I don't want you getting hurt by accident and that means you can't be round here. It's for your safety."

"Is this Kim's affair?" Will wanted to lie. He hesitated, and was lost. "It is, isn't it? For heaven's *sake*. He must sort it out right away. This isn't remotely acceptable."

"It's not that easy." He wished he could just be rude: tell her to go to the devil, send her off crying. She'd be safe that way, and wouldn't come back, and would doubtless fall into Kim's arms for comfort which would be better for everyone. "Phoebe, you said we were friends."

"I hope we are."

"Then please, as my friend, believe me and go and don't come back. Not till it's sorted out, and I don't know when that will be. Will you do that for me?"

Phoebe searched his face. Her shoulders dropped. "If you say so, but I'm extremely sorry. You will ask someone for help if you need it, won't you?"

"I'll be fine. A lot better for not worrying about anyone else."

She sighed. "All right, then, if you insist. But really, I think— Ought that motor be coming down here?"

There was indeed a motor-car nudging its way into the narrow cobbled street. They almost never got cars down here, and the roar of the engine seemed oddly loud and echoey. Will turned and saw another, coming from the other end of the street.

"They won't have much luck passing here," Phoebe observed. "The street's far too narrow. How absurd! They must see they'll block each other in."

"They're not blocking each other," Will said, to himself as much as her, as the two cars stopped and the doors opened.

"Oh shit. Get in a shop, right now! In there, use the phone, call the police! Go!"

He shoved her hard, sending her stumbling away towards Norris's shop, and lunged at the first of the two suited men who'd come from the front car, wishing he had his knife. He got in a couple of solid punches and a knee to the groin, and managed to land a couple of sharp jabs on the second man as well before someone hit him from behind, a stunning knock to the head. He went down, stumbling onto all fours, shoved himself up again, and felt a cloth clamped over his nose and mouth. Like a fool, he took in a sharp breath to swear or fight, just as a second blow descended on the back of his skull.

He didn't remember anything after that.

Will's second waking that day was a lot less pleasant than the first one.

He was lying on the floor, he realised. It was a hard floor, rough and splintery against his cheek. His shoulders hurt from the twisted way he lay. His head throbbed excruciatingly and he had a foul taste in his mouth and sore, almost scalded lips. He was very thirsty.

None of that was good. None of it was as bad as the fact that he was lying in an awkward position because his wrists were tied together.

He couldn't find the strength to test the bonds at the moment but they were there, rough and uncomfortably tight. He did not like this development at all. He tried to move his legs apart, hating the sluggish lassitude in his brain that seemed to create a yawning gap between intent and movement, and felt the restraint. His ankles were tied too.

This was bad. The only thing that could make this worse

was if they had got Phoebe. Had she got to safety? Would they have come after her? Please God, not that. He could cope on his own, one way or another. He could not let her take his punishment.

He made himself hold his breath and listen. There was no sound of anyone else breathing, which meant very little except that she wasn't in here with him. Nor, it seemed, was a guard. He needed to sit up and assess the situation, and he would definitely do that as soon as his head had stopped spinning quite so much and he was sure he wouldn't be sick. Five minutes to gather himself, he decided, and then he'd act.

The third time he woke up, it seemed to be morning.

Will blinked blearily. He had a raging thirst and an equally powerful need to pee, and he hurt all over. He'd slept on less comfortable floors than this one, but not many, and never tied into one position.

He raised his head cautiously. That hurt too.

Movement started the pins and needles kicking in, a childish name for the excruciating pain of returning blood flow to his legs and shoulders. He bit back the urge to swear aloud and made himself stretch out as best he could. After a few minutes, the agony subsided a little. Some determined wriggling like a worm, with several breaks to let his headache go down to a bearable level, brought him to a sitting position leaning against the wall. Now he could take stock.

He was in a very bare room. No furniture, no pictures, distempered walls, bare floor. It was dark because the windows were secured with shutters, and the shutters were secured with padlocks, gleaming new in this dark dingy space. They gleamed from the light outside, rather than any light source in here; he couldn't see electric switches or wiring or even a gas mantle. It was as empty as a room could be, and it seemed to be specifically empty of convenient jagged bits of metal, broken bottles, or any such useful accoutrements for the kidnap victim hoping to free himself. There was a heavy iron hasp set low on the wall next to him, secured with big bolts.

He considered his feet. His shoes had gone, and his ankles were tied with thick, tough twine; the knot had been done at the backs of his legs, which would make it that much harder to unpick if he could even get a hand to it. He wondered if he could work his bound wrists under his body and in front of him, but they had been secured quite high up the arms, which was why his shoulders hurt. He didn't have anything like the circus skills he'd need for a manoeuvre like that.

None of this was good. Will gave a moment's consideration to shouting for help and dismissed it. Whoever had arranged the kidnap, this room, and the bonds wouldn't have overlooked the possibility of sound carrying. Plus, his throat was horribly parched.

The moment he thought that, he wished he hadn't. The need for a drink overwhelmed him, clawing at his dry mouth, drowning out everything else, including the pain in his shoulders and head. He shut his eyes and tried to force it down. *At least you aren't lying in the mud with a hole in your leg this time*, he told himself.

That wasn't much help, since he had other problems. There was something brutally unfair about being desperate for a drink and a pee at the same time. If someone didn't come in soon he had a dreadful feeling he was going to piss himself.

Maybe that was the idea. He'd assumed defiance of Zodiac —it had to be Zodiac—would bring some immediate, and nasty, consequences. But they didn't have to do anything at all, did they? Just leave a man tied up for a day, or two days, or three, until he was soiled and humiliated and his thirst was blotting out all else, and then come in with a jug of water and offer it in exchange for what you wanted. Why would you go to the effort of thumbscrews when you could let your victim's body do the work for you?

Will shut his eyes and did a bit of deep breathing. Then he leaned back and began to bang his heels on the floor, a dull drumming sound on the bare boards that thumped in his throbbing head. He toyed with the idea of spelling out SOS, but that was foolish: he hadn't been left anywhere with help in easy reach. Instead, mostly to distract himself, he embarked on a lengthy message in Morse. With luck, his captors would be able to decipher it.

He'd got to the penultimate letter of UP YOUR ARSE when the door opened.

Libra had two men with him. Will recognised the gingery one as a lurker in his shop; the other was almost completely bald. They weren't wearing masks. He'd have preferred it if they were: that would suggest they feared him being able to identify them later.

"Awake, I see," Libra said. "Awake and noisy. You really are troublesome."

Will would have liked to say, *Feel free to let me go, then,* but his effort at speech was just a croak. He forced a dry cough that did no good. "Water."

"Thirsty?" Libra said. "Where's the information?"

"Water."

"You seem to think you're in a position to make demands. You aren't."

Will didn't know what to say to that; he only knew that it would not be 'please'. Libra considered him for an endless moment, then jerked a thumb. The ginger henchman went out.

"While you can't speak, Mr. Darling, maybe you'll listen. Your situation is this: The house is ours, and everyone in it is loyal. It stands two miles from the nearest building, five from a village. There is no path for walkers, and we have no casual passers-by. Nobody will hear you if you scream. Nobody knows where you are. We took you out of London by our own methods and you needn't hope they will be discovered. You aren't the first man we've brought here. None of them escaped, and nor will you."

The ginger man returned. He had a jug and a cup, and Will's entire body twitched convulsively at the sight.

"Not yet," Libra said. "We're going to reorganise the arrangements in here. When that's done, you can have a drink. If you struggle or fight, we will pour the jug out on the ground. Do you understand?" He waited for Will's nod. "We're going to manacle your ankle. That way you can eat, drink, and relieve yourself. Or you can stay trussed up without any of those privileges and see how long you last. We'd rather handle this like reasonable men, but it's up to you. Which will it be?"

There wasn't a choice. He couldn't fight: his head bloody hurt, and he doubted he'd be able to move his arms at all for the first few minutes once they were untied. A struggle wouldn't gain him anything.

You'd hold onto your defiance, a voice in his head warned him. *Now you're cooperating.*

He was, but he was also bloody thirsty, so he didn't fight as they cut his legs free. One of the men brought in a heavy iron chain, with some effort. It had a cuff on one end which they locked around his ankle; they attached the other end to the hasp in the wall with a padlock, and only then cut his hands loose. His arms hurt like hell as he moved them, and he couldn't help a wince.

"You did the right thing," Libra said, almost sympathetically. "Over a longer period, the damage might become permanent. Give him a drink. But, Mr. Darling? This is the only cup you'll have. If you break it, you'll be drinking out of your hands."

It was a pottery mug. Will didn't break it. He drank great airless gulps, letting the water sluice down his throat like life, and refilled it three times before Libra said, "Enough for now. You'll make yourself sick."

That was irritatingly true. Will swallowed a couple of times to make sure the water had gone down. "I need a lavatory."

Libra waved a hand at the ginger man, who went out again. Will wondered if his lackeys liked being ordered about that way. "You'll have a chamber pot. If you decide to break it or tip it over, it won't be replaced, and nobody will clean up your mess. If you throw your food around, there will be no more food. I hope you're grasping the principle? Behave like a sensible man, and your life will be a great deal more pleasant. Unreasonable behaviour will be its own punishment."

Will tried to keep his breath and voice even. "How long do you intend to hold me here?"

"Until the information is in my hands."

"I told you. I burned it."

"Yes," Libra said. "It's lucky for you that I don't believe you. If I did, I would not be able to protect you from the vengeance of my superiors. Take some time to think, Mr. Darling. You'll have plenty of that, and the sooner you realise your position, the better for all of us."

They went out, leaving the door standing ajar. And there Will was, left alone with a chamber pot, a jug of water, a cup, and a chain on his ankle.

He made use of the pot, had another cup of water—he was still achingly thirsty but knew he should ration himself to let his tissues absorb it—and then bent to the steel cuff on his ankle. A very little bit of tugging persuaded him there was no give in the lock, whose key had gone into Libra's pocket, or the heavy padlock that fastened the chain. The chain's links were heavy, and welded shut. The hasp was firmly set in the wall, and the heavy bolts that secured it had no give to his fingers. He tried setting his legs to the wall and heaving with all the strength of his arms and back, but no matter how hard he pulled, there was no movement. He was pretty sure the bolts were screwed into a beam, in which case he'd need a drayhorse to pull them out.

Fuck, fuck, fuck.

This could be worse, and he was sure would become so in time. He knew what Libra was up to: he'd had training on this before he started trench raiding, in case of capture. They would treat you kindly and offer you advantages if you behaved as they asked. You didn't have to betray your own side or aid the enemy: you just had to make that first little compromise of abstaining from disobedience or defiance, and it would be rewarded. Because once you'd compromised with the enemy, it would become easier and easier to cooperate with him, and from there it was a very short step to collaboration.

He'd compromised already. He didn't want to be parched and pinioned in his own filth; it wouldn't help him if he was. But it was the first step down the path to surrender, all the same.

That said, he had a pretty good defence against giving away the information for one simple reason. He didn't know where it was. The only person who knew that was Maisie.

He'd spent a chaotic twenty minutes or so the other morning hiding copies of Shakespeare in bookshops up and down the Charing Cross Road, and shed his War Office and Zodiac followers in the process as they peeled off to check what he was about. Then he'd whipped round a corner and thrust an envelope into the postbox, unseen. It had held the pages, with instructions that she was to hide them in something—drop them into a vase, sew them into a cushion, whatever she thought best—pawn whatever it was, and give him the ticket with extreme secrecy.

Will had a fair collection of items in pawn, his father's watch and his own medals among them, to be redeemed once his inheritance was in his hands. He hadn't decided whether to take the leaf-in-a-forest approach and add the new ticket to his pile, or to hide it in a book. Either way, it had seemed the best way to keep the information concealed. He still thought it was a good idea, except for the significant flaw, which was that Maisie hadn't given him the ticket.

He didn't know if she'd even done the job yet. Going to a pawnshop could be a humiliating business for anyone, and doubtless far more so for a black woman than a white man. She'd presumably visited the bookshop with her silk flowers to talk about his letter, if not to give him the ticket. But there had been too many people there for a private conversation, and Phoebe had turned up, and then Maisie had had to go to her auntie in Watford since the woman was, if not at death's door, at least leaning on the garden gate. Neither she nor Will was on the telephone, so they hadn't communicated since. Will hoped to hell she hadn't posted the ticket to him, given his post had been stolen on Monday morning.

What it came down to was, Will didn't know where the ticket was. Only Maisie could point to the information's hiding place. So if Will surrendered, he'd have to give her up to Zodiac.

That focused his mind wonderfully. The death of thousands under some dreadful manmade disease was a theoretical horror; something bad happening to Maisie Jones because of him was real, vivid, and utterly unthinkable. He couldn't betray her to these bastards. He wouldn't, no matter what it cost.

Unfortunately, that left him neck deep in shit with not one single bargaining chip. So he'd better find a way to get out, because he had to assume there was no cavalry coming. He was sure Phoebe would have called the police, and Kim, and it was conceivable that at least one of those might be searching for him, but if there was any likelihood of him being found, Libra would surely have gone for the thumbscrews rather than playing a waiting game.

Will thought about that. He thought about it a lot as absolutely nothing happened for hour after hour. At one point the bald henchman came in to refill the water jug and give him some cheese sandwiches. Will tried to speak to him and was ignored. Other than that, there was nothing. He couldn't hear anything outside except the odd chirrup of birdsong, which gave weight to the contention that he was somewhere in the countryside; he couldn't hear anything from inside the house. For all he knew, the bastards had gone to the pictures just because they could, while he was utterly trapped. They hadn't even bothered to lock the door of his room, just left it ajar. Will thought that was overconfidence at first before he recognised it as part of the torture.

The chain was too heavy to do jumping jacks so he did press ups and sit ups, five hundred of each, and another two hundred once he was sufficiently bored to start again. The sliver of light from the shutters moved steadily across the wall. Nobody had ever told him imprisonment would be so dull. He'd read *The Count of Monte Cristo* as a boy and come away with the idea that Edmond Dantès had suffered from the dark, rats, terrible food, and the cruelty of his gaolers. Now he thought about six years with nothing to read, nothing to see, and nobody to talk to, and realised that he'd missed the point entirely. Six *years*? He'd barely managed six hours.

The bald man came in again with more water and more cheese sandwiches, the same type of cheese. This time, he left a single thin blanket. Again, he didn't answer when Will spoke. Again he left, and the room grew dark, and Will sat in shadows, realising that they weren't going to give him a lamp. Or, he supposed, a bath when he'd sweated sufficiently into these clothes to make himself vile, or tooth-powder, or the privacy of a shut door. That was the point. No overt cruelty, just enough promises kept and physical needs met to make him want to cooperate just a little more, while the drip-drip effect of time and boredom and hopelessness wore away his resolve like water on rock.

But if it was Maisie sitting here instead of him, she'd be spending every second in an agony of anticipation as to what they might do to her, so fuck Zodiac and their games. Will's stubbornness had at various points in his life seen him caned, sent to his room, put on report, and threatened by the War Office. He didn't plan to give in to this lot now. But he lay in the dark as the warmth drained from the room, huddling his jacket and the inadequate blanket around him, and wished very strongly that he'd never contacted his uncle in the first place.

When he slept, he dreamed of the night with Kim. That made waking even worse.

FIFTEEN

Libra didn't come back the next day. Will did one thousand seven hundred and forty-three sit-ups, and six hundred and eight-eight push-ups. He ate six near-identical cheese sandwiches, reflecting that it was very possible to go off cheese, and that he would do murder for an apple. He spent a solid hour with the pin that had kept the sadly crumpled silk flower attached to his coat through all the ups and downs of the past days, doing his level best to pick the lock from a starting point of never having done such a thing in his life and not having the first idea of how they worked. Really, he was prodding a pin randomly into a hole for an hour, but at least it was something to do.

It was an exceedingly long day. He didn't ask for a book, or a newspaper. That would be fatal: they'd do him a favour and he'd think more kindly of them, or they'd ask for a concession, any concession, and if Will agreed, that would be a second crack in his defences. This was trench warfare, and the only way through was to hunker down and sit out the discomfort. So he did, entertaining and frustrating himself by dredging up fragments of poems he'd had to learn at school, and ones men had read aloud in the trenches. If he'd had any sense he'd have memorised the whole 'Ballad of the White Horse' when he had all that free time, or at least 'Lepanto'.

Dim drums throbbing, in the hills half heard,
Where only on a nameless throne a crownless prince has stirred,
Where, risen from a doubtful seat and half attainted stall,
The last knight of Europe takes weapons from the wall.

He really wished he could remember more than that.

Another long night passed, and another day. He listened to the birds, the occasional sounds of movement downstairs, the motor-car that drove away and returned a few hours later. He did two thousand and seventeen sit-ups, and a mere five hundred and twelve push-ups because his shoulders were feeling yesterday's exertions. At least the pain in his head had gone.

He tried hard not to think about how long he could keep this up, or how long he might have to. Zodiac were in no hurry. They could wait for a year while he sat here slowly fading into a wasted madman with a matted beard, until he begged to give them the information if only to see the sky again.

Steady on, Darling, you've only been here three days, he told himself. It sounded a bit hollow.

Half way through the fourth day, footsteps approached the door, and Libra came in. Will felt a flood of relief for which he could have kicked himself.

"Hello, Mr. Darling." Libra looked down at him, nose wrinkled. Will was well aware he was unwashed. His beard was growing and though he'd taken off his shirt and vest to exercise, he couldn't wash off the sweat, and still had to sleep in them. He was starting to smell. He'd been used to filth in the War, of course; it was funny how fast you forgot.

"Afternoon," he said. "What's the weather like?"

"Very pleasant for the time of year. I understand you're keeping yourself busy. Plenty of exercise."

"Fills the time."

"That lasts for a few days," Libra said. "You'll lose the drive soon enough. This isn't a way for an active man to live."

"Are you letting me go?"

"I'd be happy to." Libra smiled. It gave Will the impression he'd sent off a postal order for a booklet on Smiling for Beginners. "You're a determined man, Mr. Darling. Remarkably so. We could use someone like you in our organisation."

Flattery, plus an offer of companionship. Will had recent and first-hand experience of the powerful lure of togetherness when you were alone. He didn't intend to fall for that again. "You've got a funny way of recruiting people. Have you tried an application form? Might be easier."

Libra smiled again. It was perfunctory. "You're a very determined man, but a foolish one. Sitting here is a waste of your time, not mine."

Will shrugged, for lack of useful response. Libra shook his head. "You can't be defiant forever and if you are, what will it achieve? Draven wasn't the only scientist working on these ideas. Someone else will discover the same thing eventually, or something similar, and do you know what that man will do? He'll give it or sell it to his government—which may not be ours, it could be the Americans or the Russians, even the Germans. His government will develop it. Other governments will spy, and hear, and copy, or come up with still worse weapons in the name of deterrence. And sooner or later men of power will use it on cities, on London or New York or Berlin, but do you know what they'll do first?"

"Build themselves bunkers, I expect."

Libra seemed genuinely pleased by that. "I knew you had potential. Exactly so. No matter which city, or nation, or political system, the leaders will make sure they and their families and their wealth are protected long before the first gas-cylinder explodes over a city."

"Right. So?"

"So Zodiac pits itself against the corruption of wealth, and the structures of entrenched power." Libra's eyes lit as he spoke. "We want to bring it down, Mr. Darling, all of it. The palaces, whether Westminster or Buckingham. Whitehall and the White House, the Champs-Elysées and Wall Street. The whole sordid structure of capital and empire, built on lies and designed to oppress the common man. Men like you, sent to war as cannon fodder for a squabble between royal cousins, then brought back and flung on the scrapheap because the country that demanded you should bleed won't pay for your bandages. We want to sweep it all away, destroy the systems and begin again, this time with all men equal."

"Sounds good," Will said. "And that starts with spreading plague?"

"It starts with destruction. There's no choice. When the French Revolution beheaded a king, they merely created the space for an emperor. The Germans made themselves a republic and cried out for socialism, yet their new national assembly is still filled with the upper classes, the same faces as before. If Mr. MacDonald's Labour Party should be elected, how long do you think it will take before Labour members of parliament emerge from the ranks of the titled and wealthy? Power clings to power: that is the universal truth, and tinkering at the edges of the great structures of power will not change anything. We must raze them to the ground."

Will nodded slowly. The light in Libra's eyes was a flame now, the sort of flame that lit bonfires under people. He unquestionably believed what he said, and he had a good point, at that. "All right. But how many ordinary people will suffer when you raze everything to the ground?"

"How many suffer now?" Libra demanded. "How many millions died in the war? How many are dying down mines and in factories and on the streets because they can't afford the rent of a room? Why do we count the cost of change, but not the cost of the world staying the same?"

Will opened his mouth, stopped, considered. "Fair. Powerful, even. One question, though: When we sweep away all the structures of power and start off with a blank slate, what's to stop the same thing happening again? People want a leader. Say you knock everything down. What I'd expect next is a strong man to come out on top, pull an army together, give himself a nice big house and a fancy hat, and off we go, just like before. Well, just take Russia. Who's going to prevent that?"

"And that is why we need Zodiac!" Libra said, as if Will was agreeing with him. "This isn't destruction for its own sake, the childishness of the mere anarchist. Zodiac will bring a new order into being, guided by principles of justice and equality."

"There's my answer. The people setting the principles and enforcing them will be the ones on top, won't they? So who's going to be the first-among-equals of your new paradise?" Kim had mentioned one of them. Will searched his memory. "Your mate Capricorn?"

Libra's face darkened instantly, a thundercloud of anger sweeping across it. He took a step forward and Will stood up fast. He mightn't be able to defend himself that well with a chain on his foot, but he intended to stay off the floor as long as possible.

Libra visibly struggled to regain control. "You're a fool," he said. "Worse than a fool, because you could understand, but you choose to act in subservience to your puppetmasters.

First you were a soldier, nothing more than a trained dog, now you're putting yourself through misery for the sake of a nation that won't note your death, far less care. Your sort are an obstacle to progress. You don't deserve the chance I've given you. Where is the information?"

Will met his eyes and said, clearly, "I burned it."

Libra swooped down and snatched the blanket. Will grabbed the corner, and there was a brief tug of war that ended with it ripping in two. Libra held up his part triumphantly. "I'm sure your loyalty to the system of oppression will keep you warm at night."

"Oh, fuck off," Will said. "You're a whining child, fantasising about destroying the world because it's too much work to make it better. Talking about oppression like you've done a day's work in your life. Piss off to Russia with it and see how long you last there, you tosspot!" He had to shout the last bit because Libra had left the room. It relieved his feelings, at least.

They brought him water that evening but no food. The night was very long, hungry, and very cold indeed. He huddled the half-blanket round himself and spent the wakeful hours recreating the evening and morning with Kim in his head. It passed the time more pleasantly than anything else.

There was only bread the next morning. Will wondered if he should ration it, but ate it all anyway. He was still hungry afterwards, and decided it would be a bad idea to exercise, but he also knew Libra was right about his will being sapped by time. He didn't want to do a thousand press-ups. He wanted a bath, and the sky, and not to be in this fucking room any more.

They started cooking downstairs. Will could smell meat roasting. Gammon, he thought, and couldn't stop salivating.

Libra came in sometime in the middle of the day. "Hungry?" he enquired.

Will shrugged. Libra shook his head pseudo-sympathetically. "I dare say you were cold last night. I think we should begin again, don't you? I admit I lost my temper. Perhaps I was unreasonable expecting you to understand all at once. It's a hard thing to overturn one's view of the world. It takes a great deal of courage to face up to where we've been wrong, or blind, but it can be done. I believe you can do it. And, in fact, I liked that you challenged me."

"Didn't seem that way to me."

"Oh, not what you said about a great and noble man. But the fact that you wanted to know how we prevent a new king —that was right-thinking. What do you say, Mr. Darling? Shall we start again?"

"Absolutely," Will said. "Take this thing off my foot and we can have a lovely chat."

"I shan't do that. But I will give you a blanket—a thicker one, it's getting cold—and have you brought something more sustaining. A plate of ham, eggs, and potatoes? We have an excellent butcher in the village. Everything is brighter after a hot meal. A drink, even. A pint of ale to wash it down." He paused enticingly. "Just ask."

"Just what?"

"Ask," Libra said. "Ask me, 'Please may I have a blanket, and some food?'"

"If you want to give me something, why don't you?"

Libra's lips stretched. "Because I'd like a little courtesy, Mr. Darling. A little respect, an acknowledgement of your position, a give and take between the two of us. I make a concession, you make a concession. Is that really an unreasonable request?"

The roasting ham smelled glorious. The endless, freezing

night stretched out in front of him. Will called Maisie's face to mind, and said, "Go fuck yourself."

They took away the rest of the blanket then. He couldn't sleep at all that night because his feet were so cold.

There was nothing but water the next morning. Will knew giving in to despair would be the worst thing he could do, but he did spend some time with his face in his hands. That was pretty awful in itself because his hands were dirty and his face rough with itchy beard. His mouth was furry and vile and he had a hunger headache. He really hated those.

They didn't bring him anything at all at lunchtime, either to eat or drink. The water-jug was empty now. He'd have shouted, despite the inevitability of that making things worse, except he suspected there was nobody in the house. He'd heard the car go earlier, and he recognised the silence that came from absence, rather than people not making noise.

They would come back. They'd bring him food. They *would*. Or maybe they'd just decided to cut their losses and go, and he'd die here alone.

It was so quiet, and he was so hungry, that he sat up straight when he heard a faint noise from below, a tinkling crash, like some silly sod had dropped a plate.

There *was* someone here. Will started to stamp on the floor. "Hey! Hey, you bastards!" This wasn't good behaviour, it was exactly what they'd punish him for—no, he reminded himself, it was the excuse they wanted to make their cruelty his fault. They wanted him to blame himself for what was being done to him, to make him feel he deserved to starve because he didn't beg for bread.

Well, they could stick it. "Hoi! I know you're there! Are you all deaf as well as stupid, you Bolshevik wankers?"

Feet, on the stairs, very light and in no hurry. "Are you just going to stand around?" he yelled. "If you're going to leave me to starve, come in and say so to my face! I fucking dare you!"

The door creaked open wide, letting in enough light to make Will blink. A man stood silhouetted in the doorway, a slimmer shape than Libra.

"Will," he said.

It was Kim.

SIXTEEN

It was a dream. It had to be. He'd had a few of those about people coming to help—Maisie, his old CO, even Alfie Greenaway, still splattered with his own blood. Those were bad dreams to wake up from, and Will told himself fiercely to be ready for this new disappointment even as Kim sprinted across the room, skidded to his knees, grabbed his face, and recoiled.

"Jesus Christ. What the devil?"

"Kim? It is you. *Kim.*" Will grabbed his hands. He could feel the slender wrists hard under his fingers, and the tension in Kim's muscles.

"What have they done to you?"

"Get me out," Will said, voice breaking with desperation. "Please. You have to get me out."

Kim stared at him, eyes wide, then visibly snapped himself back to efficiency. "Yes. First things f...uck, is this a chain?" He tugged experimentally at the hasp. "Hell's teeth."

"I've tried breaking it. I can't. You'll need a crowbar."

"Let me see." He bent to squint at Will's ankle, and made a face. "No offence, but—"

"I stink. I know. They haven't let me wash."

"Have they fed you?"

"Not enough. And it's been bloody cold at night."

"Libra?"

"Yes."

Kim nodded slowly. "I'll have his balls," he remarked, as calm as if he were discussing the weather. "I will put his balls on a plate, and I will make him eat them." He sat back on his heels. "There doesn't seem to be anyone in the house."

"They go out. It's not as if I can get away."

"When do they come back?"

"Varies. Usually before dark."

"How many?"

"I've seen three, including Libra."

"Mph. Do I have time to call for help? If the police find you like this, there's a solid kidnapping case to be made."

Will grabbed his arm, too tightly from Kim's wince. "But if they come back—you can't leave me like this!"

"I won't." Kim scowled in thought. "We can't have them return before the police get here, and Lord knows where the nearest station is, so I agree, I need to get you out. The question is how."

"Get a crowbar."

"If there's one lying around." Kim prodded the hasp. "This won't be easy. I wonder if I can pick the lock."

"Can you do that?"

He made a face. "I've opened various jewellery cases for Phoebe over the years. She, of course, has the courtesy to carry hairpins on her person, which I don't suppose you do. I'll go and look for something."

Will didn't want him to go. He knew exactly what would happen if Kim left the room: he'd wake up and realise his rescuer never been here at all, and he didn't know how he'd get over that. "I've a pin," he said rather desperately, indicating the crumpled wreck of the silk peony.

Kim started to speak, blinked, then grabbed the flower. "You bloody fool, you've got a wire! Oh, now we're talking." He started to pull off the silk wrapping round the flower stalk, muttered an oath, and went over to where light spilled from the door. "Just give me a moment and we'll see what we can do. Anything else I need to know in the meantime? Are you hurt?"

"Just hungry. They didn't need to hurt me: they were going to keep me here with nothing to read, nobody to talk to, rotting away, and with blankets and food dependent on good behaviour. They were waiting for me to break."

Kim didn't respond to that for a few seconds. He knelt in the doorway, entirely still, and when he turned, his smile seemed like it took an effort. "How optimistic of them," he said with forced lightness. "If it was a matter of cooperation in return for food, I'm amazed you haven't starved." He came back over, stuffing the remnants of red and green silk into his pocket. "I'm bitterly sorry, Will. This should never have happened, have been allowed to happen. I don't know what I should have done differently, but 'everything' probably covers it."

"Get me out and we're quits." Kim bent over the ankle cuff with wire and pin. Will watched his dark head, telling himself *It won't work, he can't do it*. He didn't think he could bear hope now. "How did you get here?"

"It would be easier if you talk to me." Kim's voice was tense with concentration. "Distract me. Is the information safe?"

"I didn't give them anything. I couldn't: I don't know where it is. I had a friend hide it."

"Risky."

"The plan was I'd be able to get it back without involving anyone else. Didn't work. I made a mess of it."

"Impossible situation. Never mind. Come *on*, you son of a bitch, open."

"The worst thing is the dark." Will wasn't sure he wanted to blurt this out, but he couldn't stop talking, not after six full days of solitude. "They didn't give me a lamp. Hours and hours sitting here in the dark."

Kim just grunted. Will went on. "And the not washing. I'd had enough of being filthy by Armistice, and of being hungry, come to that. I'm sick of being hungry, and I'm sick of these fucking people."

"I'm dreadfully sorry to hear it," Kim said in a tone of pure, rising triumph, and there was a little *snick*. He sat back on his heels, and pulled the cuff open. "There."

"You little beauty!" Will kicked off the metal. He'd have kissed Kim if he wasn't aware of his own stink. "You bloody genius. Let's get out of here. No, let's burn the place down."

"Let's not," Kim said firmly. "I'll telephone the police, you eat something while we wait. You might even wash your—" His head came up, like a startled hare. "Do you hear a motor?"

Will's heart plummeted at the familiar note, getting louder as it approached. "Oh Christ. It's them. They're coming back."

"Can you run? Where are your shoes?"

"They took them. Let's go."

They sprinted together down two flights of stairs. Will had no idea of the layout of the house so he followed Kim into a kitchen. The window was indeed broken. Kim went to unbolt the back door while Will had a few urgent swallows of water from the tap and grabbed a hunk of bread from the table, and they ran outside.

The sky was grey but still painfully bright, and remarkably large after six days in a room. Will shaded his eyes, assessing the terrain. They were at the back of the house and it didn't seem like the motor was usually parked behind here. There was a good-sized kitchen garden, its few plants yellow and straggling in this dismal season, surrounded by a red brick wall.

"Can you climb that?" they asked each other in chorus. Kim rolled his eyes. Will grinned harshly and led the way, the ground cold and wet and sharply stony under his feet. He didn't feel hungry now, just lean and keen, as the will to survive took over his body and lent a quivering electric strength to his muscles. He'd missed that sensation. His foot was absurdly light without the chain.

Kim gave him a leg up. Will straddled the top and leaned down to give him a hand, and they jumped down the other side in a scramble.

"Copse," Will said.

"Where? Oh, trees. How disappointing."

Cops would indeed have been better. They ran for the stand of trees anyway, stumbling over thick tuffets of rank grass. The ground was wet, with claylike mud that stuck to Will's stockinged feet in heavy, cold, wet clumps and made running an experience from a nightmare. He'd often cursed his army boots, but socks were not an improvement.

"Bloody hate mud," he muttered.

They made it to the trees without incident except several sharp things under Will's feet, sticks and stones there to break his bones. He growled a curse as they ducked out of view from the house.

"Now what?" he asked. "Keep going? The hue and cry will be up any minute."

"My motor is on the other side, in the lane." Kim pointed in the direction of the house.

"Parked nearby?"

"Round a bend."

"Any idea of the terrain?"

"I passed a tiny village a couple of miles south of here. I don't know about the other way, nor do I know what happens if we continue over the fields from here. We're in the North Wessex Downs, if that helps, about ten miles north of Andover."

They might as well be in Belgium for all Will knew of the area. He shrugged indifference. "They'll find I'm gone any minute, and they'll see your motor. Either they decide the game's up and run for it or they try to get me back, in which case they'll be coming this way because they know we didn't go out the front and the trees are the obvious place to go. So we make a stand here, or we skirt round the hedges and get back to your motor-car, or we head off in search of civilisation on foot."

"But lacking shoes." Kim grimaced. "Go for the motor?"

"Works for me. Uh-oh." He pulled back behind a tree. Kim glanced over at the house and moved back as he saw the same thing: a man coming up the outside of the wall, moving purposefully in their direction.

Just one, the bald one. Kim jerked a thumb, suggesting they start moving. Will shook his head, pointed at Kim's chest, and mouthed, "Handkerchief."

Kim's brows twitched but he handed it over. It was decent, strong linen, in a delicate shade of lilac. "Ponce," Will murmured, bent to pick up a good-sized stone, and knotted it into the cloth. There was a clear track between the trees, not a path exactly but the way people walked when they walked here. Will positioned himself behind a tree on one side, indicated where Kim should stand on the other, and set himself to wait.

He'd done this before. It was all very familiar: the mud and the cold and the smell of wet wood. The hunger, the heartbeat, and the light-headed feeling of the world coming to a single, simple point. Sky above, earth underfoot, enemy at hand. Move, eat, kill.

The enemy's footsteps approached, changing from a distant squelch to a wet crunch as he came into the stand of trees. Will kept his breath shallow. In through the nose, out through the mouth. He glanced at Kim, who was frozen in place, far too tense, for all the world as if he'd never waited in ambush before. His face was set, but his hand was trembling.

Leaves rustled and sticks broke under the enemy's feet. He wasn't trying to be quiet, so he didn't need the element of surprise. He had a weapon, then. Will adjusted his intentions accordingly

The enemy was right on them now. He came forward along the path, gun in hand, turning his head from side to side. It was his bad luck that he turned it to the right as he came abreast of them, so that he saw Kim first.

They both recoiled, Kim and the enemy, just a fraction of a second's shock sending each of them back. That was the enemy's second piece of bad luck, because Will was moving forward. He brought the makeshift cosh down, using the extra swing from the knotted handkerchief to give it the greatest possible force, and the enemy went to his knees with a grunt that sounded oddly wrong. Because he was English, not German, of course. Will brought the rock down again, and this time something gave in the skull he hit. The enemy pitched forward onto his face and didn't move again.

Kim's eyes were very wide. Will said, "Take the gun. Keep a look-out."

The enemy was unconscious, still breathing but not likely to move any time soon. Will checked his feet, decided they were large enough, and started unlacing his shoes.

"Is he dead?" Kim's voice was a whisper.

"Not so far. Is it loaded?"

Kim checked with a few clicks. "Full."

Will stripped off his claggy socks, shoved them in a pocket, and put on the enemy's—they were wool, pleasantly warm from his body—and shoes. These were a couple of sizes too big, but still a vast improvement.

Kim was keeping watch with a reasonably competent air, gun in hand. "Can you shoot?" Will asked.

"Pretty well."

"Will you? If necessary?"

"Probably not as easily as you," Kim said. "Which might be for the best, as we should try not to kill anyone, or at least anyone else. Let's get to the motor, shall we?"

They went along the outside of the hedge that ran along the field, stooping low. Will went first, oversized shoes loose on his feet; Kim followed, moving quietly.

November-grey skies above, wet grass and clods of earth beneath. Smells of mud and wet sticks, the slow rot of autumn, Kim's light cologne, Will's own fusty unwashed odour, the trace of blood on the stained handkerchief. Sounds: mostly their feet, Kim's shallow breaths suggesting tension or exertion, a few late buzzing things, sparrows in the trees. Will kept an ear out for sudden cawing. He'd known crows give away a location before now, and prayed they wouldn't send a pheasant rocketing. You could hear the bloody things a mile off.

It was slow going. Will became very conscious of the hunk of bread in his pocket, and of the thirst that a few swallows of water hadn't quenched, but those had to be put to one side. There was only the long, slow, crawling progression through the mud for now, checking round the corners of the hedge, horribly aware of how exposed they were. The strain in cramping thighs, the cold ponderous weight of mud-clogged shoes, the wet chill pinching his fingers.

And then, finally, there was a line of trees and a ditch, and the road on its other side. They were perhaps a couple of hundred yards to the side of the house where he'd been imprisoned. There was no sound anywhere except birds.

Will went low to recce, going into the ditch and using cover. The road seemed empty. Kim crawled to join him in the ditch at Will's signal, mimicking his stance and movements. A bright chap, that. He'd have been useful in Flanders.

Kim brought his mouth to Will's ear, the breath warm and tickly. "My motor is just round that corner." He indicated the bend in the road.

If he was Libra, he'd have someone watching it. Maybe two. "Hand crank?" Will asked softly. If the car took several minutes to start, this might be tricky.

"Electric starter. Reliable."

Will nodded. "All right. Here's the plan…"

He made his way round the corner with painstaking slowness. You could be quick or you could be quiet, but not both. It took perhaps five minutes to traverse a handful of yards, but at least nobody was shooting at him.

A Daimler, sides splattered with dried mud, sat by the edge of the road. Libra stood in front of it. He had a revolver in one hand, hanging by his side. Will could have shot him from here, and would have, if he'd had the bloody gun.

He made his way through the undergrowth, taking it slow, mud seeping coldly through his trouser legs, and found a good position, then hunkered down to wait there. He took his borrowed shoes off while he was at it: they'd flap too noisily on the road if he had to move fast. His feet immediately felt chilled. He passed the time unknotting the handkerchief, discarding the rock, finding a couple of pebbles, and retying the cloth to put knots at two opposing corners.

A few minutes later, there was a crunch of feet on stone and Kim's voice barked, "Don't move! Hands up!"

Libra looked round sharply. Will whisked himself silently from the trees onto the road, ducking behind the Daimler.

"Hello, old man." Kim's voice was very cool. "Always a pleasure. Congratulations on your promotion."

"Secretan," Libra snarled. "You treacherous shit."

"You can't take a joke, that's your trouble. If your hands go down I will shoot you where you stand."

"You don't have the nerve. You're a *gentleman*." Libra spat the words. Will edged forward around the side of the car, stockinged feet wet and cold but silent.

"Wrong on both counts. Hand over the information."

Libra paused. "Why don't you ask Darling for it?"

"Don't play silly buggers with me. I assume he's in a shallow grave somewhere. I'll send flowers. Now hand it over."

"He's gone. You let him out," Libra said, with just a thread of question in his voice.

"Gone?" Kim repeated, incredulous. "You mean you lost him? You useless arse!"

Libra began to reply. He didn't get far, because that was when Will rose up behind him, flicked the weighted handker-chief round his neck, and pulled.

Libra flailed, one hand grabbing for the cloth. Kim was there almost at once, grappling the revolver from him. Will gripped his makeshift garotte hard, wedging one knee into Libra's back for extra leverage. Twenty seconds should do it.

"Will!" Kim snapped. "Don't kill him!"

Libra thrashed helplessly as the cloth bit into his throat. The bones would be starting to bend, the windpipe giving way. Will liked that thought a lot, and he kept pulling until the muzzle of a gun pressed hard against his temple, which got his attention.

"Will," Kim said again. "Stop."

The revolver was cold and hard against his cheek. Will turned to meet Kim's eyes, and didn't see treachery there, or betrayal. Kim was, in fact, giving him what Will's mother would call a Meaningful Look. "Why?"

"Bad tactics. Put him *down*."

Will released his grip. Libra collapsed over the bonnet of the Daimler, purple-faced and choking. Kim said, "I will give you a gun if you promise not to shoot him. I mean it, no killing. All right?"

Will grunted, but took the revolver Kim handed him, and held it to Libra's skull as Kim quickly checked his pockets. "Oh, good, handcuffs. Convenient. Let's get him out of the way, shall we?"

They hauled the gasping man into the trees on the other side of the road and cuffed him with his arms round a tangle of nice sturdy hawthorn trunks. Will fished one of his six-day worn, mud-sodden socks out of his pocket. "Gag," he said at Kim's quizzical look.

"You're annoyed with him, aren't you?"

"Should have let me kill him." Will shoved the filthy sock deep into Libra's mouth, and used the handkerchief to secure the gag. "As I expect he'd agree right now. Let's go."

"The road's too narrow to turn," Kim said as they got in the car. "We'll have to drive past the house."

Will checked Libra's revolver. "I'm ready. Step on it."

The Daimler's engine caught at once, as promised. Kim accelerated away in a squeal of tires and a shower of stones. Will thought he saw someone come running as they sped past the house, and twisted round in his seat, but the next second they were round another bend in the lane.

"Settle down," Kim said grimly. "I'm going to get this bus moving."

The motor leapt forward, pushing Will back in his seat,

far too fast for a country lane. Kim watched the road with steely concentration, mouth set, double de-clutching like a racing driver, the engine purring like a big cat in response. Will fished the bread out of his pocket. It was squashed, and he had to brush a bit of mud off, but he ate it anyway.

Kim took a turning at the next crossroads. "Where are we going?" Will asked.

"No idea. I just want to put a few options between us and pursuit."

"Shouldn't we head to London?"

"That's the last thing we should do," Kim said. "You, my friend, need to be somewhere entirely elsewhere for a few days while we sort this tangle out. Somewhere Zodiac can't reach you. I happen to know a very nice old lady with a spare room perhaps three hours' drive from here. We'll park you there."

"And then what?"

"I shall work out the next move with you off the board. I've just spent six days searching for you and it was pure chance I succeeded, so I would really prefer not to have to do that again. And I doubt Libra will play a waiting game next time he gets his hands on you, so all in all, your recapture would be best avoided."

"Then why didn't you let me kill him?"

Kim didn't answer for a moment, manoeuvring the motor round a series of tight bends. "Because you're better than that," he said at last.

"Are you serious? Do you think he'd be the first man I've killed?"

"I'm positive he'd be the first you've murdered. And that would have been murder. It's one thing to knock a man on the head while trying to escape, and another to do a professional garrotting job. Moreover, the latter would just hand Zodiac a weapon against you, because if you think they wouldn't make a complaint to police of a dangerous tramp making an unprovoked attack, you're optimistic. Don't kill anyone."

"Easy for you to say," Will muttered. It was meant to be a joke, but Kim slowed slightly, enough to put his hand on Will's leg, a brief, comforting touch.

"You've had the devil's own time, Will. I know that. I'm not asking you to forgive or forget, just to hold off so we can do this properly. Please, let me take the lead until you've had a bath, some food, and a lot of sleep." He paused. "Maybe two baths."

"Sod you."

"Try to see it from my point of view. I had the upholstery cleaned only last month."

Will shook his head, making himself smile. It was funny, in its way, but the battle-excitement was ebbing from his veins and his many physical and mental discomforts were rushing back.

"I'm thirsty," he said abruptly.

"There's a village coming up. Hold on."

Kim drove through it and parked the motor a little way beyond, around a bend to avoid being seen. Will sat in it and waited for what seemed an unconscionably long time while Kim went to get supplies. He returned after an age with two pewter tankards and a brown paper parcel.

"I paid for the tankards," he said. "Drink off the tops so they don't spill, and we'll keep going."

Will did that, draining about a pint between the two mugs, then attacking the parcel, which contained thick-sliced ham and pickle sandwiches. Not cheese, thank God. He devoured the lot in a couple of minutes, sluicing it down with ale. Picnicking in a Daimler while chauffeured by a lord and dressed like a tramp.

Thirst quenched and hunger staved off for now, he dozed

off, despite the roar of the engine and the cold. It was an uneasy slumber, not a real sleep, one that felt feverish, and he kept twitching awake at the sound of Libra's voice or the sensation of a weight round his ankle. Kim spoke to him reassuringly, with words Will forgot as soon as he heard them, but a tone that said, *You're safe*. In his half-dream Will believed him, and the miles rolled away.

SEVENTEEN

I t was dark when they arrived at a little cottage on the outskirts of a village. They could have been anywhere in Britain for all Will knew. He stared through the windscreen, dizzy with exhaustion and hunger, as Kim went to the front door, returned, and tugged at his arm. "Come on, old man. Out of the car now and say hello to Nanny. Nanny, this is my pal Will. Will, this is Mrs. Mungo."

"My goodness." The woman framed in the cottage door was about five feet tall and a good seventy years old, with cloudy eyes in a wrinkled face. "Master Kim!"

"I did say, Nanny. He's had a bad time."

"So I see. Come along in, now. Goodness me."

Will staggered into a cottage that was far too neatly kept for a man in his state. He stopped at the parlour door, unable to make himself go in to the sanctum sanctorum. "I'm filthy."

"I can see that," Mrs. Mungo said tartly. "Into the scullery, right now."

"I'll organise the bath," Kim said. "Can you dig out something for him to wear, Nanny?"

"I suppose he's about Tom's size. Might as well have some use of them."

"And he's starving and thirsty. If you've anything in the larder..."

Will sat on a hard chair eating a dense slice of fruit cake, while Kim set water boiling over a fire, just like a normal man who didn't have servants or machinery to do every task for him. They didn't speak. Will couldn't think of anything to say, and Kim seemed not to feel the need. He stayed, though, even when the bath was ready and Will had started the laborious task of peeling off his borrowed, muddy socks.

"Going to scrub my back?" he enquired, as he pulled off his vile shirt.

"I'd like to be sure you won't fall asleep and drown in the tub."

"It's a hip bath," Will said. "I'd need to be a contortionist."

Kim nodded. "Then I'll leave you to it."

It wasn't a huge tub and the water cooled quickly even in front of the fire, but Will didn't care. He scrubbed every inch he could reach, enjoying the harsh yellow soap as if it were the sort of luxurious unguent Phoebe doubtless kept in her bathroom, finally kneeling in the tub to dunk his head under water.

When he pulled his head out, Kim was there, watching.

He stood with a pile of material in his arms. His eyes were very dark in the dim light, and he looked—it was hard to identify that look. It held something of the expression you saw in church sometimes, when people were lost in the invisible, and the pain in their minds was edged with hope.

Will knelt up, very aware of his nakedness, and Kim's gaze. "Enjoying the view?"

Kim didn't answer for a second, then he gave a quick smile, as if shaking off his mood. "Very much.

Notwithstanding, here's a dressing gown and pyjamas. They belonged to Nanny's grandson, so treat them carefully, if you would."

Past tense. "War?"

"Jutland. Navy man."

Will wondered how Nanny felt about Kim's war record. He decided not to ask, and instead stood, water streaming off him. Kim's eyes flickered down his body, but his expression didn't change as he held out a towel.

Will took the rough cloth he was handed and set about drying himself. He took his time and didn't bother to cover himself up as he did it. Kim stood, watching. Neither of them spoke.

"Better?" Kim asked once he was in pyjamas and dressing gown.

"Much."

"Nanny's put out food in the kitchen. I'm starving, so..."

They ate at the kitchen table: veal and ham pie, heavy filling bread, cheese that tasted a lot better now he wasn't in chains. There was ale too, dark and nutty.

"Is Mrs. Mungo your old nurse?" Will asked once he was properly full.

"She used to take care of me, yes. A long time ago."

"Are we near your..." Will waved a hand. "Family home?"

"Not far."

But they hadn't gone there for refuge. Will considered that as he cut another slice of bread. "How did you find me?"

"Luck, desperation, elimination. And Ingoldsby, actually. He's had a few hints of suspicious activity in that area over a couple of years and let me know discreetly that Zodiac might have a nest around there. I tried six houses over two days before I happened on that one. I was coming to the conclusion that he'd lied to me to get me out of the way, but clearly I wronged him."

Will frowned. "So was the War Office trying to find me?"

"No," Kim said. "The leak, remember? It wouldn't have helped to send a detachment of agents off to an address if one of them telephoned Libra with an advance warning. That could have got you killed. Ingoldsby extended his cooperation in a private capacity."

Will put down his fork. "Look, I'm still not clear. Are you War Office or not?"

"Not. I have lent a hand on occasion but I'm an amateur."

"An amateur what?"

"Busybody. Jack of all trades. Let's say I extend my assistance when it's needed or requested."

"And why did Libra call you a traitor?"

"Ah, that." Kim grinned. "I did a spot of infiltration a little while ago. Learned a certain amount about the organisation before I was rumbled. Trusting me was the error of judgement that got the previous Libra removed from his position, and this mortal coil."

Will raised his brows. Kim shrugged. "Zodiac is unforgiving."

"But they didn't come after you?"

"They haven't yet. I will give them this: they're practical. Waging war on individuals is a pointless and distracting waste of resources. They'll doubtless kill me if I get in their way again—"

"You just have," Will said. "I told you I should have finished Libra. Now he knows you were involved and they'll come for you."

Kim sighed. "I do have some small amount of experience in this business, Will. Give me a little credit? When it comes to lurking around trees and ambushing people, I happily bow to you."

Will couldn't find an answer to that, or at least not one

appropriate to the circumstances. He yawned instead. It was past eight, and he was bone-tired.

"Bed," Kim said. "You need to sleep. I'll show you the room."

It was a very nice spare room, simply furnished, with a fire blazing in the small grate and a big bed with a patchwork quilt. It was also, Will was pretty sure, one of just two bedrooms in this tiny cottage.

"Where are you going to sleep?" he asked.

"I can stretch out downstairs."

"The bed's big enough," Will said. "We can share." It was entirely unremarkable for two men to share a bed in these circumstances. Nanny Mungo wouldn't think anything of it, he was sure.

Kim hesitated, then gave a little shake of the head. "You need a good night's rest. I'll go."

"Don't."

Will hadn't meant to sound like that, as if he were pleading, but he did. Kim's lips parted soundlessly. Will took a step closer. He put out a hand, ran a finger down Kim's jaw, felt just the first hint of stubble.

"Stay," he said softly. "I'd like your company."

Kim's expression was almost painful, as if nobody had told him that before in his life. Will brushed his fingers down his neck, up over his fine cheekbones, into his hair. "It's been a rough few days. When you turned up—I've never wanted to see anyone more."

"You don't need to be grateful to me."

"Bugger gratitude. I'm *appreciative*," Will said. "I said that I didn't think you were a shirker, and I was right. You came to get me, Kim. For all the pissing about before, you did that."

"Don't underestimate the pissing about." Kim's voice was strained.

"I'm not, but don't underestimate saving my life either. The other morning you said nothing had changed. Well, it has now. Maybe it doesn't alter anything in the grand scheme, but..." He let his hand drop to meet Kim's, catching his fingers. "We don't have to do anything. I'd still like you to stay."

Kim's hand tightened convulsively on his. "You won't thank me tomorrow if I do. No, really. You're exhausted, and I'll need to get moving at dawn and—well. Common sense is required." He held up a hand as Will began to speak. "Don't take this as a no. I can't tell you quite how much I'd like to stay with you now; I'd strongly prefer not to go back to London at all. Oh *hell*."

He tugged at Will's hand, pulling him forward, and their mouths met with desperate need. Will kissed him back, and Kim's hands came up to grip his face, flexing convulsively against his skin. He had the oddest feeling that they were both trying not to collapse against the other one.

"I was terrified," Kim mumbled against his mouth. "Six days, Will. All my fault. I really thought you were in that shallow grave I spoke of."

"I wasn't so good myself." He rested his forehead against Kim's, the two of them leaning together like a pair of cards.

"Something of a week all round."

"Damned right."

They stood together a moment longer, then Kim stepped back. "And now I am going to be sensible. I shall sleep downstairs, and you will get the good night you desperately need. Stay here for—say a week? I really do want you out of sight, out of London and Zodiac's clutches. I'll be in touch."

Will nodded. It *was* sensible. He tried not to feel rejected, or to let the clawing longing show on his face. It was just reaction to the time alone; he'd get over it. "All right, if you say so."

"Good man. Sleep, eat, recover, and let me try to sort this out as best I can. I'll leave Nanny funds for your sustenance, so indulge all you like. Don't contact *anyone*, and wait here for me, will you? No coming back to London early. You've done your part."

Will nodded. He was too tired to argue any more. "Kim?" he mumbled. "Thanks. For everything."

Kim gave a little, painful twitch of a smile. "No more thanks, please. Just take care of yourself, for once."

Will slept until past eleven the next morning, by which time Kim and the Daimler had long gone. Mrs. Mungo cooked him a large breakfast, interrogated him about his family, marital status, village of origin, education, employment, and war, and equipped him with a set of clothes of roughly the right size. "My Tom's," she said. "My grandson. I've no more use for them, and he'd have wanted to help a soldier. He always liked Master Kim."

"You worked at, uh, the big house, is that right?"

"Holmclere," Mrs. Mungo said. "The family seat. Four miles up the road towards Rathbury, you'll find it. Do you know the house?"

"Never been in this part of the world." Will hesitated, wondering if he could ask the obvious question.

Mrs. Mungo gave him a sharp look. "And now you're thinking, why did Master Kim come to Nanny in trouble and not his own home?"

"Well. Yes."

She clattered at the sink. "He was always the clever one, Master Kim, not like his brothers. So sharp he'd cut himself, and where he got that I couldn't say but not from the marquess, that's certain. A clever boy with secrets. Were you like that?"

"Not really," Will said. "I mostly climbed trees and played football."

"That was my James, and Tom after him. Master Kim was always different, even before the trouble," Mrs. Mungo said ruminatively. "And after—well. But I'll tell you this, young man, he asked me a few years ago not to believe anything he hadn't told me himself, and I haven't and shan't. So if you want to know why he didn't go home, it's because not many people know him like his nanny, and them as should, don't. But if I needed help, there's nobody in the world I'd turn to before Master Kim. You remember that."

"I will. Thank you, Mrs. Mungo."

She sniffed. "You may as well call me Nanny, like everyone else. Now make sure you finish up your plate. I don't know what you've been up to, nor I don't want to, but Master Kim told me to feed you up, and feed you up I shall."

She was as good as her word, providing an enormous late luncheon and supper. He earned them with a few deeply relished walks out in the fields, getting reacquainted with fresh air and the sky, and sat with her that evening, reading while she knitted, remembering his own grandmother and cosy evenings long ago when the world had been a very simple place.

He slept like the dead that night, replenished and rejuvenated. Good food, exercise, peace. What more could you reasonably ask? Maybe he ought to sell the bookshop when probate came through and move back to the countryside.

That was the first day. By the morning of the third, he was bored stiff.

It felt like he was still under house arrest, that was the problem. Six days of forced inactivity had been bad enough without adding more by choice. If you could call it choice. He wanted to know what was going on, and what Kim was up to. He wanted to find Libra, and beat the daylights out of him in an approved and civilised manner. He wanted to know Maisie was all right, to be sure he hadn't caused her trouble.

The last was the most urgent. He was almost convinced that his plan hadn't got her in trouble, and he knew logically that if it had, he'd be far too late to help. He still couldn't settle without knowing, so he gave up, borrowed a shilling from the money Kim had left, and went to the post office to find a telephone.

He called Villette's and asked to speak to Maisie Jones, claiming to be her cousin with a family emergency. She came to the telephone a moment later. "Hello? Vincent?"

"It's me."

"Will!" Her voice hissed down the crackly line. "Are you all right? Where have you been? Why didn't you get in touch?" She sounded as though she were about to cry.

"Long story. I'll tell you soon, I promise. Are *you* all right?"

"Of course I am. Why shouldn't I be?"

"That damned ticket. I was a fool to involve you. If you still have it, you need to get rid of it right away."

"What? Will—"

"I'm serious, Maisie. It's dangerous for you, and you have to be very careful. Now, I need—"

"Will!" Maisie said in strangled tones that suggested she wanted to shout. "I haven't got it. *You* do."

"What?"

"I gave it to you." Maisie spoke with extreme meaning. "Remember? When I last saw you? I gave it to you, but you'd said not to say anything that could be overheard, so I sent you a note that night to say you should keep it safe!"

"Keep..." Will stared at the wall of the telephone booth without seeing it, feeling his stomach plunge.

The flower. The silk flower Maisie had carefully secured in his buttonhole. She must have folded the pawn ticket small and made the flower around it with silk and wire. A brilliant, perfect place of concealment.

And Kim had taken it to pieces. Will could see the image now, as bright and vivid as any Pre-Raphaelite painting. Kim crouched in the doorway, unwrapping the wire. Going absolutely still for that long moment as Will had recounted his miseries.

He'd thought Kim had been affected by his words, that it had hurt him to hear Will's pain. Whereas in fact...

He'd found the pawn ticket, hadn't he? Found it, worked everything out, parked Will here with a pack of lies, and gone off to London to retrieve the information. The unbelievable shit.

"Will?" Maisie's tinny voice demanded. "Are you there?"

"I'm coming back," Will said. "See you soon."

It wasn't quick. He had to thank Nanny properly—it wasn't her fault that her precious Master Kim was a manipulative lying toe rag—and then embarrassingly, take some of the money Kim had left to pay for his stay. He had to get a lift by cart to the nearest railway station, and two changes of train to reach London, and then the Tube. It was quarter to five when he arrived in Lexington Street. He nipped into Villette's, caught Maisie's eye, and kicked his heels irritably until she came out.

"Will!" Maisie grabbed his hand, eyes wide. "What on earth is going on? What *happened*? Phoebe came to see me, she said you were kidnapped!"

"I was," Will said shortly. "Tell you on the way."

"The way where?"

"To the pawn shop you used."

He explained what had happened as she led the way. It took a while. Maisie gasped, squeaked, spluttered and, as he concluded, gaped at him. "You—but— They can't *do* that!"

"Well, they did. It wasn't much fun."

"And you think Lord Arthur stole the pawn ticket after he rescued you?"

"*While* he was rescuing me, the shifty swine. That's what we're going to find out, but yes. I do."

She frowned. "But if he only wanted the ticket, why would he bother with the rescue part? All the running and fighting and finding you a safe place sounds like hard work to me."

"If he'd taken the flower and left me there, I dare say I'd have put Libra on to him. Or maybe I wouldn't but he couldn't risk it. He was safer not leaving any clues. And sending me to stay with Nanny, Mrs. Mungo, got me out of the way and gave him a free hand to get the information."

Maisie narrowed her eyes. "I'm not sure that's quite fair. Phoebe came to see me two days after you went off. She said he was awfully worried and he'd gone to find you. It does sound like he wanted to help."

"Maybe he did, but he wanted the ticket more. We'll know in a minute," Will said. "If whatever it was you pawned has been claimed, we'll know Kim found the ticket and stole it in front of my face and lied to me *again*. And if he did that…"

He remembered standing dripping and naked, Kim's eyes on him. He'd all but pleaded with the bastard to share his bed in part because of how Kim had been then. Kim had wanted him, and Will had wanted him right back: his warmth, his sardonic tongue, his rare smile. The way his eyes lit at Will's pleasure, the way they found a rhythm together so easily, fucking or fighting or running for their lives. The way he looked when he came, stripped of his defences for a few brief seconds.

You won't thank me tomorrow if I stay. Well, that was true. The only thing that could make him feel stupider now would be if he'd spent *another* night in bed with a man who fully intended to screw him in a much less pleasurable way. He should probably thank Kim for his restraint; he should definitely learn his lesson.

He'd wanted to believe Kim had come for him because he mattered. Because they could have been friends, and more than friends. He'd wanted to believe there was something meaningful between them, and perhaps there had been, but the minute the ticket had fallen into his hands, Kim had once again proved that he would burn it all to the ground.

"He doesn't care for anyone," he said aloud.

Maisie glanced up. "Phoebe loves him."

"Phoebe," Will began with exasperation, and turned it into, "Since when are you two on first-name terms?"

"Oh, she's marvellous," Maisie said, eyes lighting with a warmth Will recognised, because Phoebe seemed able to evoke it from far less generous souls. "Isn't she lovely? She came to the shop and bought four hats and took me to tea. We had such a good talk. I like her."

"I expect everyone does."

"Do you?"

"Of course."

Maisie hesitated. "I did wonder, when she came to see you in the shop, all 'darling' this and that—"

"Nothing like that," Will said, possibly too hastily. "She's an Honourable, for goodness' sake, and engaged. She's just very friendly."

"Yes," Maisie said thoughtfully. "Very. We're here."

The pawnshop was a dingy sort of place, its shelves and cases cluttered with dusty relics of a thousand people's better times. China ornaments, trinkets, fading clothes, once-valued objects that were now worth what their desperate owners could get for them. Will had a sudden sharp urge to get his own things out of pawn: his father's watch, his mother's locket, his medals.

This shop was like all the others he'd used except in one respect: there was a woman behind the counter. She was dark-haired with deep-set dark eyes, and she smiled at Maisie with a lot more humanity than Will had ever been shown by a pawnbroker. "Hello, miss."

"Hello again. How have you been?"

"Well enough, thank you." The woman's smile faded a little and she glanced at Will, a quick professional assessment.

"Oh, he's with me," Maisie assured her. "No secrets. I've just come to check something. That vase I left with you the other week, has it been redeemed?"

"Well, yes. A gentleman came in with the ticket and paid in full. That's the law, ticket for goods."

"Of course," Maisie said. "Could you remember what he looked like, do you think?"

The woman's brows drew down. "I hope there's not a problem, miss?"

"If there is, it's not yours," Maisie said firmly. "He had the ticket. Only it would be an awful help if you could tell me anything you remember about him, there's a dear."

The woman paused, thinking. "Well—tallish. About your height, sir, but thinner. Willowy sort of fellow. Well dressed. Very dark eyes, almost like mine." Hers were sloe-black, a point of beauty in a face worn by life and work. "And a purple handkerchief in his pocket. He came in, oh, two days ago, and paid with a ten-shilling note."

"I know the man," Will said. "Thank you very much. I

don't suppose you took anything out of the vase while you had it? No, never mind."

"I'm sorry if there's any trouble caused," the woman said, sounding a little worried. "He had the ticket. If you like, I can make a note of it all now, for if it comes to the law."

"You're a love," Maisie said. "And it's not your fault in the slightest. Thank you."

Will exhaled hard as he left the shop. "You struck gold there. The only kind-hearted pawnbroker in London."

"I'd looked at five shops before her, trying to find a woman. I don't know how you go in those places. They're so bleak."

"I don't by choice," Will said. "I don't suppose Kim has set foot in one before. Nice experience for him, the swine."

"I'm so sorry. This is my fault. I needed to tell you what I'd done with the ticket, but you'd made such a point of not letting anyone else know, and the shop was full of people— and I did have to go and visit my auntie, you know, she's not well, and—"

"It's not your fault in the slightest. Putting it in the flower was a stroke of genius, and it was rotten luck how things played out. It's no more your fault than hers in the pawn shop. The only person in all this who's had meaningful choices is Kim. Well, and Zodiac," Will added as an afterthought.

"And you're not half as annoyed with them."

"Oh yes I am. Just differently."

"So what are you going to do?" Maisie asked.

"I'm going to pay Kim a visit. I'm going to get my property back if I can, and if I can't... Well, I'll have some words for him."

"Are you sure this is a good idea? He is a lord."

Will exhaled. "It's all I've got."

EIGHTEEN

He went home first. That was trying in itself, since his front door was still nailed shut. He'd left the back unlocked, he remembered, when he'd come out to speak to Phoebe that very long week ago, and as he scaled the back wall for the umpteenth time, he braced himself to find the place ransacked.

Surprisingly, it hadn't been. He took a cursory glance round and could see nothing missing at all. That was a credit to the neighbourhood, or possibly an indictment of the local youths' work ethic. He changed out of the borrowed clothes and shoes—he'd bring them with him to Kim to return to Nanny, he decided—dressed in the best he had, and washed the travel-stains off his face. Might as well go into this looking sharp. Shame he didn't have a flower for his buttonhole.

He hesitated over whether to go armed. If he inflicted damage on Kim it would be with his fists, but the Messer might be an aid to persuasion. If Kim believed he'd use it. He remembered the feel of the revolver against his face when he'd been close to murder: it had been a shock but he hadn't honestly felt a threat. Maybe he should have.

Better to have the Messer and not need it than vice versa. He attached the sheath to his braces and made sure his jacket covered it.

It was nearly seven. He pocketed three rather wrinkly apples that had survived his absence and set out again to Kim's flat, munching them as he went.

He'd worried that the doorman at Kim's building might be an obstacle, but the man greeted him with a courteous "Evening, sir," and a nod of recognition.

Will gave him a wave. "Is Lord Arthur in? He's expecting me."

"Yes, sir, he's at home."

Will went up the two flights and knocked at Kim's door. There was no response. He waited a few moments, knocked again. Still nothing.

This was just rude. He knew the bastard was in. If Kim was fucking someone else—sucking Ingoldsby off after handing him Will's property, perhaps—he could bloody well stop and answer the door. He slammed his fist against the wood, loud, heavy thumps, and added a few kicks, the last of which didn't connect as the door was jerked open.

Kim stood there with words on his lips that died unspoken. He stared at Will, eyes wide.

"You shit," Will said, in lieu of greeting.

"Go away," Kim said, and tried to slam the door.

Like he hadn't seen that coming. Will put hand and foot to the door, forcing it right back open. "Son of a bitch."

"Please," Kim said through his teeth. "Not now. Go *away*."

"Fuck you!" Will slapped his palm into Kim's chest, sending him off balance for a second, and barged his way in, dumping his bag with Nanny's clothes on the floor. Kim planted his feet and stood his ground so they were facing off in the little anteroom that constituted the flat's entrance hall. The door to the sitting room was ajar and Will caught a flash of colour that might be clothing. Maybe Kim did have a man here. Well, he could find out what he was getting into, and if it was Phoebe she ought to know too.

"You lying bastard," he said. "You shit. Every time I think I know what a shit you are, you make it worse." He'd thought in some detail about what he was going to say on the way over, a proper measured denunciation that clinically dissected Kim's moral failings. Now he was here, he couldn't remember any of it. He just felt an immense rage and, worse, hurt. "How could you do that? I was chained up in a *prison*, and all you could think about was stealing from me! How can anyone be that cold?"

"Keep your voice down," Kim said low and savagely, staring at Will with an odd, hard look as he spoke. "It's a game, and you lost. Stop whining and go."

The contempt in his voice burned. Will almost recoiled at it. He'd at least expected shame, not this unconcealed, uncaring malice. "The hell I will. I'm not leaving until you give me what you stole from me."

"It's gone to the War Office already. You're wasting both our time."

He'd passed on the information. After all the twists and turns and miseries, Will hadn't managed to keep it out of anyone's hands. The failure descended on him like a leaden shroud and it was all Kim's fault. Or his own, for seeing something in Kim that wasn't there.

He couldn't bear it. He could *not*.

"I don't believe you," he said abruptly.

"Why would I keep it? My job was to get it and hand it over, which I did. Now get out. I'll call the doorman or the police if I have to."

"Bastard," Will said, and shoved him with both hands.

Kim went stumbling back. Will shoved him again, pushing the door open, thrust him backwards into the sitting room ignoring his shout of protest, strode in after him, and stopped dead as the muzzle of a gun connected hard and cold with his temple.

Libra was holding the gun, his eyes boiling with malice. There was a nasty deep purple line of bruising round his throat. Will stood, frozen, and Libra whispered, "You." His knuckles around the gun stood out white against his skin.

"My neighbours will be complaining about Darling's approach to doors as we speak," Kim said. "The moment you pull the trigger, they'll come running. Do you really want to kill him more than you want the information?"

Libra didn't react at all for the longest three seconds of Will's life, then he stepped back, giving himself a bit more space, and jerked the gun at the settee.

It was already occupied, by Captain Ingoldsby, his face drawn with tension and fury. He was glowering at the fourth man present: his lackey, the pink-faced man called Price, who stood against the bookshelves of the opposite wall holding a revolver. It was pointed at Ingoldsby. That made no sense, until it did.

"Shit," Will said.

"Quite," Kim agreed. "I did try to make you leave."

Libra smiled unpleasantly. "Loose ends. Sit."

His voice was a whispery rasp. Will's handkerchief garotte had clearly done him serious damage. His hand was steady on the revolver though, so Will followed the direction of its jerk and took one of Kim's armchairs.

Kim sat next to Ingoldsby, expression decidedly sour. "Can I observe this will do nothing but add a third person to the newspaper list of Bodies Found In Holborn Flat? I am loath to indulge in such clichés as 'you'll never get away with it', but you really won't. And your masters won't be grateful for this level of attention."

"Shut up," Libra wheezed. "Information. Now."

"As we were discussing before we were so rudely interrupted," Kim said. "I believe I asked you why I should hand it over when you're going to kill us all anyway. You have so far failed to give me an answer. If I'm about to die, I'd rather do it in the knowledge that you will too, whether on the gallows or at the hands of your masters. And you will, because I assure you, if you shoot us, you won't have enough time to search this place before the superintendent arrives. They take noise awfully seriously here."

Libra looked at him, then at Will. "Don't—have to shoot."

The half-smile faded on Kim's lips. Libra took a slow step forward, eyes on Kim, gun on Will. "Give it up. Or watch me —throttle him."

"Don't give it up," Ingoldsby growled.

"You can come and try it," Will said. His heartbeat sounded loud in his chest, and his hand was already curving to the shape of the Messer. One more enemy, one more kill, and he'd let himself enjoy this one. "Hand to hand, you and me. I'll make you shoot me."

"In which eventuality, as I have already remarked, it's all over," Kim added.

"It's over anyway," Price said. His voice was clipped and Will saw something rather wild in his eyes.

"Not—yet," Libra whispered.

"Nasty throat you have there," Will remarked. "Flu?"

Libra gave him a look of loathing. Will put his hands round his own throat and stuck out his tongue in a caricature of strangulation. Libra's lips drew back over his teeth like a dog's.

"I think it is over, you know," Kim said. "You'll notice we've found the leak, Darling. I say 'found', but he rather gave himself away when he pulled the gun. Terribly unfortunate—for the War Office, of course, but also for Price himself, and Zodiac. He had *such* a promising career at Ingoldsby's right hand, trusted and unsuspected. A pity to waste such a well-placed traitor for this." His eyes flicked to Libra. "But you are quite desperate now."

"Shut up," Libra rasped.

"Just making sure we all understand the situation. I regret to say Price had Ingoldsby utterly fooled. Once the War Office had the information, I dare say he'd have helped himself at his leisure and become Zodiac's new hero. But Libra's needs were urgent, so he's sacrificed Price's cover to get the information, and if he doesn't bring his masters their bone this time, they'll put him down like the dog he is. And doubtless Price with him, pour encourager les autres." Kim's smile at Price was a masterpiece of unpleasantness. "Bad luck, old man."

Libra swung his arm and levelled the gun at Kim's head. "So—nothing to lose."

"Yes, that is the stalemate," Kim agreed, seemingly unconcerned. "If you don't get the information you're dead, so you might as well kill us all. If you're going to kill us all, we might as well not give you the information, in which case you're dead. There's a rather pleasing symmetry, isn't there?"

"Just a minute," Will said. "Who the hell is 'us'?"

Every eye flicked to him. Kim said, "What?"

"This is nothing to do with me. I'm not a spy or a War Office lackey. I never wanted the bloody information in the first place. *And* I had it safe till you stole the ticket. You're the arsehole who decided it would be better to give it to the War Office, and see where that's got everyone."

"If you'd listened to a word I'd said at any point in the last weeks, it would now be held securely," Kim snapped. "It's a pity you're constitutionally incapable of that."

"Quiet," Libra said. "Hand it over. Or watch me hurt..." The gun barrel moved between Will and Ingoldsby.

"Oh, shut up," Will said contemptuously. "Like he says, it's not a threat if you're going to kill us anyway. Christ, the lot of you are useless." He leaned forward, jabbing a finger at Ingoldsby. "You with your smug superior talk, bullying and shouting, and all the time you were harbouring a traitor right next to you, like a wanker. You, Secretan, if you'd just *once* told the truth instead of lying whenever you had the chance, we might not all be in this mess. And as for you, standing around threatening people— Get that gun out of my face!" He waved his hand angrily at Libra. "As for *you*, you missed the information when it was sitting on a shelf in my shop, you missed it when I had it on me in your prison cell for six days—*six days*, you cretin—and you're missing it again right here in this flat. Dear God, you're thick."

"Darling," Kim said, tensing visibly.

"Shut up. I'm tired of this. I've had nothing but threats, lies, abuse, and treachery, and for what? I'm not going to be cannon fodder any more. The lot of you can rot." He turned to Price. "I'll give it to you."

"No!" Kim and Ingoldsby said at once.

Will met Price's wide eyes. "We've both been shafted by the officers. Am I right? Ingoldsby would have left me to rot; Secretan's a son of a bitch; Libra's blown your cover and he'll take you down with him. Sod the lot of them. Let's make a deal."

"Darling!" Ingoldsby roared.

Will ignored him. "I give you the information and walk out of here unharmed. You hand it over to your people and get the credit. You leave me alone afterwards, and I'll forget everything I've seen this evening. And as for these three— well, do what you like. I'd lock 'em all in a room and see who comes out alive. My money's on Secretan. He's the nastiest of the lot."

"You don't know where it is," Price said, over Libra's strangled noises and Ingoldsby's angry shout. "You just got here."

"He and I spent days talking about where to hide things while he was playing secret agents. Of course I know where he's put it," Will said. "It's in this room."

Ingoldsby sprang to his feet. Libra stepped forward, jabbing the gun to his chest, and he stopped, but the words hissed out savagely. "You damned filthy traitor!"

"Takes one to know one," Will said. "What do you say, Price?"

"He'll give it straight to Libra, you fool!" Ingoldsby shouted.

"No, he won't," Kim said. "The old order changeth, yielding place to new. Price will take care of himself. You rather miscalculated this, didn't you, Libra?"

"You can bloody talk," Will told him. "Shut up."

Price's eyes darted back and forth. "I'll take it back to the House and explain the full situation. They'll make a judgement." That was addressed to Libra, whose cheekbones were stained red. "Fetch it, Darling, and you can go."

"I'll tell you where it is while I'm standing at the door," Will said. "No offence, but I don't trust you that much."

He could see Price making calculations. Libra with a gun; a roomful of desperate men. "You say it's in here. I could shoot you now and search the room."

"Not before someone knocks on the door to ask what's going on," Will returned. "And if I were you, I wouldn't let Libra get behind you while you're searching."

Price's jaw firmed. "Hand it to me, and I'll let you go."

"He won't," Kim told Will savagely. "You could identify him. And when he shoots you, you'll deserve it."

"I've been shot at plenty of times," Will said. "Never had much thanks for it. I'll leave you to your business, Price, if you'll leave me to mine. Do we have an agreement?"

Price nodded firmly. "Give it to me and you will walk out of here unharmed. You won't hear from me, or my people, again. Your safety is guaranteed, my word on it."

Their eyes locked. "Your word," Will said at last. "Fine."

"Then get up. But don't play the fool," Price warned.

"I'm not planning to." Will flicked a thumb at Libra. "If he shoots me, you'll never have it."

"He won't," Price said. Libra's mouth moved silently.

Will got up carefully, no sudden movements, and went to the bookshelves that lined the wall. Behind him, Kim inhaled audibly.

"Keep them covered," Price told Libra, for all the world as though he was the boss now. He came close to Will, breathing hard.

Will turned to scan the room. Libra was dividing his attention, flicking his gaze from Kim and Ingoldsby to Will. Ingoldsby was watching Price, the skin stretched tight over his angular features. Kim was watching Libra.

Will pulled out *The Book of British Birds* but didn't open it. He turned to the room. Every set of eyes was on him now except Kim's.

"Here we are," he said, and opened the book wide to reveal a paper covered in spidery handwriting. Price made a noise in his throat and reached out for it.

Will tossed the heavy book into his face, caught the wrist of his gun hand, and wrenched it sharply upwards. Price yelled, and the revolver went off, shockingly loud in the enclosed space, along with a flurry of movement and crashing behind them. Price grabbed at Will's wrist with his other hand, trying to free his arm, leaving his torso entirely exposed.

Will pulled the Messer from under his coat and struck upward. The blade slid into Price's ribcage like butter. He took the revolver from Price's suddenly limp hand, shoved him away, and swung to face the room as Price slumped to the ground.

Kim and Ingoldsby had got Libra on the floor. He still held his gun, though at least Ingoldsby was holding his outstretched arm down, and he was thrashing and fighting like a wild beast, bucking under Kim's weight, careless of the arm twisted behind his back.

Desperation was always dangerous. Will walked over and gave Kim Price's revolver. "You might want this."

"Thanks." Kim took the gun, and jammed it into the back of Libra's neck. "I really would enjoy shooting you. Give me an excuse."

Libra roared and flailed. "Take the damned gun off him!" Kim snapped.

"Trying!" Ingoldsby snarled back.

Will went over, put a foot on Libra's wrist, and applied his considerable body weight, forcing the edge of his heel into flesh and bone till Libra's fingers convulsed. He scooped up the gun. "Got it."

Ingoldsby leapt to his feet. "Price!"

Libra took the chance to try and buck Kim off. Kim ground the revolver into his neck with an exasperated noise. "Get me something to tie him with, would you, Will? A dressing gown cord should do it. Back of my bedroom door. The red one, please, *not* the purple velvet."

Ingoldsby gave a snort of disgust. "Call a doctor first. And get me a towel. This man's bleeding to death."

"When are your blasted neighbours turning up?" Will enquired of Kim.

"Twelfth of never. You could fire a Maxim gun in here

without adverse comment. The chap at number twelve once brought a pig in."

This seemed to annoy Libra. Will left Kim to manage that while he went to the bathroom, grabbed a towel, and tossed it in Ingoldsby's direction. He picked up the phone and asked the operator to summon an ambulance. Then he went to get the cord.

"The red one, Will," Kim said again as he left the room.

Kim's bedroom was much as he remembered it, all warm lamps and luxury, except that the bed was neatly made and it didn't smell of sex and male sweat. It should have. Will paused at the door where Kim had stood that Monday morning, asking to part on good terms. He remembered the way Kim fucked, the noises he made, the need and pleasure and wariness in his eyes.

He didn't want to look for what he'd come to get now. He didn't want another false hope; he didn't want to be wrong. His heart thumped unpleasantly, in a way it hadn't when he'd been readying himself to kill.

Deep breath, in and out.

Kim's purple bathrobe was hanging on top of the other. Will moved it aside, put his hand into the pocket of the red one, and touched folded paper. He pulled it out, and there it was. Two pages of Shakespeare, scribbled on in Draven's familiar hand.

Will leaned against the door, pressing his face against the smooth purple velvet that smelled like Kim. He let himself do nothing but feel for a moment, a chaos of hurt and gratitude, anger and deep, profound relief. Then he pocketed the papers, extracted the red cord from its loops, and went back out.

In the sitting room, Ingoldsby knelt over Price, pressing the towel to his abdomen. It was soaked with blood. Kim still had Libra prone, one arm twisted behind his back, revolver pressed into his neck. Will dropped the red cord onto Libra's back.

Kim's dark eyes met Will's in a silent moment before he spoke. "Can you tie him for me? As you see, my hands are occupied."

"So they are," Will said. He pulled out the papers, walked to the gas fire, and thrust them into the grate.

"What the— Darling!" Ingoldsby bellowed. "What are you doing?"

Libra turned his head, saw what was happening, and thrashed wildly. This time he caught Kim napping. Kim went over sideway, dropping the gun, which skittered across the floor; Libra leapt to his feet and ran for the door.

"Ingoldsby, stop him!" Kim bellowed.

"This man's bleeding to death!"

Kim clambered to his feet as Libra's footsteps rapidly retreated, and turned on Will, who held up the Messer warningly. They stared at one another as the papers flamed in Will's hand.

"Get those damned papers off him!" Ingoldsby called out.

"You do it," Kim said. "I don't like that knife."

The pages were down to a couple of inches, starting to heat his fingers. Will dropped them into the grate, where the unburned paper caught instantly and fell as a flaming mass onto the tiled hearth.

Kim stamped on the remnants, then stooped to check and made an exasperated noise. "It's gone. All burned. That's rendered a great deal of hard work entirely pointless."

"You found your leak," Will said. "And Zodiac didn't get the information. Two out of three's not bad. Shame you let Libra go, though."

Kim started to reply to that in uncomplimentary terms as Ingoldsby's voice rose furiously. Will ignored them both. He found a cloth to clean his knife, and took a seat, waiting to find out what would happen next.

Medics—doctors, rather—came and removed Price. Ingoldsby spoke angrily, near rather than at Will. There was a certain amount of discussion in low voices, but nobody seemed inclined to arrest him. So he went home.

He was a bit nervous about encountering Libra on the way. He hadn't expected Kim to let the man go. Probably he had his reasons for doing so: Will didn't know what they were, and didn't care. If he found Libra lurking at the bookshop bent on vengeance, he'd use the Messer again.

Libra wasn't there. The shop was cold and dusty, but it was safe, and Will had a fine night's sleep in his rickety bed.

NINETEEN

Will put his back into work the next day, sorting and tidying as best he could. He started to clear space in one of the upstairs rooms in the hope of one day making it a proper living space. He dropped round to see Maisie at lunchtime and agreed a date to take her out for dinner and the full explanation she made it clear he owed her, and went back to do more work.

Nobody official came to interview him. Presumably Ingoldsby was putting a lid on the events around Price's treachery, or perhaps there was a storm brewing and about to break. Will just worked through the day, and the next one. Working, planning, thinking, waiting.

Kim turned up on the third evening.

Will had closed up and pulled the blinds against the dark by then. He could only see a silhouette at the door, but Kim's outline was imprinted on his mind now. He went to the newly mended door to let him in.

"Hello," Kim said, slipping inside. "I thought we should speak."

"I dare say." Will went to his desk and indicated the spare chair. Kim hovered a moment, then took it.

"So what's new?" Will asked, when he seemed unwilling to start.

"Price has died." Kim spoke neutrally, watching his face.

Will nodded. "I should expect the police, then?"

"No, you shouldn't. It's being handled internally, as they like to say. Ingoldsby agrees you acted with impressive initiative in a difficult situation—I quote him directly—and more to the point, nobody from the WO wants you standing in a public dock, explaining that Price was engaged in ongoing treason. The matter will be dealt with at Horse Guards Parade, and the family given a story."

"So much for Price?"

"No flowers by request," Kim agreed. "So you needn't worry about official repercussions. His demise is generally agreed to be for the best, in the circumstances. Of course, it's a shame he expired without regaining consciousness because a number of people had questions for him, but you can hardly be blamed for that. Except in a very literal sense, of course." He paused. "I'm not sure if I should offer reassurances."

"What about?"

"You killed him. Do you need to hear that you had to do it?"

"I know I had to do it: that was why I did it. I don't stab people by accident."

"Indeed not," Kim said. "And I couldn't see another way out, so I'm glad to hear you aren't racked by remorse. Can I take a moment to applaud your speed on the uptake, by the way? A flawlessly executed divide-and-conquer strategy."

"Well, you told me everything I needed," Will pointed out. "Let's call it a pincer movement."

There was a glimmer of a smile on Kim's lips. "You enjoyed it, didn't you?"

Will grimaced. He'd shared a trench for a while with a senior lecturer in mathematics who insisted that equations could be beautiful. Will's school experience of algebra didn't support that in the slightest, but he'd sometimes had a vague inkling of what the fellow meant. When you lost yourself in work; when you could operate in perfect harmony with someone; when you had that soaring sense of everything clicking into place and the world running on well-oiled tracks, however briefly.

Kim gave him that, so Will said what he would not have done to anyone else. "Yes. I did."

"And yet the Army let you go, the damned fools. Talking of which, you should know that Libra—his name was Martin McLean—is even now practising scales alongside Price in the choir invisible. He was pulled out of the river yesterday."

Will whistled. "Zodiac?"

"Undoubtedly. They don't like mistakes, and wasting an asset like Price with nothing to show for it was the last straw. McLean looked like they had made that point to him, over some hours."

Will studied his face. "Did you know that would happen? Is that why you let him go?"

"I let him go so he could report that the information had been burned, in order to get Zodiac off your back. The rest was incidental."

"But you knew they'd get him."

Kim shrugged. "He lost any claim to mercy when he chained you up like a dog."

And he'd promised to have Libra's balls for that, and now Libra was dead, and Will was, perhaps, safe. He nodded. "So Draven's horror is gone, Zodiac know it, and the War Office is covering up. Does that mean it's all over? At least, over for me?"

"I think so. Zodiac has sustained a heavy loss, and their very sensible habit is to regroup, not to throw good money after bad. Ingoldsby—well, he's not happy about you burning the papers, but he has other things to occupy him. He recommended Price for promotion twice, you know. Thought of him as a son."

"Poor sod," Will said, with an unexpected surge of sympathy.

"You think so?"

"It's not much fun to trust someone and then find out they've played you for a fool."

The words hung in the air. "No," Kim said after a moment. "Indeed."

"You stole that ticket in front of me while I was chained up. That was shitty."

"It was, yes."

"I really don't understand," Will said. "You're better than that. You're clever and brave and determined. You ought to be a man whose family are proud of him, with friends who trust him. Why aren't you?"

"Your ability to inflict damage with words as well as knives is noted. Can we agree I behaved appallingly and get on to the part where I apologise and remove myself from your presence?"

"Not yet. You stole the ticket from me, but first you spent six days searching for me. Was that just in the hope of finding the information?"

Kim shut his eyes. "Will..."

"I want the truth. I *deserve* the truth."

"Yes, you do." Kim's face was blank, but his knuckles were white. "I...was not looking for the information, no. I came after you because I couldn't do otherwise. Knowing they had you—that if I had done better, you could have trusted me, and we might have worked together—I had to find you. And if I hadn't managed it..." He stopped there.

"What?" Will demanded.

"I'd have burned Zodiac to the ground," Kim said simply. "However long it took. Whatever it cost."

Will breathed out, feeling a band loosen around his lungs. "But you still took the ticket, for all that."

"Of course I did. I had you safe and well, or approximately so, and it fell into my lap. An unexpected bonus." There was a nasty twist in his voice on that last.

"You took it off me and got the information and used it, and then you told me where the pages were. You stole them from me, and you gave them back. Why?"

"Because they should have been destroyed, and nobody else had the balls to do it. Not your uncle, not Draven, and certainly not me. I'm glad you did. Some other soulless bastard who looks at humanity through a lens will doubtless come up with a similar evil in due course, but I don't have to facilitate it. I should have reached that conclusion a long time ago."

"Yes, you should."

"In fairness, it was also rather urgent to find the leak," Kim added. "I needed the information to dangle as bait, force Libra's hand while he was desperate. I could have told you that, of course, and asked you to trust me with the information. I didn't."

"Why not?"

"Because you'd have said no, of course."

"Christ, you're trying," Will said. "Hold on. Is *that* why you wouldn't let me kill Libra before? Because you wanted to use him to get at the leak? Not that stuff about 'you're not a murderer'?"

Kim rolled his eyes. "Oh, please. You know who you are,

and you wear it well. I really don't know why you listen to me."

"Nor do I, you corkscrew-tongued bastard. Jesus wept. You could open wine bottles with that."

"I do my best." Kim's eyebrow flickered suggestively, then he made a face, as if recalling himself. "Anyway, there you are. Finding the information was not my priority, but when it fell into my lap, I took advantage. Is that what you needed to know?"

"As far as it goes, but I've another question and I want a straight answer, with no dancing around. You owe me that."

Kim's face tensed, but he nodded. Will said, "All right. Did you fuck me under orders?"

He might as well have struck the man. Kim's nostrils flared. "What a remarkable fist I have made of my life, that it is quite reasonable for you to ask me that."

"I need to know. Did you do it because you were told to? Or to get me to trust you? Or—" He could see it hurt and he didn't care. He couldn't let Kim off this hook. "To have something on me?"

"Christ. No, Will. None of that." He paused, then shut his eyes again. "Or, at least, not the first time. I can safely say that my professional judgement didn't come into it at any point that night: it was just me and you. But when you came to my flat for that bath—granted I brought you there because I wanted you there, but once I'd guessed what Draven had done with the information, I decided to keep you there by fair means or foul. I am aware that was contemptible. I knew it at the time."

"Would you have gone through with it?"

"I don't know. Probably. Or perhaps not. I don't *know*. I can't say I was looking forward to the prospect. I fucked for professional reasons a few years ago—as a matter of national necessity, I mean, not the other profession. It did my self-esteem no good at all, and that was a man I had no moral qualms about deceiving. And yet, when the opportunity arose, I fully intended to do it to you. So there you are."

"You're a bit of a mess, aren't you?"

"My friend, you have no idea."

Will ran his hands through his hair. "I did some thinking. All the blowing hot and cold, all the times you said no. You were trying not to fuck under false pretences, weren't you? You stole from me when I was at my weakest, but you wouldn't share a bed at Nanny's house once you'd done it. I don't understand you."

"I didn't *enjoy* betraying you. I did it, repeatedly, but it's really not a hobby. And I didn't want to fuck under false pretences because…" He exhaled. "Because I wanted so much to do it under real ones."

Will wasn't sure how to respond to that. Kim managed a smile. It wasn't a marvellous smile, but he managed it, and even met Will's eyes. "I like you, Will, enormously. Your certainty and courage. I don't know anyone with whom I'd rather execute an ambush in a muddy field."

"I've done a few of those. You were pretty good."

"And you're exceedingly hard to resist," Kim said softly. "Your eyes, your smile, your strength. Your hands."

"My—" Will couldn't help looking down at them. They were toughened and battered, scarred with thin white lines and thickened knuckles. Ugly working hands, not like Kim's elegant manicured ones.

Kim was looking at them too. "Beautiful. Like English oak." His eyes flicked up and met Will's. "As I say, hard to resist, and I failed to on several occasions, which caused us both a great deal of unnecessary pain. The night I spent here and the one you spent at my flat were two of the best I can remember, entirely because of you, and I wish I hadn't tainted them. I wish I had done better by you."

Will could wish that too. "Thanks. That helps."

"It's not remotely enough and we both know it. I made such a bloody mess of everything. And it was all my mess, no fault of yours. I'm sorry. Especially since we worked rather well when we were on the same side."

"It would help if you were more reliably unreliable. At least I'd know where I stood."

"Sorry."

They both sat in silence for a minute, listening to the old bookshop creak and settle around them.

"So what now?" Will said at last.

"For whom? I continue doing what's required of me, attempting to arrange the pieces of my life into a shape that has some meaning. You run your bookshop and court your flower-making beauty—"

"Sorry, what? What are you talking about?"

"Your young lady. The ingenious and adorable milliner of whom I hear so much."

"I never said a word to you about her!" Will protested.

"Didn't you? Maybe it was Phoebe. In any case, I trust the assessment of her callipygous pulchritude is correct and that you'll be very happy."

"That's as may be," Will said severely, since he had no idea what that meant, "but first off, she's not my young lady, and second, I didn't mean 'what now for the rest of both our lives'. I meant..." He shrugged. "Drink?"

Kim looked completely nonplussed, for once. It was rather satisfying. "Drink?"

"Two blokes in a bookshop. One of them has a lot on his plate and the other one says, you've had a bad day, let's get a drink. So they go to the Black Horse on the corner. Does that sound familiar?"

"It sounds like the start of a joke," Kim said, and then, a little less waspishly, "Or at least, a story."

"It sounds like a good idea to me. Pub, couple of pints, chat. Coming?"

Kim's eyes met his, deep and dark and definitely unsettled. "What do you want to talk about?"

"I don't know. The football results? Politics. The pictures. Why the blazes you're called Kim when your name is Arthur."

"My name, since you raise the topic, is Arthur Aloysius Kimberley de Brabazon Secretan. What would you do in my place?"

"Leave the country," Will said wholeheartedly. "You poor bastard, you never stood a chance."

"Not much of one." Kim's lips twitched, just a little. "Pub, you say?"

Will stood. "Black Horse. And you're buying."

"Oh, *now* I see the motive." Kim stood too and shrugged his coat on. "The gin there is abominable, by the way."

"So drink beer. Is it always Kim, or does anyone call you Aloysius?"

Kim picked up his hat. "Not if they want to live."

It could be the start of a story or the end of one, Will thought, as they headed out together into the cold, dark street. It could be a farewell, or the foundation of a friendship. It could be an awkward drink in a crowded pub with an upper-class man wound tighter than a neurasthenic's pocket watch, or just possibly something else entirely, something precious and fragile that Will didn't want to look at straight on in case he jinxed it. It could be anything.

He might as well find out what.

Kim Secretan and Will Darling return in THE SUGARED GAME

THE WILL DARLING ADVENTURES

A m/m romance trilogy in the spirit of Golden Age pulp fiction. It's the 1920s and tensions are rising along with hemlines. Soldier-turned-bookseller Will Darling finds himself tangled up in spies and secret formulas, clubs and conspiracies, Bolsheviks, blackmail, and Bright Young Things. And dubious aristocrat Lord Arthur 'Kim' Secretan is right in the middle of it all: enigmatic, unreliable, and utterly irresistible.

Slippery Creatures
The Sugared Game
Subtle Blood

For more 1920s romance by KJ Charles, this time with magic...

Spectred Isle

Archaeologist Saul Lazenby has been all but unemployable since his disgrace during the War. Now he scrapes a living working for a rich eccentric who believes in magic. Saul knows it's a lot of nonsense...except that he begins to find himself in increasingly strange and frightening situations. And at every turn he runs into the sardonic, mysterious Randolph Glyde.

Randolph is the last of an ancient line of arcanists, commanding deep secrets and extraordinary powers as he struggles to fulfil his family duties in a war-torn world. He knows there's something odd going on with the haunted-looking man who keeps turning up in all the wrong places. The only question for Randolph is whether Saul is victim or villain.

Saul hasn't trusted anyone in a long time. But as the supernatural threat grows, along with the desire between them, he'll need to believe in evasive, enraging, devastatingly attractive Randolph. Because he may be the only man who can save Saul's life—or his soul

ABOUT THE AUTHOR

KJ Charles lives in London with her husband, two kids, an out-of-control garden, and a cat with murder management issues.

KJ writes mostly historical romance, mostly queer, sometimes with fantasy or horror in there. She is represented by Courtney Miller-Callihan at Handspun Literary.

For all the KJC news and occasional freebies, get my (infrequent) newsletter at:

kjcharleswriter.com/newsletter.

Pick up free reads on my website:

kjcharleswriter.com

Join my Facebook group, KJ Charles Chat, for book conversation, sneak peeks, and exclusive treats.

facebook.com/kj.charles.9

twitter.com/kj_charles